THE
DEADLIEST DECEPTIONS

THE
DEADLIEST DECEPTIONS

A COLLECTION OF MIRIAM BAT ISAAC SHORT MYSTERIES

JUNE TROP

Author Photo Credit: © Michael Gold: The Corporate Image

First edition

ISBN: 978-1-68512-275-1

Cover art by Level Best Designs

This book was professionally typeset on Reedsy.
Find out more at reedsy.com

For my Paul

Contents

Praise for the Miriam bat Isaac Mysteries

"June Trop brings to life a fascinating figure in 1st Century CE Alexandria, Miriam bat Isaac. Despite its ancient setting, the actions, conflicts, and characters come across realistically, even vividly. You will feel very much there as you witness crimes of murder, jealousy, and greed." — The Amazing Kreskin

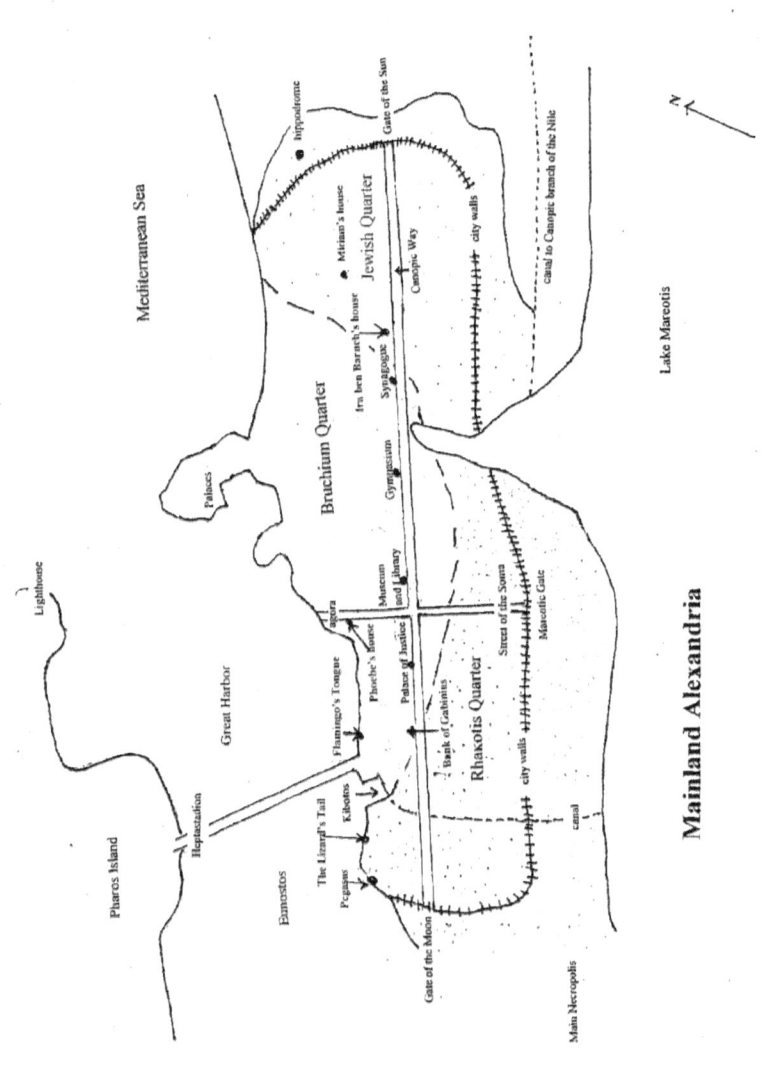

Adapted from Sly, D. I. (1996). Philo's Alexandria. *London: Routledge.*

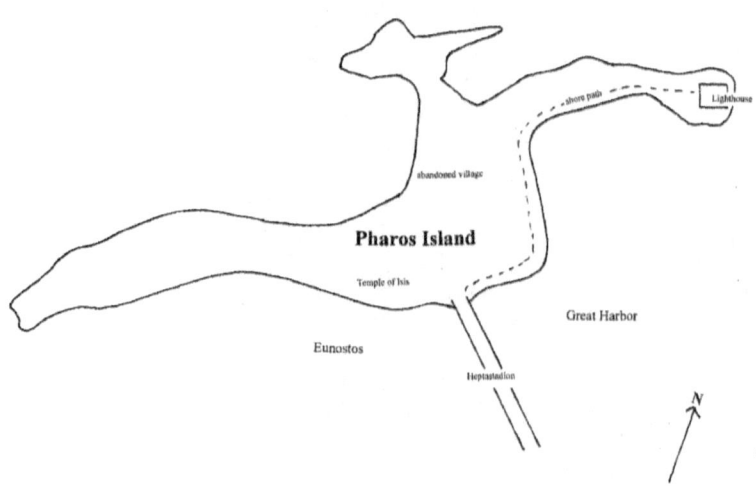

Pharos Island

abandoned village

shore path

Lighthouse

Temple of Isis

Great Harbor

Eunostos

Heptastadion

N

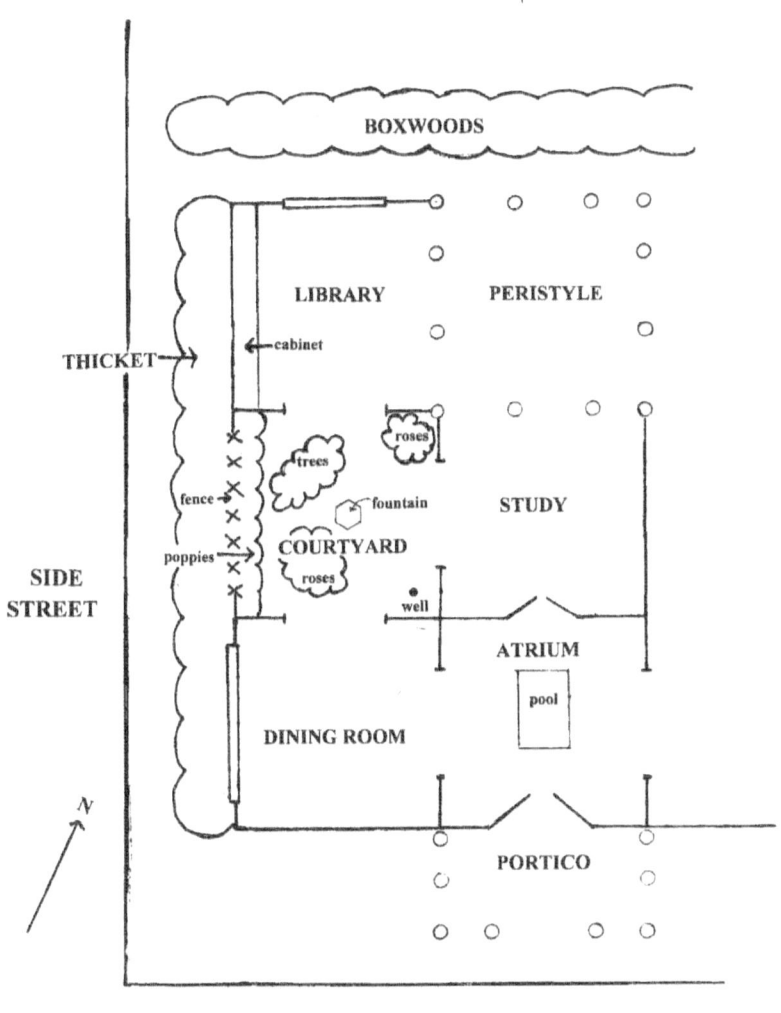

Miriam's House: Public Rooms

Introduction

You are about to enter the world of first-century CE Roman-occupied Alexandria and participate in the perilous adventures of Miriam bat Isaac, budding alchemist and sleuth extraordinaire. Join her and her deputy Phoebe as they struggle to solve nine of their most baffling cases.

Alexandria has already been in existence for nearly 400 years as a strategic crossroads between the western cultures of the Mediterranean and those of Egypt and the rest of the Near East. In 332 BCE, the Egyptians welcomed Alexander the Great to liberate them from Persian oppression. Then, with the help of an architect from the city state of Rhodes, Alexander designed the city that would become second in the Empire only to Rome.

But Alexander died before he could realize his dream. One of his generals, Ptolemy, declared himself king and established a dynasty that would reign for 300 years. Ultimately, the last of the Ptolemies, Cleopatra, was unable to maintain control of the city and lost her power to the Romans at the Battle of Actium in 31 BCE. Three years later, the Roman Senate bestowed on the victor, Octavian, the name Augustus, meaning the revered one, and declared him the first emperor of Rome. The Miriam bat Isaac stories in this collection take place about a hundred years later during the reign of Nero, the fifth emperor.

Join Miriam and Phoebe as they wrestle with scoundrels capable of the deadliest deceptions. But be careful. They will take you into Alexandria's malignant underbelly. The first story, "Believing is Seeing," is a locked-room mystery in which Miriam is baffled by not just who killed the sailor but how he could have died. As she explains to Phoebe, "He couldn't have died from any natural cause, but suicide and murder were also out of the question." Then comes "The Brother," about a bizarre scheme to steal a rare manuscript. And next is "Revenge," the story of two cousins dying suddenly from the same familial illness, or did they?

"The Fire" is an investigation into the death of a coquettish Roman woman. "The Guest" recounts the effects of one man's simmering grudge against another. And in "The Mistress," as Miriam overhears a stranger tell his companion that he plans to commit a murder, she and Phoebe try to thwart his scheme.

"The Recollection" is about a man who, awakening on a pile of rubble in a rutted alley, struggles to recall who he is. "The Dagger" features Phoebe, eager to solve the murder of a retired gladiator whose throat was slit in a sleazy waterfront inn. And in the last story, "The Missing Widow," Phoebe risks a pair of antique Etruscan earrings and her very life to solve the disappearance of her next-door neighbor.

Each adventure stands alone, but if you read the stories in order, you'll see how the major characters develop and the minor ones earn a place in later stories. But most of all, whether or not you can help Miriam and Phoebe solve the crimes, your blood will flow faster as you escape to that world of adventure we all long for. Enjoy!

June Trop

Believing is Seeing

The Eighth Year of the Reign of
Nero Claudius Caesar Augustus Germanicus [Nero]
62 CE, Early March
Alexandria *ad Aegyptum*

"But Miriam, how could someone be dead when every way he could have died was impossible?"

"That's why the death of Calix was my most baffling case. He couldn't have died from any natural cause, but suicide and murder were also out of the question. I had no explanation until I mixed some intuition in with the facts."

As usual on Shabbat, Phoebe had taken a break from helping Bion, her cherubic-faced husband, in his shop to pay me a lunchtime visit. Given the unusual warmth for an early spring day, I asked her to join me under the linen canopy of my family's third-floor Egyptian-style roof garden.

We were sitting at a marble table across from each other on teak benches banked with cushions of cerulean and turquoise silk. Under the pinpricks of light, a rush of air grazed the nape of my neck and rippled Phoebe's Chinese silk outer tunic, puffed out the ruffle along the lower edge of her inner tunic, and lifted the wispy feathers of dark hair that shade her brow. She giggled as she patted down her skirts with her dumpling-like hands, her fingers laden with massive rings glittering with precious gems in keeping with her status as the wife of a prosperous shopkeeper.

"So, what made you think of Calix today?" I asked. "That case was so long ago."

"Bion hired an apprentice who is occupying our upstairs apartment with his younger brother. I already told you about that, right?"

I wasn't sure.

"Well, the brother had been staying at that inn, you know, The Pegasus, where you solved the case of that jackal-faced slave who was bludgeoned to death in his own locked room."

"Oh, that greasy place! Even the soup would saw off the roof of your mouth."

"Well," continued Phoebe, "both deaths—the slave's and Calix's—defied explanation, but I wasn't paying much attention in those days. Little did I know you'd make a vocation out of this sleuthing business. So, when I was walking over here and saw a beggar with something like the face of a jackal, and then I passed the house on the corner—that's where Calix was killed, right? The place with that neat little walk—I made a connection between the cases and wondered how you happened to get involved in the one about Calix."

"You passed the house of Ira ben Baruch—"

"Yes, the house that used to belong to his father, that elder of your synagogue, the one who was crucified during the Riots."

"Well, Calix was killed maybe ten years after the Riots. At the time, Ira ben Baruch was living downstairs in the front of the house, and his father's elderly maid, Rhea, was staying in the room behind the kitchen. He'd rent out the two single rooms upstairs to sailors when the ports were closed for the season. Calix was one, and his shipmate—"

"So, how did you get involved in that case?"

"It was early in the morning, a chilly February morning. The household was still asleep, but I'd been up working in our library on my formula to enhance the luminosity of precious stones. I remember how I shivered like a frightened horse when I opened the door. Mr. Baruch's bearers stood before me, their bodies rigid, the taller one with a face as white as a fish's belly, the other's coursed with purple veins and glittering with moisture.

"My mouth hinged open as I drew in a quick breath. 'Yes?' I said in a barely

4

audible tone. The very sight of them standing there thickened my tongue."

"'It's Rhea, Mr. Ira's maid.' The white-faced one spoke, his words getting tangled as they rushed out of his mouth. 'She found the sailor this morning. Late, she said, for his appointment. So, she unlocked his door, saw him dead on his sleeping couch, and flew out of the room, screaming for us to fetch you. Said she didn't know who else to call, Mr. Ira being away in the Holy Land. Said you'd know what to do.'"

"So, what *did* you do?" Phoebe asked, tilting forward, her eyes vivid with excitement. The passing years hadn't dulled her taste for sharing a juicy story.

I closed my eyes until the case returned to me on a wave of memory.

"Well, are you going to tell me or not?" Already Phoebe's voice was thin with impatience.

"Give me a chance. I haven't thought about it in years." I waited a while and then shook my head. "I couldn't make any sense of it—"

"Until you did—"

"Okay. Until I did, but it was a challenge."

And so, I told Phoebe the whole story, letting the events wash over me as I relived every detail beginning with changing into my walking shoes, grabbing my himation, and sprinting out the door while tucking my satchel under my sash.

* * *

"Once I folded myself into the litter, Mr. Baruch's bearers swept me southward into the crescendo of the awakening city as it braced itself for the harangue of hawkers, the bickering of moneychangers, and the haggling of vendors. After they dropped me off to park the litter in the outbuilding where they lodge, I elbowed through the onlookers, their wagging tongues, sighs, and creased foreheads gathering at the curb, and watched my shadow pull me up the narrow walk to the metal-studded, sun-bleached oak door. Like the door to a fortress. No wonder. The fear of another Riot waits like a coiled spring in the bowels of those who lost so much.

"Rhea opened the door before I had a chance to knock and greeted me with a tear-stained leathery face atop a spindly neck and a baggy tunic girded at the waist around her scrawny frame. Dusted with cornmeal, she smelled of kitchen grease and dill. 'Oh, Miss Miriam! It's you. Thank Jupiter, you got here.' A little pulse jumped at one corner of her lipless mouth as she pulled me in with an icy hand gnarled with arthritis.

"'Were you expecting someone else?' I asked, turning around to survey the marble atrium. Fingers of a winter sun were poking through the door, stretching across the onyx floor, and dusting the paneled walls frescoed with swirling vines and flowers.

"'Well, with that gawking mob outside—like a pack of dogs—I've never seen such rabble—good-for-nothings, ruffians, like they're at the games waiting for a handout. What's this world coming to? Mr. Ira would be so upset. He'd fret no one'll ever rent here again. But Lycus says they came because they heard me screaming—'

"'Lycus?' I asked.

"'Calix's friend. He rents the room across the hall from, well… Calix is the dead man.' She'd lowered her voice to a whisper as if she might awaken him. Otherwise, her shrillness stabbed my ears like an icepick. 'Calix was a perfect tenant, polite, neat, regular habits, and ever punctual with not just the rent, which, of course he was, but with everything else. And he would tip me on the calends to bring him at seven o'clock every morning some chopped dill stirred into a bowl of gruel to ease the pain in his bowels. Of course, I never told Mr. Ira about that. He'd say he wasn't running a boarding house and it wasn't my business to take money from the tenants. But that's why at precisely seven—well, near enough—I went upstairs to knock on Calix's door just like I always did, but this time he didn't answer. Not a sound. So, I knocked again and again, even calling his name a few times, something I hated doing. If the bearers in the outbuilding slept as lightly as Calix, I knew I'd awaken them too. But that's how frantic I was.'

"'Do you know whether his room was locked?'

"'We all lock our door from the inside with a bolt just above the doorsill in case someone forgets to secure the front door. And all the tenants have a key to both the front door and their room, to lock or unlock it from the outside. But Mr. Ira and I have a duplicate of each tenant's key.' Her bony arm reached inside the bodice of her tunic and withdrew a long, silk cord with several L-shaped latch lifters. I counted four, each with an iron shaft and a unique pattern of teeth.

"'So, what did you do next?' I asked.

"'Well, of course, I did the right thing. I unlocked Calix's door, and there he was just as I pictured him: on his sleeping couch, motionless—'

"She said more, but the blur of words was lost as her features crumpled, her shoulders caved, and her hands flew up to cover her bloodshot eyes and the thousand wrinkles that ringed them. I guided her to the wall to lean against a panel as the tears trickled through her twisted fingers and slid down her hollow cheeks.

"Waiting till her pain ebbed, till she finished wiping her eyes with the heels of her palms and only a watery sheen remained, I prompted, 'You were telling me about Lycus.'

"'Calix and Lycus are friends—I mean were—I don't know what I mean—but they've been renting for the season, till the ports reopen.' She stopped to clear her throat and then continued. 'They're shipmates, came in on the *Sirius* last November.'

"Although I wanted to hear more about the friends and their routines, I was anxious to examine Calix's body and inspect the room before the authorities arrived."

* * *

"Well, so far, the case seems ordinary enough. This Calix either died a natural death—he did have bad bowels—or he was murdered by someone who entered the house, right?"

"Phoebe, Phoebe, Phoebe, you've been with me so long! Those were my very thoughts. I was even ready to dismiss Rhea as a suspect, that's how genuine I thought her grief was except she was, after all, the one who found the body."

"So, what did you find out when you went upstairs?"

"Hold on. I'm coming to that."

* * *

"I followed the bedraggled gray braid that trailed down Rhea's back as it led me to the foot of the sweeping, lantern-lined marble staircase.

"'Wait!' She cried, stopping so abruptly I almost knocked her over. Then, turning to face me, her hand gripping mine like a vice, she sputtered, 'Please understand, Miss Miriam, I cannot go up there. I just can't.' She was trembling like a terracotta puppet controlled by invisible strings. 'I'd heard there was a curse on that room, but now Calix's death is proof.'

"'A curse?'

"Rhea nodded her head several times and swallowed hard. 'That's the room where Mr. Ira's father slept, the room at the top of the landing. In fact, he was sleeping on that very couch when the mob stormed the house and carried him away. Even Mr. Ira refuses to use that room.'

"'So, you think Calix died because he slept in that room?'

"'Well,' said Rhea, cocking her head, 'Can you come up with a better idea?'

"I was certainly going to try."

"So, stooping on some of the steps to pick up shards of pottery speckled with dill, I mounted the stairs and landed in a hallway smelling of polish and punctuated by mahogany doors."

"I stopped at Calix's room, suddenly my senses on alert. Its door had been smashed. Struggling against the urge to rush into the room, I paused to inspect the locks. A latch lifter of the kind on Rhea's cord could certainly have worked the shoulder-high lock. I also examined the keyhole for scratches, but no one had tried to use another key to persuade the lock to give way. Then, when I stepped over the debris to enter the room, I could see from the splintered woodwork that the inside bolt had been wrenched from the door jamb; even its bracket had been split."

* * *

"Oh, Miriam, did you really think the room was cursed?"

"Certainly not in the beginning. I was looking for a rational explanation. But as a solution became ever more remote, I too began to wonder about the curse, even to the point of engaging that oracle by the Gate of the Sun."

Phoebe rubbed her hands together with glee.

"You know the one," I continued, "the blind cyclops named Polyphemus." *Who says Phoebe is the only one with a flair for theatrics?*

"Oh, Miriam!"

"But seriously, I wondered how Rhea got into Calix's room in the first place. She herself said the tenants use the bolt just above the doorsill to lock it from the inside, and she certainly wouldn't have had the strength to breach that bolt let alone smash down the door."

"Okay. Tell me more."

* * *

"I didn't need to walk far into the room to know that Calix was dead. The room itself reeked of death, as if the sour smells of feces and urine had seeped into its very walls. He lay presumably as Rhea found him, on his sleeping couch curled on his left side, his head and body facing the wall. When I leveled his body, I saw that despite its stony stillness, his face was of a once-handsome man. His strong jawline, splendid forehead, and deeply sculpted cheeks were weakened by only the worry lines fanning his eyes.

"His throat had been punctured with a short but sharp blade and with enough force to prevent air from reaching his lungs. Moreover, he must have died quickly because only a ribbon of blood had trickled down from the gash to stain his chest, tunic, and bedding.

"When I lifted the skirt of his embroidered tunic and pressed my lips to his abdomen, his body still felt warm. His arms were only a little cooler judging from the inside of his wrists. So, he hadn't been dead long, perhaps an hour but not more than two. He probably died around the time Rhea brought him the gruel, which we can assume was around seven o'clock, certainly not much before. But there was something else too, an odor to his skin, somewhat like chocolate but with a fishy edge. I couldn't place it then, but when I looked it up in my copy of *De Medicina*, I learned it was opium, the kind from China.

"Still, I had lots more to figure out. Why had Calix gone to bed in his tunic? Had he worn it to go out the night before? And if so, where had he gone, and why hadn't he undressed?

"By now, the morning sun was slipping through the room's one window, the northern rays scissoring through the louvered shutters above Calix's sleeping couch and painting stripes on the polished wooden floor. Its opposing panels were fastened with a hook-and-eye latch, no doubt to keep out the nighttime chill. When I swung them open and looked down, I saw the window was too high for anyone to have entered or left that way, and no tree or building was close enough for someone to have jumped. And then, when I tried to open the window, I confirmed that no one could have passed through it anyway, certainly not recently. An intact vertical web spanned the windowpane, and sure enough, an expectant spider hiding at its edge was guarding its handiwork.

"Next, crouching down, my nose to the floor, I saw that the floorboards, smooth with wear, fit together snugly. Then, lurching to my feet, my muscles aching from the stress, my joints straightening reluctantly, I rapped on the walls. *Solid*, I said to myself, *with no breaks to provide any other way to enter or exit the room.* So, I concluded no one could have entered except through the door.

"Next, I scanned the room's spartan furnishings: the sleeping couch headed by a wicker chair, its wicker seat topped with a thin cushion, and a night table with an earthenware candlestick, a few candles, and a striker and trimmer. Across the room, I noted a flanged chamber pot; a basin and pitcher on a tripod washstand with a razor, comb, and polished bronze mirror; a seaman's chest; and a cedar wardrobe. A lantern hung on the blind wall.

"The wheels of an oxcart grumbling in the distance warned me that the authorities must be on their way, that I would need to hurry to avoid becoming a suspect myself. Still, I took a chance and went right to the wardrobe hoping for a clue as to why he wore a tunic to bed. As expected from the tidiness of his room, his clothes were hung neatly on hooks. He had one other tunic, a blue wool with a geometric border print, and two Indian cotton nightshirts. Next were his himation, a cloak with a hood, and a pair of shoes tied together. Above the hooks was a shelf with his sandals, a purse heavy with coins, a scroll, a seaman's knife, and a bundle of letters. But, as I was about to open the scroll, the stamp of horses' hooves alerted me that the magistrate's soldiers had just turned into Mr. Baruch's street."

* * *

"Oh, Miriam, what did you do?" Phoebe looked at me with a sudden arrested attention.

"I listened to my heart pounding like a sledgehammer."

"But what did—?"

I held up my hand to silence her. "Give me a chance, Phoebe!" I took that moment to gather some more shreds of memory until I could once again hear the clop of the horses turning the corner and the soldiers' hobnail boots scratching the pavement in front of Mr. Baruch's house.

"Remember I had my satchel with me, that I'd tucked it under my sash when I ran out?"

"Oh, no, Miriam. You didn't!" She said, gripping the edge of the bench and leaning forward.

"I had no choice. Any minute the authorities would come pounding up the steps, and still I had no answers. In fact, based on the likely time of Calix's death, Rhea had to be my prime suspect. But how could such a timid old woman have even broken down the door? Besides, what could her motive have been? I could only wonder whether she'd accurately reported the event to me. But again, I couldn't figure out a motive for her lying either.

"Even more to the point, I felt a duty to Mr. Baruch. The only asset his poor father could leave him was the house itself. Everything inside had been plundered during the Riots. And, as if that wasn't enough, the looters smashed the shutters and hurled their torches through the open windows. It took years for Mr. Baruch to rebuild. So, the only way he can pay his taxes is to keep lodgers, who certainly won't rent when they hear rumors of a curse and an unsolved murder.

"So, I did what I had to do. I thrust everything—the letters, knife, scroll, and purse—into my satchel and clattered down the stairs shouting to Rhea that I'd be back later. The door clanged shut as I raced down the walk, and turning the corner, I dove into the tide of shoppers."

"Well, I'm dying to know about the letters. You said Calix was handsome. I'll bet they were from some mysterious woman he met on an exotic voyage!" Phoebe's whole body wriggled with excitement.

"Don't worry, I'll get to that. But first, to calm myself, I wended my way toward the local plaza. As long as I had my satchel, I figured I may as well pick up some raspberries from our vendor. You remember Nestor? He was standing by his cart—"

"Miriam!"

"Well, okay, I did skip the fruit," I said feigning irritation. "But if you'll stop interrupting me, I'll tell you all about the letters and everything else I took from his room."

* * *

"I got home from Mr. Baruch's house around noon. Tiptoeing into the library, I held my breath like a common thief before dumping the contents of my satchel onto the cherrywood table and putting all but the bundle of letters in the back of the lowest shelf of the hutch. You probably remember my cubbies there, where I used to keep my souvenirs and the figurines that belonged to my mother.

"Then I untied the letters and skimmed through them. Right away I could tell they were all from the same person, a woman who wrote with the strong slant and even script of an innocent schoolgirl. She'd signed them 'Your faithful Helen.' Presumably she was his fiancée, and the letters were her half of a lengthy and ongoing correspondence in which she longed for their coming wedding. She praised his maintaining his connections with the traders he'd met on his voyages and saving the money to open a spice shop upon their marriage.

"After that, I swapped the letters for his scroll and purse. The purse held ten drachmas (about $500 in US currency), a considerable amount of walking around money. It was the scroll though that surprised me. According to the entries—it was a ledger of sorts—he'd been making sizeable deposits at the Bank of Gabinius, his winnings from playing knucklebones at the Lady Luck, one of the sleazy saloons lining the waterfront. Already he'd accumulated a hefty sum, over a thousand drachmas, more than enough to buy a barrow for his business and a slave in his prime to help run it. Finally, I slid the knife out of its sheath and examined it: nothing remarkable, clean and sharp, the kind of short straight blade every seaman carries to cut rope."

* * *

"So, what did you make of all that?" asked Phoebe, her forehead crinkling like a fan.

"Well, I had some facts, but I still didn't know who killed Calix and more baffling, how the murderer got in and out of that room. I only knew it couldn't have happened as Rhea reported it. Calix's doorsill lock had been engaged, and she couldn't have broken down the door by herself.

"By this time, of course, I'd already concluded that suicide was impossible. He'd died almost instantly with no bloody knife near his body, or, for that matter, anywhere he might have flung it. His upcoming marriage, his plans to establish a business, and his having continued to save money toward those goals merely confirmed my judgment.

"It was murder all right, and now I had a lead for a motive. Who'd been gambling with Calix at the Lady Luck? So, my next priorities were to sneak the items back into Calix's wardrobe and ask more questions."

"Oh, Miriam, I wish I could have been on that case with you. Remember in Caesarea when I spotted—"

"*Shsh.* That mission was dangerous enough and could still have dire consequences. But you were fearless, the bravest scout anyone could have. Ever!"

Phoebe's long jeweled earrings jingled as she wriggled again, this time with pleasure, and then shifting the cushions, she leaned back for more of the story.

* * *

"The authorities left Mr. Baruch's front door unlocked when they took Calix's body away. I knew that because after threading my way past the few remaining loiterers still milling about as they speculated on the morning's events, I was able to slip into the house easily. The clang of pots and the smell of scorched pans told me Rhea was busy in the kitchen. The house seemed otherwise empty, so I let my swift light feet carry me up the stairs and stepped over the debris that still littered the hall in front of Calix's room.

"My body stiffened as my gaze swept the room. It looked as if it had been burgled. The wardrobe doors were flung open, the garments in a heap, and the contents of the seaman's chest (a pair of deerskin boots, tattered blankets, and some smaller items I didn't have a chance to inventory) were strewn about along with the things that had been on the tripod stand and the now-toppled night table. The stench of dung from the soldiers' boots and the ever-present stink of their beer, sweat, and arrogance brooded over the chaos.

"I held onto Calix's items, but more than ever, I had to speak with Rhea.

"Refusing to listen to my inner voice urging me to calm down, I scuttled down the steps and barged into the kitchen.

"'Rhea, what happened to Calix's room?'

"Turning around while wiping her hands on the towel about her waist, she stared at me in horror. 'What do you mean?'

"'It's been burgled!'

"Fear hardened her eyes into dark pebbles. 'I told you there's a curse on that room.' Her voice had risen to a metallic shriek. Then, perhaps reining in some of that fear, she added with a deep sigh and mellower voice, 'I've told you everything I know.'

"*Easy, Miriam,* I thought. *She's your principal witness. Don't turn her into your principal adversary.* 'I know you have, but maybe you'll remember more if we talk a while.'

"'Like what?' She snapped. But then her shoulders melted, and she pointed with her chin to a pair of wrought iron stools under the workbench adjacent to her oven.

"I pulled out the stools but kept them close together. With our knees nearly touching, I could gauge her emotions. I still had so many doubts about her.

"'This morning, when you found Calix,' I asked, 'what was he wearing?'

"'Why a nightshirt, of course!'

"'But when I saw his body, he was dressed in an embroidered tunic as if he'd gone to bed wearing it. How do you explain that?'

"Her eyes flew open. 'Well, I'm not his wife! How in the name of Jupiter should I know what he wears to bed!'

"'Rhea, you were the first to discover the body. Your observations are crucial to finding Calix's killer. You want to do that, don't you?'

"She bowed her head and nodded over and over.

"'I know you do. That's why you sent for me. You were frightened. What frightened you?'

"She murmured to her knees. 'He didn't answer the door like he always did, even though he was such a light sleeper. He always met me at the door. Instead, I stood in the hall holding his bowl of gruel, you know, with the dill for his bowels. It was so quiet, so very quiet inside his room. And I knew he had an early appointment at the bank—'

"Her legs twitched, her features convulsed, and then clumps of sound gushed out of her in a rising howl. 'I saw him with my own eyes, but how can you expect me to remember what he was wearing? And then the bowl fell to the floor. I tell you, the curse did that! Probably just when Charon was ferrying his soul across the River Styx. Oh, I wish I'd never brought him that gruel this morning! Seeing him like that, lying on his back, cold and stiff, that ghastly pool of blood, his skull crushed, his face bloated with death, his eyes bulging, will haunt me forever.'

"'You poor, poor dear,' I said, patting her knee as she hiccupped with sobs. But now I no longer had to wonder how she breeched Calix's doorsill lock.

15

She simply didn't.

"I waited for Rhea to calm down, but the truth is I needed the time myself to digest her answer. When at last her tears dried to a crust, I asked my other question. 'Rhea, can you tell me where Calix went last night?'

"'Not exactly. They'd been—'

"'They?'

"'Lycus, him and Lycus. They'd been drinking. Must have been. But how would I know where sailors go? All I know is they came home late, so late I'd already gone to sleep. But even so, they woke me. And even from my room at the back of the house, I could hear Lycus's uneven footfalls as he helped Calix up the steps.'

"I almost believed in Rhea's curse because at that moment I too heard uneven footfalls mounting the stairs. And I shuddered."

* * *

"Okay, so she answered your questions, but she must have told you something else because I can tell you're holding something back from me."

"Remember, Phoebe, I told you I couldn't solve the case until I used my intuition?"

"So?" Phoebe rolled her hands forward like little wheels.

"After I spoke with Rhea, I was able to do just that."

"You mean you figured it all out?" Phoebe sucked in her lower lip, frowned, and then drummed her fingers on the table. "But I still don't get it. What am I missing?"

"Well, I haven't finished yet. I had one more person to interview."

* * *

"His little cage of a room exhaled the stench of ripe clothing and the acrid grease of tallow wicks. Low-raftered and with a sagging wooden floor, it had space for only a trunk, a chamber pot under the washstand, a pallet—really just a puddle of straw—and a couple of benches against the windowed wall where we sat. The other walls were paneled in a dark wood that sucked up whatever was left of the late-afternoon light.

"'Okay, I know how you did it, but I don't know why, though I have a pretty good idea. Was it because of money?'

"He was so quiet, so deep in thought, that I began to wonder whether he even heard my question. But then his face collapsed in despair, and his brooding eyes stared down at the bitten-back nails of his ropy hands while mine surveyed his room.

"His meaty shoulders sank. 'Sort of. Yeah, money was a big part of it.'

"I waited for him to find the words to continue."

"'Calix was saving money for a new life with his girl, Helen, so he wouldn't have to go to sea no more. But never in all the years since Ephesus, did he mention rewarding me for saving his life.'

"I looked into the weathered face of this bullnecked sailor, his burly chest pressing against the contours of his tunic, his arms as substantial as battering rams, his calloused hands knotted with snaking veins. His torso ended with a left thigh as solid as a tree trunk, but his right one looked as spindly as a sapling."

"'His life?' I asked.

"'Yeah. Calix loved to gamble, and he was good at it too. Maybe too good. We was best buddies, him and me, see?' I saw the memory twitch behind Lycus's eyes. 'And we'd go to The Dionysus. That's the tavern in Ephesus where all this happened. They had this backroom—probably still do—where you could play knucklebones all night. And he was winning big time when this granite slab of a man waved his cudgel and accused my buddy of cheating. There must have been several thugs there. Okay, maybe just two or three. So, we got into this brawl. The one with a bull-dog face and a swag of fat over his belt. I must have broke his jaw the way his mouth flapped open and his eyes rolled back."

"'I smashed the other's face too. He went down with a groan, flat on his back, smacked the floor so hard it felt like an earthquake. That's when Calix snatched his money and ran, which left me to fight it out with Granite Slab. I remember him swinging that cudgel. Oh, he worked me over real good.

Polished it on this here right leg of mine. Busted the bone in a thousand pieces. I can still hear the sniggers as I hopped away on the good one.

"'Oh, he patted me on the back all right, Calix did. He'd been listening for me in the latrine next door. So, he hired a litter—big deal—to take us back to the ship and paid some slave to wrap my leg. But after that, I could never earn the wages he did. Wrenching pain unless I have my helper right here.' He patted the leather purse fixed to his belt. 'But the worst of it is this here wobbly leg of mine. When the *Sirius*—she's our ship—is heaving and swaying and the foam is reaching out to throw me overboard, my good buddy just guffaws, having a high old time chasing the froth around the deck.

"'But like I said, he never offered to compensate me for the leg I lost that night. Never even asked! What a buddy! By rights, some of his money is mine.'

"Then, closing his eyes and shaking his head, he bit the corner of his thumb and spat out a sliver of cuticle. 'You know, I wouldn't have killed him if the pieces hadn't fit together.'

"'The pieces?'

"'Well, we went out to the Lady Luck last night. I knew I shouldn't 'a' gone, but what am I supposed to do? And yeah, he gambled a lot. Me? I just watched. I knew I wasn't in his league. Never was. But when he hunched over the table and winced, I went over. 'What's the matter, buddy?' I asked. He said, 'Nails in my bowels. You got something?' He meant the opium I always carry for this here leg. I fished a pinch out of my purse and gave it to him. Anyway, that was the first piece.

"'His grimace soon softened into a tentative smile, but he could barely stand up. "Time to go," I said as I stuffed his money into his purse, about ten drachmas. He was in no condition to object. So, I hired a litter to take us home, eased him up the stairs, took his key ring, unlocked the door, helped him in, and slipped the key ring back on his finger.

"'I was about to leave when he asked for another pinch, bigger this time to get him through the night. "The nighttime chill is stirring up my bowels again," he said. Or maybe I offered. I forget. Gave him all I had with me just to shut him up. His moans—like they were scraping his throat—really got to me. Anyway, I heard him bolt the lock above the doorsill as soon as I left, but the second dose probably kicked in before he got undressed for the night.

"'Of course, he never did engage his outside lock last night, though the doorsill bolt was still fastened. But that half-wit Rhea would never have gone in anyway. Claimed his room was cursed. So, there she was early this morning, screeching for Calix like a caged fowl awaiting the butcher's knife. Then, thinking he was dead instead of stoned, shrieking for the bearers, she dropped that bowl of swill. If her shouts hadn't yanked me out of my stupor, the shards clanging down the steps sure did.

"'But I'm getting ahead of myself. When I left Calix's room last night, I went to bed. That was when the pain, probably from helping him up the stairs, hit like a bolt of lightning and hurled me back to that night in Ephesus smelling Granite Slab's stink. Tears flooded my eyes, enough to drown him, but that grotesque image of Calix running out of The Dionysus burrowed into my brain instead and rekindled my bitterness. That's the piece I meant to tell you about before I told you how Rhea woke up the neighborhood.

"'The doorsill lock was bolted so I busted down the door. At the time, I half expected to see him dead. Thought I'd take his purse. You know, he owed me for getting him home safe. But when I saw him sleeping, his mouth slack, breathing deeply as only the drugged can, I took out my knife. It was as easy as cutting through air. I wanted to be quick—Rhea was calling for the bearers but could come back any minute—so I figured I'd go back for his purse later. I should have realized the authorities would beat me to it. Those vultures are worse than the tax collectors! I know. And then later, when I came back for the purse, I rifled through his wardrobe. Really tore the place apart. Nothing. Not a drachma. They'd taken everything. Anyway, I didn't really kill him for the money. I killed him because he was just so cheap. Like when he took my opium, he didn't offer to pay for that neither.'"

* * *

"So, Miriam, whatever happened to Lycus?"

"Well, I agreed not to report him to the magistrates. I had no proof anyway, and he'd have that wasted leg forever. But I did make some demands: That he tell me how to find Helen. I wanted to send her the letters, the purse with the drachmas Calix won that night, and his ledger, which listed his deposits at the Bank of Gabinius. And as important, I demanded that Lycus leave the city immediately and dedicate his life to helping the poor."

"And did he do that?"

"I think so. Once in a while, he pays a scribe to send me a message. At first, he was assisting in the soup kitchens of Rome, but last I heard, and that was several years ago, he was working in a leper colony there."

"All that sounds fair. You're not the Roman Law, after all, and Isis knows they've sent enough men to the lions to let one go free."

"Well, for a while I worried that I might have failed Mr. Baruch because the murder was never officially solved. But by the next winter, given the exorbitant rents here, he had his pick of sailors whether or not they'd heard about the curse, or the murder committed there."

"Well, I still have one more question. I can see how and why Lycus killed Calix, but I still don't understand how you figured it out."

"I didn't know, at least not at first. I thought Rhea killed Calix, but I was looking at only her facts. She said she found the body. He was killed at about that time. I hadn't yet thought to assess her reliability as a witness until, quite unexpectedly, she described Calix with his skull crushed. Remember I saw only a ribbon of blood. That's when I knew she hadn't really seen him. But I also knew, given her details, that she thought she had. You see when someone as punctual as Calix—and with an important meeting besides—didn't answer her call as he had so many times before, she believed he was dead. It was a case of 'believing is seeing' rather than the other way around."

"Oh, Miriam, you're the best, but I still wish Rhea had been hiding an exotic woman in the kitchen."

"Speaking of the kitchen, I hear someone on the stairs, and if I'm not mistaken, she's bringing us a Shabbat lunch of cold lamb in a fragrant plum sauce and a salad of wild greens and berries."

The Brother

The Eighth Year of the Reign of
Nero Claudius Caesar Augustus Germanicus [Nero]
62 CE, Mid-March
Alexandria *ad Aegyptum*

I t was almost noon on the Ides of March when my house servant, Minta, recognizing the frantic jingle of bells as those on Phoebe's litter, rushed into the late winter chill to greet her at the entrance to our townhouse. "Miriam! Miriam!" The urgency in Phoebe's voice rang through the house.

A moment later, my best friend was plunging through the ceiling-high, double mahogany doors of my study. I looked up from my desk and had to remind myself to breathe.

Her cheeks flushed, her shoulders rigid under her crimson *stola* and the matching silk himation, she stared at me with wild eyes before dropping into the *sella* opposite me. To calm my own blood hammering like a clapper inside a bell, I focused on the scent of alarm in her perspiration.

"Tell me, Phoebe."

Wringing her hands together, she squeezed out the bitter words. "It's gone, absolutely gone. Menander's *Dyskolos*. The edition Bion brought me from Athens. We'd been keeping it on display in the shop to attract customers. You remember—"

For an instant I caught a nascent glitter in her eyes as she reminded me that Bion had picked out this play for her because in the story, Sostratos falls instantly in love with Knemon's daughter just as he fell in love with her.

"When, Phoebe? When did it disappear?"

"I'm not sure. I hadn't been to the shop lately. I only went this morning to help rearrange the shelves for a shipment due this week."

And then with tears flooding her cheeks, her eyes a little bigger as they fixed me with a searching look, I felt the question in her gaze.

"Of course, Phoebe. And we'll find it. That I promise you."

* * *

I entered the shop on a shaft of afternoon sunlight slanting under the *stoa*'s portico. Bion, maneuvering his paunch with the skill of a sea captain, sailed around the half-empty boxes of scrolls and stationery supplies to greet me. His easy smile turned his gold-flecked eyes into fringed slits and his chubby cheeks into pomegranates.

When Bion met Phoebe, he was a public slave repairing scrolls in the workshop of the Great Library. Eventually he was sold to a Jewish sandal-maker and bibliophile in Caesarea who liberated him after six years as is the custom with our people. Along with the quitclaim, his master gave him enough money to establish a business repairing and selling rare scrolls. Now Bion owns a thriving *bibliopōleion* in the agora, where he deals in rare classical manuscripts as well as the contemporary works of scholars like Thrasyllus of Mendes and engineers like our very own Hero.

"Oh, Bion, I'm so sorry!"

"I see Phoebe's already told you. She mentioned when she was here earlier that she'd stop by to see you. She's quite upset. Actually, we both are. But let me show you where it was displayed."

I followed his stubby shadow as it looped around the stacks of manuscripts and knots of customers buzzing about the counters, tables, and shelves until we reached the empty vitrine at the front of the shop.

"How much could that scroll be worth today?"

His voice dropped to a whisper. "About 2000 drachmas, enough to buy the grandest house."

A fishy reflux rose in my gorge.

"Quite rare," he continued. "An almost complete edition of what is still regarded as the best example of Athenian New Comedy."

I pinched my lips. *By now, it could be on a ship headed anywhere.*

"It was right here." Bion, in a characteristic gesture, pointed with his chin. Then he threw up his hands in despair.

After swallowing hard, his face softened, and he jerked his head toward the young man walking toward us. "But wait. I'm forgetting my manners. Let me introduce my new apprentice, Varius. Surely Phoebe's told you he and his brother are lodging with us."

Rare for me, I had to look up to meet the deep-set dark eyes of the trim, immaculately dressed man before me. Cleanshaven, baldheaded, and with the immovable face and bearing of a military officer, he exuded the somewhat sweet leathery scent of the labdanum that oiled his body.

"Welcome to Alexandria," I said.

He seemed pleasant enough. When I asked him how he happened to come here, he answered that he and his brother were eager to escape the stench of Nero's Rome. "It hovers over the city like a fog, enough to make even the dogs sneeze." He spoke our Greek smoothly but with the limestone-edged consonants of a Roman.

"So how did you find Varius?" I asked when Bion and I had taken our usual places in his office behind the scrim at the back of the shop.

We were sitting across from each other at the rosewood table that stretches across the room. Facing the marble-topped cabinets that frame the lone, east-facing window, I had a chance once again to admire the tidy elegance of his office. No careless piles of scrolls or sheets of papyrus shingled its surfaces. Instead, the busts of classical dramatists, poets, and philosophers peered out from their niches.

"Actually, he found me. He answered the ad to let our upstairs apartment that Phoebe had posted at the East Gate. He wanted it for himself and his brother, and when I saw how learned he was, that he'd even studied rhetoric and grammar with the disciples of Pliny the Elder, I invited him to be my apprentice as well.

"You know Thoth and Galen have been with me for years, ever since

Caesarea, but I just felt we needed the energy of someone younger. Even with Phoebe's occasional help, we barely keep up with shelving the new supplies as they come in. As you can see for yourself," he added with a rueful smile and a sweep of his arm.

"His brother had been staying at The Pegasus—"

"Oh, no! Not that slimy box of depravity—"

"—And working as the night watchman at the warehouse behind the Flamingo's Tongue. Actually, I've never met brothers more different. There's a family resemblance to be sure—both tall and swarthy—but otherwise they're completely different and not just in appearance but in personality and accomplishments too. Dario—that's his brother's name. Did I already mention that?"

I offered Bion a crisp shake of my head, but with unfocused eyes, he was already organizing his impression of Dario.

"He carries his head cocked to the right as if he were balancing a barrel of henket on his left shoulder. And, oh yes, his hair is thick—like a hedge of curls—and grows low on his brow before crawling down his cheeks and flowering out of his nostrils and ears. And—forgive me for saying this—he smells like a stable.

"Well, Varius signed the lease for both of them on the calends, and they moved in right away, Dario sometime that day and Varius that evening."

"Let me ask you this, Bion: When did you notice the manuscript was missing?"

"I wish I could say for sure—I've been in and out of the shop arranging credit for the next shipment—but surely within the last couple of days. *Hmm.*" And then pausing with half-closed eyes as if reading the information on the inside of his lids, he declared. "Yes, it was yesterday. Had to be. That's when I told Phoebe."

"And is there a key to the vitrine?"

"Yes, four, one for each of us," he said, ticking them off on his fingers. "Phoebe and me, Thoth and Galen—No, make that five. Varius has one too. I had a key made for him just this week. And, of course, we kept the cabinet locked. Besides, my regulars knew the manuscript wasn't for sale, and it was much too expensive for anyone coming in off the street."

I nodded.

"Please, Miriam, do what you can to find it, especially for Phoebe."

"It'll be okay. You'll see," I said in that phony singsong I use whenever I want to sound more confident than I feel. I knew it wasn't going to be easy, but I could never have imagined what was in store for Bion and me.

* * *

It was the next day when looking up, I saw Bion standing at the threshold of my study framed in the bloom of late-morning light.

"Miriam, something bizarre has happened."

I put aside my reagents—I'd been perfecting the fabrication of pearls—got up from my workbench and slid into the chair behind my ebony desk. Bion flopped into the *sella* across from me.

He looked past me for a while, beyond the purple-tied-back drapes, as if intent on watching the light finger its way between the columns of the peristyle. He didn't speak until the incessant squawking of a crow punched the stillness.

I hinged forward.

"Listen, I'm sorry to bother you again, especially after yesterday, but Varius told me this morning that Dario didn't come back from the warehouse after his nightshift. That's when they have breakfast together." Confusion and worry competed for purchase on Bion's face. "Do you think this could have anything to do with the manuscript?"

"I think you need to alert the authorities."

Bion sighed with exasperation.

* * *

"You were loitering outside a brothel this afternoon." The twinkle in Judah's luminous green eyes belied his flinty tone as he regarded me over the rim of his wine goblet.

25

"Well, yes, and not just one." I replied, leaning forward, raising an imperious eyebrow.

"Look, I knew when I married you that you were *unusual*—"

"I hope you mean—"

"Okay. I should have said *special*, but I hardly expected to hear that you'd be passing your afternoons outside brothels, saloons, latrines, soup kitchens—"

"Oh, that must have been Aspasia who spotted me. For a while this afternoon, I was near her apothecary. And then she must have stopped by your shop."

"Spoken like an astute detective. But don't you send Phoebe to do your undercover work?"

"This time I couldn't. Bion needs her in the shop right now. Besides, he doesn't want her involved in our latest investigation. Too upsetting."

I saw through the windowpane shadows of the leaves shivering in the wind as Judah and I sat in our dining room. Waiting for Minta to serve us boiled capon in a honey glaze with a platter of cucumbers garnished with dill, we snacked on a tray of olives and deviled eggs. A spike of pepper tickled my tongue and sharpened my memory of that first encounter with Judah, that unexpected ache when I'd walked into his jewelry shop to collect the mortgage payment, he owed my father. As he leaned toward me to hand me the envelope, close enough for our air to mingle and for his hand to brush against mine, he ignited my embryonic fantasies of love. Now, sixteen years later, his eyes are still framed by a dreamer's lashes, but his wreath of black, glossy curls is lit with silver.

"So, tell me about your investigation."

"Bion and I are trying to recover a scroll stolen from his *bibliopōleion*. At the same time, the brother of his new apprentice, a night watchman at one of the warehouses, didn't return home after his shift last night."

"You suspect a connection?"

"Well, I don't believe in coincidences, and his brother could have known about the manuscript and, at least indirectly, had access to it."

"So, you and Bion went searching for the brother today."

"And Varius—he's the apprentice—he checked some places too."

I gave Judah a thumbnail description of Dario based on Bion's report, that he's hairy, cocks his head to the right, and smells like a stable.

"Well, with a description like that, he shouldn't be too hard to find."

"Spoken like the deputy to an astute detective," I said, "especially when you have a friend like Aspasia, but I believe Dario must have absconded with the manuscript by now."

Such was my opinion at the time, but I couldn't have been more wrong.

* * *

I waited anxiously for any news of Dario or the manuscript. I heard nothing, not a word despite slogging every day through the tide of vehicles, dodging bullying oxcarts and getting trapped behind clots of hawkers and gawkers. Nothing, not a word despite my daily rounds to every barber shop, tavern, brothel, soup kitchen, latrine, moneychanger's stall, and port official. When I went to the warehouse behind the Flamingo's Tongue with Bion's description of Dario, even the guards claimed not to know him.

But I got an update a week later when Bion stopped by to tell me about the two granite-faced soldiers who'd swaggered into his shop.

"They barged in, flaunting their red-crested helmets and iron cuirasses as if they were going to arrest us all. I heard only their hobnail boots scrape the tile floor—which they carpeted with filth by the way—until one of them summoned me by name."

Bion described him as pear-shaped, the other as lanky. The pear-shaped one handed him a cylinder of parchment sealed with a puddle of wax bearing the magistrate's signet. Then Bion watched the backs of their scarlet capes billow and snap as they passed under the portico, mounted their horses, and vanished in a geyser of dust.

His fingers trembled as he tore through the seal to read the memorandum and then pass it to Varius. The substance was that Dario's body had been found floating in the canal that crosses the *Rhakotis* quarter.

"'Oh Jupiter, how can this be?' Varius asked, his hand to his cheek as though he had a toothache. 'And where on Earth is this canal and this

Rhak—whatever-it-is?'"

Bion then explained to his stunned apprentice that *Rhakotis*, our oldest residential quarter, is in the western section of the city, where most of the Egyptians who work in the shipyards and on the quays live. He tactfully refrained from adding that the quarter is blighted by poverty, pestilence, and violence and that murderers lurk there to prey on the nameless and dump their corpses in its malignant canal.

"But," Bion added, "it was even harder telling Varius that the authorities wanted the next of kin to identify the body. I thought he'd want to—you know, his chance to say good-bye, his filial duty and all that—but no, he boggled as soon as I mentioned it.

"'Could you do that for me?' he asked.

"My mouth hinged open. 'Look,' I said, 'I'm just his landlord, and not for so very long at that. I saw Dario a few times running down the steps, rushing to the warehouse—oh, and that one morning when he came to the shop to tell me you'd be late—but as his brother, your word would be beyond dispute.'

"'But you know him—I mean *knew* him,' he pleaded. I tell you, Miriam, his voice was pitiable. 'And I can mind the shop while you're gone. Really, I can. I just don't think I can bear to see my brother like that.' His hand felt like a claw as he gripped my wrist.

"Well, you know what a pushover I am. I told him I'd do it providing I could get you to accompany m—"

"Me? You must be kidding."

"Miriam, dread was consuming him like a fever."

"You want me to vouch for the identity of a man I've never seen?" My voice came out like the rasp of metal on stone.

Bion's cheeks turned crimson. "Listen, the truth is corpses surface in that canal every morning, more than anyone can count, let alone investigate. I was notified simply because I reported Dario missing. But that doesn't mean I can make sense of a body that's been putrefying maybe for days in that nasty scum. That's why I need your help, you know? Besides, you're a Roman citizen, so I figured your statement would be more persuasive than mine alone."

"Well, I do want to get to the bottom of this—at least to recover the manuscript—and Dario, or what was once Dario, may be our only clue. So yes, I'll go with you."

And then, as the corners of my mouth lifted, I asked with a hint of mischief peppering my voice, "If we hurry, do we still have time to get to the morgue today? It's inside the Palace of Justice."

Bion pointed his chin toward our side street where his litter waited.

* * *

We cruised southward and then westward in a grim silence. Blades of the late-afternoon sun spilled through the colonnades, porticoes, and arcades; stabbed my eyes; and forced them to the pavement, where I saw torch lighters refreshing the wooden staves with a mixture of sulfur and lime.

Knowing the importance of spectacle, the Romans had designed their Palace of Justice to be a perfectly proportioned repository for their official records. From the vine-covered, wrought iron gate to its twin marble columns, we mounted the long flat steps to its double-arched doors.

An albino guard in scarlet livery squinted at the fibula that distinguishes me as a Roman citizen and scrutinized the seal on the parchment Bion presented. Then he called to a flat-faced soldier to escort us to the morgue. Crossing a grand hall redolent of exotic perfumes, pomades, and unguents, we passed the high arched windows that splashed long slants of sunlight across the mosaic floor and dusted the clerks with glitter. Finally, we followed the soldier's easy stride through a tangle of corridors to a narrow flight of stone steps. Claiming two portable lanterns from a stand in the landing, igniting them with his fire steel, and handing one to Bion, he opened the thin sheet of mica on his lamp to direct an amber beam down the steps and into the low-raftered chamber that was the morgue.

The thud of his military boots and the rhythmic clang of his sword against his thigh filled the stairwell.

The air exhaled a chill.

The stench, a hideous brew of decay and human waste, rushed up the stairwell, growing closer and heavier as we made our way down. A fit of retches ripped through Bion, his face turning a bright pink before he covered his nose with the tail of his himation. My own skin turned clammy as a foul taste collected on my lips. Worsened by underventilation, the stink hung over the chamber like a mist.

Excusing himself in a coarse Latin, the soldier left to fetch the body. The clip of his heels on the stone floor returned a feeble echo. Otherwise, we waited in the gloom watching the lantern lick at the darkness while the time passed with appalling slowness.

My heart fluttered with expectancy as he rolled the gurney toward us. The corpse lay on his back. First, I checked the tag tied to his toe. It read *Rhakotis*, the date, and Dario's name.

His flesh was half gone. What remained was bloated, bloodless, and bleached to a pale yellow with clumps of algae in his eye sockets. The cause of death was not obvious until I lifted his skull and found the rear portion had been crushed into a spongy mass, the result of a savage blow. One-by-one I called out these observations to Bion, who was standing behind me, his shoulders bunched, still recovering from his fit. The soldier stood in a far corner rocking on his heels.

"I need you here, Bion. Tell me whether you recognize Dario."

Bion edged up to the gurney on trembling legs, coughing as he tried to suppress another retch. "You know, I don't think there's enough left of him for me to know. *Hmm.* The build seems right, though. Can you straighten out his limbs so I can get a better idea? Here, I'll help you lift him."

"Look, Bion. He's missing a hand, his left. Was Dario missing a hand?"

"No. Certainly not. But maybe he lost it when he was killed."

So, I examined the stump and removed what was left of his tunic to see whether he'd suffered other traumas. Meanwhile, Bion stared at the ceiling, now and then closing his eyes.

"The scarring around the stump is old. Look how white it is compared to the rest of his arm. Not even any redness, which means the injury occurred years ago."

Bion pinched his face and nodded.

"And here's something else. There's a fuller's mark on his tunic."

"So?"

I turned to Bion with a single nod. "That must have been how the authorities identified him as Dario. They recognized the fuller from his mark and then checked his customer list against your missing person's report. Still, regardless of the fuller, I'm convinced this man couldn't be Dario, not with that missing hand."

"Me, too. So, I'll call the soldier. Let's sign the statement, and then we can tell Varius the good news."

"But now we have two new questions: What happened to Dario? And why was someone else wearing his clothes?"

* * *

We folded ourselves back into the litter and headed toward Bion and Phoebe's house and Varius's apartment. Our shadow crawled alongside us as we passed arcades and monuments flecked with the last shards of daylight. I wrapped my arms around my chest to fend off the evening chill and clamped my jaws shut so my teeth would stop rattling like a backroom dice game. At the same time, a bead of sweat trickled down my spine. And then the bearers stopped and lowered us to the pavement in front of a three-story limestone townhouse, prim, solid, and respectable, with a dim yellow light shining through a window veiled in lace.

My arms swung with lightness as we carried our good news through the red marble atrium, its walls veneered in the latest style and its mosaic floor patterned with scenes from *The Odyssey*.

"Where's Phoebe?" I asked.

"Her shift tonight at the soup kitchen. Let's go right upstairs to see Varius. The news is worth interrupting his dinner if we have to." I could hear the relief that had seeped into Bion's voice.

He took the oil lamp from the window and led the way up the curved marble staircase to the second floor. From there, we took a narrow wooden staircase to a hallway punctuated by the thick oak door that was the entrance to the brothers' apartment.

Bion knocked gently at first, but with no response, he became more insistent until he was pounding on the door, calling Varius by name.

"Gee. Where could he be?" I asked.

Another shrug, this time in despair. "He should have come back from the shop already, and it's too early for the saloons, not that he's the type. He could have ordered dinner from a cookshop, but surely he'd have brought it home to await our news."

"Do you have a key?"

"Oh, Miriam, I couldn't do that, invade his privacy like th—"

"He won't even know," I pressed. "We don't have to touch anything. I just think these are exceptional times. And if something did happen to his brother—and I'm convinced it did—that same thing could be happening to Varius."

Bion put up his hand to stop me, but I could see him debating with himself. "I don't kn—"

"And look. He is, after all, more than just your tenant. He's your apprenti—"

He threw up his hands. "Okay, okay. I'll unlock the door."

* * *

We entered the apartment like thieves. Holding our breath, dragging our shadows behind us, we tiptoed along the polished oak floor of a square room tucked under the eaves of the house, its one heavily draped window facing the harbor. The mournful ring of a buoy and the groan of an oxcart slipped through the drape.

Bion's lamp painted the gloom with a watery light.

"*Whew*! What is that?" A menacing stench was seeping into my nostrils.

"Holy Isis, that's an animal stink."

"Have they been keeping animals here?"

"Not that I know of. Why would they?"

We looked at each other in bafflement as Bion swiveled his head from side to side. His eyes widening, his words tumbled out in a thin, high pitch.

32

"This place is all but empty, just the furniture that comes with the apartment. Look, even the shelves are bare."

"Only one sleeping couch?"

"They're here together only at breakfast. But did you hear me? The place is empty!"

And then I felt a pinch in my gut and could taste the tang of acid in my throat. "Wait! What's that?" I gasped, pointing to the washstand, my arm twitching like a branch in the wind.

"What? This? The head? It's a wig holder. Made of wood. Phoebe has several."

I exploded with barks of laughter that I could stop only by stuffing my knuckles in my mouth. "Yikes, I thought it was Varius, his head I mean. But didn't you tell me Varius is bald, and Dario's hair is thick? You said 'like a hedge of curl—'"

"Quick, Miriam!" He gestured me toward him with a series of arm rolls. "Over here, by the cooking furnace. The smell is even stronger."

"Oh, Lord!" I slapped my mouth with an open palm as I edged toward the counter above the furnace. "These are hoofs. They've been making glue from the hoofs of horses!"

"But why?" Incredulity spilled from Bion's voice.

"We have to search the apartment."

"But they have rights under their lease. You said we wouldn't touch anyth—"

"The manuscript is here, Bion. I know it is. You search the washstand, wardrobe, and sleeping couch. I'll check the rest. And don't forget to look for hiding places in the walls and floor around them."

I found nothing in and around the shelves and table and chairs, so I hunkered down and inched along the floorboards, oscillating my head, my eyes raking the strips for any gap, any disruption in the grain of the wood. My palms extended, my fingers fanned, feeling the sting of dust chafing my fingertips, I paused only to pick at a drop of dried spill and dislodge some grit from the corner of my eye.

Then staggering to my feet, wiping my palms together, calming my skirt, and brushing the grime from my hem, I rapped on each wall, my ear flush with its surface, listening for any hollowness. At the same time, I heard the dry complaint of the wardrobe doors as Bion swung them open and their wheeze as he slammed them closed.

"Miriam, the wardrobe is bare, like they were never here and never coming—"

"Take your time around the sleeping couch. Check under the bed linen, mattress pad, and pillows."

Between the slaps of my own footsteps, I heard the crack of his knees as he skirted around the sleeping couch, his weight shifting as he snapped the sheets, his himation swishing as he beat the blankets and pounded the pillows.

Bion took a step back. "Nothing," he said, with a hiss of exasperation.

"Are you sure? It has to be here. Let's move the wardrobe."

"No, I'll do that. It can't be very heavy."

A creak and then a whine as Bion slid the wardrobe away from the wall.

Blinking slowly, he caught his breath and released a sigh so extravagant that the track of lamplight trembled in the gloom. "Oh, bless me, Isis! I can't believe it! It's here, been here all along, hanging from a hook behind the wardrobe. And look, its sheathed in the very same linen I stock."

Silent tears streamed down his cheeks as he pulled me toward him. "Miriam, how did you know? How did you know the manuscript was here? And that Dario took it?"

* * *

"There is no Dario. I found that out when I went to the warehouse. No one knew him. Also, Varius claimed his brother was working there when he rented your apartment, and I knew that was impossible because the ports had yet to open. True, some days have been mild this winter—that's probably what misled Varius—but the ports never open here before March 10th."

"If Dario never existed, then who was the other man staying with Varius?"

"There was no other man. Varius assumed both identities. And by claiming they were brothers he could account for any resemblance. But if you think about it, their differences were superficial, something Varius could create with a little glue and a lot of imagination."

"So, he planned to steal my manuscript all along! I feel so foolish, but why, after all that deception, did he leave it behind?"

"He knew he was in danger when the authorities found a body they thought was Dario's. See, Varius had staged his brother's flight so he could blame him for the theft. That's why he threw away Dario's things. Of course, we'll never know, but my guess is a one-handed beggar took the clothes and was wearing them when he was killed.

"But I'm rambling. To answer your question, if Varius had been found with the manuscript, he could have been accused of murdering Dario to get it. So, he had to leave it behind. And he left the wig holder behind because it was too conspicuous to carry along with the rest of his things. Besides, he didn't need it anymore. Anyway, seeing the wig holder and finding the glue confirmed my theory."

Bion stared into space and then furrowed his brow. "Well, should we just let the scoundrel go?"

"Well, at least we got the manuscript back, and he's gone. But, unfortunately, without proof, we can do nothing more. Let's just hope he thinks we identified the body as Dario's. That, more than the authorities, ought to keep him running for a long, long time."

"The Brother" appeared in the anthology, Crime Pays. *(Hellbound Books, January 2021).*

Revenge

The Eighth Year of the Reign of
Nero Claudius Caesar Augustus Germanicus [Nero]
Vernal Equinox
Alexandria *ad Aegyptum*

Chapter 1

P hoebe and I were in the Flamingo's Tongue about to peruse the luncheon menu when I let out a shriek. Even a stifled yawn would have been uncouth in this, our most fashionable restaurant east of the causeway to Pharos Island. But a shriek? Boorish under any circumstances but especially today, the Vernal Equinox, when our table was pressed against those of other revelers who, spicing their food with merriment, were celebrating the return of life and the official opening of our sailing season. With an unobstructed view of the Pharos Lighthouse and the hundreds of ships berthed in the Great Harbor, we were accompanied by the shouts of jostling waiters shouldering silvery trays of grilled fish, smoked meats, and fried fowl.

"What's the matter, Miriam? Don't tell me the noise is getting to you."

But I could only shake my head and point repeatedly at the window with the bowl of my spoon.

"The Lighthouse?"

I extended my reach while inhaling deeply to regain my composure. "That ship, the *Oceanus*, the one moored next to the trireme."

36

"So? Dozens of ships are setting sail today."

"But this is the only troop carrier. And the stevedores are loading its supply vessel now. Nero must have ordered another expedition."

"Okay, I'll bite. How on earth would you know that?"

"The *Oceanus* has the capacity to transport exotic plants for the imperial gardens and wild beasts for the games so Nero can assure us all of the power and reach of the emp—"

"I can see that," snapped Phoebe, "but I meant how do you know what its mission is now, and why the outburst?"

I closed my eyes to resurrect a memory from some seven years ago. I was in my twenties then, Phoebe had just gotten married, and I'd walked into Aspasia's apothecary for some white hellebore to treat Papa's constipation. I can still remember being ushered in with a wave of her knotted hand. The bundles of herbs hanging from the ceiling feathered my nose as I met the liquid blue eyes and pleated mouth of my frail-boned friend.

"Well, while you were beginning your new life, Aspasia referred one of her customers to me, this artisan who lives near her shop. He makes and sells those little bronze casts tourists buy for souvenirs, you know, of the Lighthouse, the Temple of Serapis, places like that. She said he was driving her crazy with the same questions over and over about poisons: how fast the various concentrations work, how they affect the body, whether they're detectable, where to get them, things like that."

Phoebe's widely spaced eyes glittered with excitement as she inched forward rubbing together her bejeweled, dumpling-like hands.

Phoebe had joined our family as the Greek foundling my mother reared as our domestic slave. When I was five and Phoebe ten, my father engaged a tutor and invited Phoebe to study with me. And so, she became my big sister, stubbornly girlish best friend, co-conspirator, and eager assistant. Then eight years ago, in anticipation of her marriage to Bion, a former slave himself who became the prosperous owner of a thriving *bibliopōleion* in the agora, she agreed to her manumission so their children would be free. So now, she trumpets her new station in life by sporting Chinese silk and adorning herself with sparkling gems.

"I have a hunch you're going to tell me he was planning to kill his wife's lover and escape on the *Oceanus*."

"Well, you're close," I fibbed. "Not that I expect my intrepid and loyal scout to be anything less than clever."

Blushing with pride, she tipped her head back but not before unwrapping a dimpled, life-loving smile.

"I have to say that strange case still leaves me shuddering, and it all happened because Nero sent the *Oceanus* on that expedition."

"How could I have missed that story! You must tell me all about it!"

"Okay, but let's start with the chopped flamingo tongues, the ones smoked and served with citron peel."

Nodding, Phoebe put her menu aside and sat back to listen.

Chapter 2

"So, you were telling me about this souvenir maker who was asking Aspasia a million questions about poisons." Phoebe, having just plucked an olive from her salad, popped it into her mouth and pushed the dish aside.

"Yes, his name was Giovi. He sent his breathless messenger to press me to come that very afternoon to his house near Aspasia's apothecary. He's her regular customer, mostly for that salve she compounds for burns. Anyway, I called for the sedan chair straight away with no idea of the adventure to follow."

Phoebe drained half her wine goblet as if she'd been lost in the desert, and then, rolling her hands like two wheels turning, said, "Well?"

"Don't rush me, Pheeb." With a trace of annoyance, I let a silence hang between us until it roared in my ears. "He lives on the corner near the agora, that stout, three-storied townhouse with those bright brass fittings on its cypress door.

"You'd think it would look grand with the sun sweeping over its graduated marble steps, but something depressed me about the place, as if a mute sadness, a gloominess, was seeping out of the ivy that shrouded the front. Or maybe it was the heavily shuttered arched windows that made the house look so forlorn."

I nibbled on a floret of pickled cauliflower and washed it down with a sip of wine.

"Well, what was he like? I'll bet he was scary."

"Actually, he was rather ordinary looking, a rangy man tall enough to fill the doorway when he received me. A stray sunbeam caught the thinning white hair atop his long, tapered head and settled on his overlapping front teeth while another, curving around him, spilled into the atrium to pierce the gloom.

"He rushed me through a narrow apron of light, past the planters of lilies that surrounded the pool, and into his office, a small square room to the left of the atrium. Entombed in shadows, it was curtained from the peristyle by an embroidered tapestry of the Trojan War, which leaked thin creases of light along its edges.

"Flanking his desk were a stool and his carved oak armchair, the only surfaces that weren't encumbered with piles of scrolls, sheets of papyrus, and boxes of souvenirs. Pointing me to the stool, he folded his body into the cushion of his seat, stretched his lanky legs into the canyon of clutter under his desk, and turned to face me.

"Then, after a few pleasantries including an apology for having called for my presence so urgently, he got right to the point. 'With your experience distilling exotic substances, Aspasia recommended I contact you.'"

Of course, I assured Phoebe in a whisper that neither he nor Aspasia knew of my alchemical practice, a pursuit that could send us all to eternity in the company of a score of granite-faced soldiers, a few dusty spectators, and a swarm of flies.

"'My son was my only offspring. Since his death several months ago, my life has lost its meaning. My only mission now is to find out how he died and see that the killer suffers the same misery.'"

"I don't understand. The authorities concluded that your son died of apoplexy, that he was in the agora—near your shop as a matter of fact—when he was stricken, that he died just like your cousin Rufinus about a year before, that the illness is familial—"

"'Miss bat Isaac, that cannot be true. First of all, there is no history of anything like that in our family. Second, Rufinus was not a blood relative. In fact, he didn't even look like any of us. He looked more like Caligula and was just as hairy except Rufinus's barber would pluck him hairless leaving only those swirls of carrot-colored curls to tumble over his forehead. No, he was my uncle's son by adoption. And perhaps most importantly, the authorities couldn't identify the cause of Rufinus's death. Only when my Dion died, did they attribute the cause of both deaths to some rare family weakness.' Giovi's fine-boned, liver-spotted hands stirred the air as he spoke.

"Grief dragged down the corners of Giovi's mouth, but he managed to continue after a deep sigh. 'Both men died in a crowd, my Dion in the agora practically in front of my very eyes and Rufinus on the Canopic Way. In both cases, witnesses reported remarkably similar observations: a sudden collapse, the victim's head rolling back, his features fixed in a malignant expression of fear and horror, his limbs swelling, his wide-open, sightless eyes—'"

Phoebe raised a hand to interrupt me. "Please, Miriam. No need for the details. I can already picture—"

"Well, you need to grasp the elements common to both cases. Oh yes, and each man died a few hours later, raving in a state of sheer madness. No wonder the authorities believed the cause had to be some rare familial weakness. There were no signs of violence. Not even the bite of a venomous snake or insect known in the region could have produced such grotesque symptoms."

Despite the din—the buzz of conversations, the rattle of tableware, and the chink of goblets—I tried to reconstruct where I'd left off in the story.

"You mentioned the father's—"

"Yes, yes," I said, nodding. "Giovi rejected the magistrates' findings. He believed both his son and Rufinus had been poisoned, but when he questioned Aspasia about such a poison, she scoffed. She knew of no substance, ordinary or exotic, that could have such an effect. Instead, she claimed to know of many familial conditions that can cause sudden death in even apparently healthy men. That must have been when she recommended, he contact me.

"By the way, Aspasia also knew Rufinus. She described him as a well-heeled, retired legionnaire, a handsome bachelor with the charm of a ladies' man. He'd come all the way to her shop from his estate on Lake Mareotis, and not just for her natron, which she packages in colorful glass amphorae, but for her upscale products. He swore by her unguent to prevent baldness—some blend of the fat from a crocodile, lion, and serpent—other ingredients too, but she keeps them a secret. Anyway, he said her products would be worth the trip even from Rome."

"Well, what did you think they died of?"

"Wait. I have more to say about Giovi." I took a deep breath and another floret of cauliflower to fortify myself. "Pheeb, I have never seen such naked sadness in a man, as if the flow of tears had carved the lines in his face. It wasn't as if he was sobbing or anything, but, believe me, grief lay on him like a weight. Even his breath smelled sad."

I could see tears thickening in Phoebes eyes.

"He spoke about his son. He was so proud that Dion, only twenty-five, had so much to live for, that he was a legionnaire who worked as an engineer to maintain the canal and tunnels that bring us water and all our upcountry goods from the Nile. Very important, Pheeb. 'And, as if that wasn't enough,' Giovi said, 'my son was the envy of all his friends. Here he was engaged to marry the local beauty.' This time when his hands stirred the air, his nostrils were flaring."

"I could see why this Giuvianu—"

"Giovi—"

"Okay. I could see why this what's-his-name would reject a familial illness as the cause, but why was he so sure it was a poison when no one, not you or Aspasia, could link the effects to any you knew?"

"Oh. He told me that one physician at the medical school, Professor Jason, happened to be present at both Rufinus's and Dion's autopsies. He too disagreed with the magistrates, saying that there was no evidence of disease, familial or otherwise, that in both cases the internal organs were perfectly healthy. And so, he offered poison as a hypothesis but admitted he couldn't defend his opinion."

"So, what did you tell the father? Two similar deaths but no agreed-upon cause, and although the victims and their families knew each other, there was apparently no other link between them. In fact, one—that would be Rufinus—was some thirty years older."

"Of course, I told him I'd take the case. And I'll tell you what happened, but first let's see whether the soup is as good as everyone claims."

Chapter 3

As soon as the waiter turned to serve the next table, I attacked the soup, a fish chowder served with buttered caraway muffins. The flavor was strong with spikes of hot pepper that flowered in my chest. Then, just in case anyone had observed my gluttony, I followed with a dainty twirling of my goblet, a genteel sip of wine, and a refined tap of my lips with my napkin.

When I peeked at Phoebe, she'd already raided the basket of muffins and was bending her face over the soup either to study its contents or tickle her face with its steam. Then brushing the crumbs off her bodice, she threw back her wine, smacked her lips, and wiped the corners of her mouth with her thumb and index finger. Next, she realigned her rings, so each stone caught a ray of the fading afternoon light and smiled at the world with a beam that rivaled moonlight on the Nile.

"So, Dion had everything to live for. He had a secure position in the Legion, he was engaged to marry, and some day, he'd be heir to a modest fortune. He certainly had more than most," said Phoebe, stabbing the air with the bowl of her spoon as she ticked off each advantage.

I pointed toward the carafe of wine. Did she want more? She nodded. I filled the ladle and served her.

"And don't forget he was the envy of all his friends," I added.

Taking the last of the caraway muffins, Phoebe ripped off a hunk, bit deeply, and chewed thoughtfully. "So, who was this dream girl?"

"Exactly what I asked Giovi. I could tell he wasn't pleased with the match. The way his face hardened I knew he thought his son could have done better.

Her family lived in the *Rhakotis* quarter—"

That's when Phoebe dropped her spoon. "Oh, Isis! Don't tell me they lived in one of those piss-soaked tenements near the canal!" Despite the veil of noise around us, the diners buzzing like a roiled beehive, the clink on the floor tiles swiveled every head.

Phoebe slapped her palm against her lips, but a squeal leaked out anyway.

"Pheeb, it's okay. But yes, that's where she lived. Her father—Giovi liked him by the way—he was a shipbuilder, a woodworker skilled in mortise-and-tenon joinery. Wait a second. I'm trying to remember his name." I coaxed another sip of wine across my tongue. "Ophelos! That was it, and his daughter was Korinna. So, he—Ophelos—did well enough. Financially, I mean. At least that's what Giovi thought except he complained about the girl's dowry. 'Meager,' he said. 'No landed properties.' But yes, he liked the father, felt bad when he died, some time before Dion as a matter of fact, not that there was any connection. Between the deaths I mean. Ophelos died of muscle spasms. Started in his jaw. After that, Korinna and her mother moved away.

"But it was the girl and her mother he didn't like. Describing the girl, he said, 'She was an empty-headed little thing, giddy and vain, you know the type, always fishing for compliments about how she looked, her hair, her dress, always complaining about the other girls trying to steal her boyfriends.'"

"I'll say he didn't like her!"

"Giovi and Dion first met her at a banquet Rufinus held to celebrate his appointment to the Emperor's Grain Commission. That was after he'd retired from the Legion and served as a *quaestor*. I'm going back maybe three or four years."

"And her mother? What about Korinna's mother?"

"As I said, he liked the father, but he absolutely loathed the mother. Listen to what he said about her. 'Tanis was a domineering manipulator, a social climber with the face of a shrew who led her daughter around by the nose. I warned my son about the connection between them, the girl and her mother, but my poor besotted son wouldn't listen.'"

"So, what happened next?"

"Well, that's about it, what I learned from Giovi anyway. He believed some kind of exotic poison was used, which was why he consulted Aspasia, but he had no idea what it was or how, why, and who used it. His only contribution was that both men were bachelors who knew the girl. To what extent Rufinus knew her Giovi didn't say, but she was beautiful and attracted lots of malicious gossip, especially from the girls her age."

"Well, knowing you, you probably went to the medical school to talk to the physician who participated in the autopsies."

"Oh, Pheeb, you know me so well. And as you will see, that was my first step in a dark tale that still stipples my skin. But if I'm not mistaken, here's our waiter carrying a platter brimming with smoked flamingo tongues. I can already smell the citron."

Chapter 4

It was mid-morning of the next day when I got to the campus of the Museum and the site of the medical school, a massive limestone building that radiated the promise of wellness. My bearers, Orestes and Solon, zigzagged me through the clamorous streets. Passing the statues and temples, barrows and booths, colonnades and arcades, fountains and sphinxes of the Canopic Way, I inhaled the odors of sweat and manure while I rehearsed the questions to ask. I'd sent Orestes earlier that morning with my request to discuss the autopsies and was assured the professor would see me.

Despite his leper-white skin, an otherwise soldierly built man emerged from the shadows of the plane trees at the building's vine-covered gate. The sunlight formed a changing pattern on his worn, thin-lipped face as he greeted me with an energetic courtesy.

"Thank you for seeing me, Professor, especially on such short notice. I'm here to speak with you about—"

"*Shsh.* I know why you're here, Miss bat Isaac, and I'm comforted that someone of your stature is finally looking into these curious cases, albeit unofficially."

"I hope to learn—"

He stopped me with a raised hand, saying "Let's wait to discuss this in my office."

As we threaded our way along a tree-lined arcade, I peered into the surrounding park, its botanical gardens and ornamental pool with the statue of the Muses. Soon enough, we reached a sweep of steps to a narrow but symmetric building tucked between the scholars' dormitory and refectory. Passing through its hallways flanked by vivisection laboratories that exuded a faint fecal odor and storerooms that shelved flasks of every shape and size, he stopped at a rude plank door. He unlocked the door and ushered me in.

We seated ourselves across from each other at a wobbly table in this small, strangely angled office. Turned toward the Muses, the east-facing window flung a lemony trapezoid of sunlight onto the stone floor. The rest of the room was in shadows.

He knotted his hands in his lap and leaned forward. "Excuse me, Miss bat Isaac, for bringing you to this humble office, but I still regard my conclusions on the autopsies as a delicate matter. You see, my appointment here is funded by the government, and as such, I enjoy many privileges, not the least of which is an exemption from the poll tax. And, as I'm sure you know, I failed to endorse the magistrates' latest findings."

"Yes, I understand the position you'd be in to challenge their findings publicly."

While he rubbed his temples as if to recall the details, I took the moment to glance about the room. The cubbies on each wall were crammed with dusty scrolls, files, and folders. To store his other items, he had a single sideboard, darkened with age, probably a cast-off judging by its cracked marble top, warped doors, and peeling veneer.

I wondered whether he'd been transferred to this modest office as a warning.

"As you know," he began, "the authorities concluded after Dion's death that the two, his and Rufinus's, were related, that the men suffered from the same rare familial illness, which resulted in their dying of apoplexy. But let's start with Rufinus's death, since that's when they first contacted me.

Because he died in such a horrific manner—and don't forget he was a rising bureaucrat—the magistrates called on me to do an autopsy no doubt with the expectation that I'd come up with a cause of death. But I was unable to do so. And so, the postmortem was initially recorded as inconclusive."

I nodded.

"The trouble started about a year later, when Dion died. Because the manner of his death was so similar to Rufinus's—and perhaps because he was also prominent as a legionnaire—they asked me to perform that autopsy as well. And so, I did."

"But your findings differed from theirs."

"Exactly. I could not concur that both died of a familial illness. First of all, despite Rufinus being up in years, fifty-five as I recall, his organs showed no sign of weakness, let alone of disease. And as expected given his youth, Dion's organs were likewise free of any such imperfections. Of course, I might have been more inclined to attribute their deaths to a familial illness if they'd died at approximately the same age. But they did not. So, I could not endorse the magistrates' findings. Instead, I concluded both were poisoned. My problem was that while I believed and still believe that, I could not name a single substance that would produce such grotesque symptoms."

"So, why then were you so sure they were poisoned?"

"Well, now I come to an observation they redacted from my report."

The thrill of anticipation coiled throughout my body.

"I found a needle prick on Dion's upper arm, a puncture ever so small. Only then did I remember seeing one on the back of Rufinus's hand. At that time though, I'd disregarded its significance, attributing the mark instead to a barber overzealous with his tweezers."

* * *

"Well, Pheeb? Do you get it?"

Phoebe, leaning back and tugging on her lower lip, frowned with concentration. "You mean the professor confirmed the poison hypothesis?"

"Yes, but there's more, much more. The substance was so unusual that

46

even experts in Alexandria could not identify it. And it was administered to both men the same way. So, it's likely they were killed by the same person, someone who'd been to or at least had a connection to an exotic land.

"And look, they were killed a year apart. That means the killer simmered with a motive. So, I was looking for someone who had an abiding grudge against both men. I didn't know who it was, but my meeting with the professor ignited a glimmer of hope that I'd find him."

Chapter 5

"Oh, Miriam, look what's coming now!"

"I'll bet it's the smoked fish."

Phoebe rearranged our cutlery and goblets to make room for the platter. As soon as the waiter brushed the crumbs from the tablecloth and removed our empty dishes, she dipped her pinky into the sauce and then her mouth. Closing her eyes to focus on the taste, she said, "*Hmm.* It has that perfect lingering hint of salt." Then, wiping her pinky on her napkin, she asked, "Well, how did you go about finding someone who could sustain a hatred that long?"

"Well, I thought about the men. Yes, they were well-established bachelors and legionnaires. And being distantly related, they had some common relatives. But given their age difference, I thought it odd for them to have the same friends. I certainly wouldn't have expected a girl from the *Rhakotis* quarter, regardless of her beauty, to be included in either social circle let alone both. So, I began by looking for anyone who knew her or could tell me where she lived."

* * *

I certainly dreaded going into the *Rhakotis* quarter. Alexandria's third residential district is all that remains of the old fishing village, pirates' nest, and Egyptian outpost Alexander the Great recognized as having the potential to become his great city. But today, it's blighted by poverty, violence, and despair. People are robbed, beaten, and dumped in the canal there, and some years back, I myself had been left for dead in a blood-soaked alley beside an old slaughterhouse.

Branching off the main grid of the *Bruchium* quarter, passing the last of its warehouses, Orestes and Solon brought me to a knot of narrow, tenement-fringed lanes, shoulder-to-shoulder ramshackle buildings, and boarded-up street stalls. The grimy buildings clung together so tightly that even a blade of the early afternoon light couldn't slip between them. The fungoid stench of the canal confirmed my guess that we were in the neighborhood where Korinna likely had lived.

With orders to keep watch, Orestes and Solon dropped me off to follow a pigtail of smoke and the scent of fish roasting in a courtyard. There I encountered a huddle of toothless, thickset women and approached the one whose eyes locked onto mine. She had a squashed face covered with boils. When I mentioned Korinna's name, she suppressed a smirk and directed me to look for a hooked-nosed woman with fish-like eyes named Legeia, who'd been the family's next-door neighbor.

I found that woman on a nameless claustrophobic lane clotted with weeds and studded with unidentifiable debris. Despite her gnarled arthritic hands, she was playing knucklebones by herself as she squatted on the stoop of her mudbrick, six-story tenement drinking *posca*, a cheap, watered-down, sour wine. I could disregard the scuttling rats, mangy dogs, and old whores, but I gagged on the smells of rancid urine, fresh scats, and fried grease.

"Is your name Legeia?" I asked astride the gutter that trickled past her stoop.

"What's it to you? Can't you see I'm busy?" She croaked in a voice scarred by misery and rotgut. The slur in her words told me she'd been drinking most of the day.

"I was hoping to chat with you for a few minutes."

"Oh, yeah? Holy Jupiter! I got nothin' to say, not to you, not to nobody."

"I wanted to ask you about Korinna and her mother. I know you were friends." I might have been stretching the truth, but if they weren't friends, I might learn even more. Then with some ceremony, I dug out a bronze coin from the draw-string purse tied to my belt. Holding it up, I climbed the steps and offered it to her.

"Well, what do you want?" Her voice softened as she took the coin. Then she scrutinized it with narrow eyes and tucked it under her sash. "Yeah, I knew 'em. I still see the girl. Mother's dead. Father died first though. Folks say she nagged him to death."

Was that a snicker or did she have a scratchy throat?

"Died right before they moved away."

"So sorry to hear that." I tried to sound consoling. Instead, I sounded like a bad actor reading a stale script.

"Well, they had to move, you know. Those rumors! Everyone said the girl was cursed. Korinna couldn't even get a litter to take her around town. And no cookshop would serve them. 'Scares away the other customers,' they said.

"She came to me cryin'. I mean Tanis the mother did. Said no one would do their laundry. I told her to forget about it, that it would all blow over, but she couldn't stand those pointin' fingers and waggin' tongues, all that gossip behind curved palms. Anyway, the girls disliked Korinna even before those gentlemen died. Said she was stuck up. Jealous they were and played nasty tricks on her."

I let her prate on about how hard it was for them to find work after the father died and what a good neighbor she was. I don't remember much else until she mentioned something quite unexpected.

"But her mother and I knew that couldn't be true, that she was cursed, I mean. She once had another suitor, a serious one. Local boy. Still livin', I believe. Woodworker on the docks like her father. But she dropped him like a hot coal. Gone like a summer storm, he was. That was right after she met that older guy, the red-haired gentleman, the one who dropped dead first. Too old if you'd'a' asked me, but nobody ever did."

This time I was sure I heard her snicker.

"And then that young legionnaire. Fell for her faster than a fire licks hay. And he died like the red-haired one. Dropped dead, this time in the agora. Just like that." Legeia snapped her fingers. "Before, she had more suitors than a pomegranate has seeds. After that, nothin'."

"So, you say you still see the girl?"

"Not the mother, of course!" Legeia said after yet another snicker.

"I'd like to meet her. Can you tell me where I can find her?" I was tempted to dig out another bronze coin, but I could see she was eager to talk, would have talked away the entire afternoon.

"She lives on Pharos Island, not far from the Abandoned Village. Just go past the cobbled courtyard and follow the path. She lives in one of those flat-roofed houses."

* * *

"Well, did you go right away, Miriam, or were you afraid Korinna might really be cursed?"

"Oh, Pheeb! Don't be silly. Of course, I went—Wait a minute! You ate all the fish!"

"Sorry, Miriam." She belched softly. "Don't be angry." A wary little smile played on her lips. "I just got carried away. Besides, something better is coming next. And please, you first. Take as much as you want." With that, Phoebe clamped her jaw shut and covered her mouth with her palm.

Chapter 6

"You owe me, Pheeb."

"What do you mean?"

"The broiled mushrooms topped with these spicy breadcrumbs are good but not nearly equivalent to the fish." I pushed my plate aside and feigned annoyance.

"Okay. Okay." Phoebe patted down the air with her palms. "I thought the squab stuffed with pine nuts would be next. So, my offer stands for the squab too. Take as much as you want."

I retrieved my plate with an extravagant sigh, bit daintily into a mushroom, and scooped up a few more.

"So, what about Korinn—"

"*Shsh.* Give me a minute more. I'm still eating."

After a long chewing silence, Phoebe said with a full mouth and a drip of olive oil on her chin, "Good mushrooms." Then she put down her spoon and leaned forward on her elbows. "Can you tell me about Korinna now?"

I plucked one more mushroom from the platter, this time with my fingers, and savored the zesty flavors as they burst on my tongue. "Okay, I'm ready."

* * *

I bought some *tiropita* from the pastry shop near Aspasia's, and then Orestes and Solon ferried me across the causeway. When the road degenerated into a narrow, twisting path, I knew we were close.

With my bearers' help and a good guess, I found her house among the few dozen mudbrick shanties huddled together. One in particular bore the marks of prolonged neglect. Most of the paint on the door had peeled off to expose the silvery wood underneath.

"Korinna? Korinna are you home?" I shouted from the concrete stoop.

"Back here. In the yard," a high voice answered.

"Hi. Who are you?" she asked. I found her stirring a washtub of woolen garments and stale urine in the shifting shade of garments swinging from a web of clotheslines. Around her, the ground, baked into hard, sun-stricken fissures, was a riot of brambles.

I saw some hint of beauty in her pale blue eyes ringed with a lush fringe of dark lashes, but hardship had already scored her brow and outlined her eyes in red. Most dreadful were her hands: chapped raw, the cuticles bleeding, and the nails dirty and ragged.

"Legeia suggested I stop by and say hello. My name is Miriam. She says you don't get many visitors out here."

"Legeia." Her face pinched into a frown. Then as if her old neighborhood came back to her like bubbles floating up to the surface of her mind, she said, "Oh, sure." A moment later, she jerked her head toward the washtub and added, "I was just finishing this load of dry cleaning. Well, not exactly, but I need to let the clothes soak a while."

51

"Oh, and I brought us some *tiropita*."

With a smile that began in her eyes, she took off her apron and hung it on the lip of the tub. "Come inside," she said as she brushed an unruly lock of coppery hair from her face, "but be careful on the steps. Some of the concrete is loose."

Indeed. When she opened the groaning door, it scraped against the landing adding to the crumbs of concrete already scrunching under my feet. Despite the faint smell of rot as I entered, I found myself in an immaculately clean, heavily raftered room, a dim sepia light filtering through the one north-facing window.

I did a quick inventory but found only the usual: a chamber pot, an oil lamp, and a washstand and basin flanked by a short stack of tattered towels. A charcoal-burning furnace for cooking and a pallet draped in a light woolen blanket filled opposite corners of the room. A raw pine shelf against the back wall held some cutlery and crockery, an amphora of oil, and two more amphorae joined by a rope for hauling water. Hanging from hooks under the shelf were a bleached linen tunic, a himation, and a pair of low boots. The only hint of indulgence was a vial on her washstand of opopanax, one of my favorite perfumes because of its long lasting, sweet-balsamic undertones, and the only hint of cheer was a multicolored hooked rug in the center of the room highlighting a rustic round table and two cane chairs.

When I sat on the nearer chair, it squealed like a feral cat.

"Oh, don't mind that," she said with a nervous laugh. "Here, let me get us some plates for the *tiropita*, and we can have a little *posca* with it." The streets of *Rhakotis* lived in her voice. "Is it okay if we eat it with our fingers?"

"That's fine. Please don't go to any trouble. I just want to chat a while."

"Oh?"

She concentrated on dividing up the triangles of pastry onto two tin plates and serving the *posca* in cups. Then she sat down and looked me over.

"Yes," I continued. "Legeia told me you might be able to help me find this man. All I know is he's a woodworker you once knew."

"Oh, Jupiter! I haven't seen or heard from him in ages!" Her backstreet clip of consonants sounded vulgar to my ears. "And with my life the way it is now, I wouldn't want to, me being more common now than he ever was."

I thought she was going to roll her eyes, but she didn't.

"Right after my father died, my mother moved us out here. We barely made a living what with taking in laundry, odd jobs like that, and then a month later, she goes and dies. So here I am living the life of luxury!" This time her laugh was shrill.

"Can you tell me what you remember about—?"

"What are you some long-lost relative who inherited a treasure chest from an uncle or somethin'?"

Was that a flame of suspicion darting from her eyes?

"No, nothin' like that." I was starting to sound like her. I hoped she didn't notice and worse yet, think I was making fun of her. "No, nothing." I repeated with emphasis on the *g*. "I know he was a woodworker. Did your father introduce you?"

"As a matter of fact, he did. My father liked Yam a lot. I'll bet you never heard a name like that. He was an orphan from the streets of Palmyra. That's why he had only one name." Her eyes closed as she got lost in a memory. "My first boyfriend. Said he loved me, and I knew he meant it. I was keen on him too, but my mother warned me not to waste my youth and beauty on a dullard like him, that he'd only leave me with children and spend his money on drink, gambling, and whores. Well, you can't exactly tell now, but I was once very pretty." For the moment, a vertical furrow cut into her brow. "My mother wanted me to do better than her. She even snuck money from my father's purse to have fancy clothes made for me. Cost a fortune. She called it an investment. Ha! Look where it got me? Anyway, I did what she said, but I cried afterward."

She bit off a hunk of the pastry and then licked the crumbs off her fingers. "*Hmm.* Thanks so much. A real treat."

I waited until she swallowed. "Life is like that. You can never tell the future."

"My mother sure couldn't."

* * *

"Miriam, did you think this Yam could be the killer?"

"He had a motive, I guess, but it was too soon to know. In any case, I had a name. I could have asked her for a description—and maybe I should have—but I didn't want to press her in case I needed to interview her again."

"I know how dogged you can be. So, tell me what you did next."

"Oh, Pheeb. You promised me more than my fair share of the stuffed squab, and I intend to collect on that first."

Chapter 7

As the waiter cleared away the squab, I asked Phoebe, "So, what would *you* have done?"

"I would have sent me to the waterfront saloons to see whether anyone knew Yam. Remember how I used to scout for you?"

"Well, that's exactly what I did, except I sent myself."

"You're kidding, right?"

"I had my bearers take me to the Lady Luck, the saloon nearest the waterfront. Of course, I'd given them strict orders: Solon to guard the sedan chair in the alley and Orestes to come in ahead of me and take a seat at the counter.

"I decided to dress as a prostitute. Why else would a woman go there? So, I painted my lips and cheeks with red ochre, blackened my lashes and eyebrows with ashes, and plaited my hair with ribbons into one thick braid to trail over my shoulder. I shrugged into that flashy blue tunic—the one you always hated—and hiked up the hem so any opals of phlegm on the floor there wouldn't stain my skirt. And you know what?" I asked with a chortle. "When I checked my reflection on the surface of the pool, I saw my blue eyes, dark hair, and tall frame, but I still had to throw a wave to make sure it was really me."

"I still say you should have asked me," said Phoebe. Her pout reproached me more than words.

"My bearers would have agreed with you. When they came to pick me up, they looked at me with squinted eyes. Solon whistled air in through the gap between his teeth, and Orestes coughed primly. A moment later, with faint smiles curving their lips, they lowered their eyes like Vestal Virgins."

"So, what happened when you got there?"

"I'll tell you that in a minute, but let's ask the waiter to skip the melon and give us some time before serving dessert."

"I knew you ate too much squab."

***

I arrived at the Lady Luck just as the darkness was absorbing the evening shadows. Its door was propped open with a pile of mudbricks and a thickset man parked on a stool. A scar puckered the right side of his face, and the hilt of a dagger protruded from the scabbard on his belt.

"What do you want?" he barked. The scar pulled at the corner of his mouth as he spoke.

"L-l-looking for a friend." I stammered while leaning against the doorpost to steady my knees.

He half turned toward me and responded with a curt nod, which I interpreted as an open invitation to elbow my way in.

The saloon was mean looking, a long and narrow room under a low planked ceiling and a ring of sputtering oil lamps. Its deeply stained walls exhaled the hot breath of unwashed bodies, rancid grease, and henket, a cheap Egyptian beer. A few heads swiveled in unison like a line of dancers, and I heard a few rude propositions, wisecracks mostly, but then this old guy—his name was Erasmos—came up to me, but not like what you're thinking. He was protective, sort of avuncular. Or maybe he was just curious because with a tilt of his head, he beckoned me to sit with him at a table near the backroom.

You should have seen Orestes! I never saw him spring up so fast. He leaped forward with the hiss of a viper, planted his feet, and cocked his fists ready to land a sledgehammer blow. But with a waggle of my head, he sat right back down.

Anyway, here I was at a table, the dim overhead lamps throwing a flickering shadow on the faded eyes that peered out from droopy lids. He took a swig from the bottle on the table. His lips trailing a thread of spittle, he closed his eyes and shivered before setting it down with a thud. Then he held it out to me. As much as I wanted to calm the pounding in my chest, I shook my head.

He leaned back in his chair and said with a half-laugh, "You ain't no prostitute, that's for sure."

"Oh?" I said, feeling a blush race up my neck.

"Plain as day. You're dressed like one, but your hands are too smooth and your boots too new."

"Oh."

"So, what you here for?"

"I'm looking for somebody. Maybe he's here. A woodworker. Name is Yam."

"What you want him for?"

"Maybe he inherited some money." I was trying out Korinna's idea.

"Yeah? Already heard that one."

"A friend of mine is looking for him—"

"Ain't here—"

"Says she knows him from the old days, hasn't seen him around, thinks he might have fallen on hard times."

"Your friend's right. If he's not gone already, he's been going dead, wasting away from this fever, but really from that silly-assed girl. I remember him from years back when he was a regular. Told everyone he was gonna marry her. But then that minx—she couldn't have been more than fifteen—jilted him. Really that bitch of a mother. Didn't think Yam was good enough for her princess. Gold digger, simple as that. So, the girl dumped him, left him with nothing but a hand and a hard-on."

"I can see you knew him well."

"Listen, lady. I know everyone. Been around for years. But him was special, meant something to me, like a son. I used to visit him. Bring him opium for that cough. But I haven't seen him for a while, not feeling so good myself these days. So, like I said, I don't even know if he's alive anymore."

"Still, I'd like to find him."

"Squatting in an abandoned tenement just outside the Gate of the Moon."

* * *

"Ready for dessert now, Miriam? My eye is on the *dulce domestica.*"

"How is theirs special?"

"Like everyone else, they chill the dates; soak them in wine; and stuff them with currants, spices, and cake crumbs; but then they serve the nuts in a pyramid on the side."

"Sounds good, but I don't think I can eat all that. How about if I just take a bite of yours?"

"Oh, Miriam, I don't think that'll work. I'll tell you what though: Let's order two, and I'll eat whatever you can't finish. But first, tell me what happened when you went to see Yam. You did find him alive, didn't you?"

Chapter 8

"You asked if I found him alive?"

Phoebe nodded slowly with contracted brows.

"That's a matter of opinion. He was thrashing on a pallet in an abandoned, rat-infested tenement, his bedlinen smeared with mucous and blood, a throw covering his body, and a fever glazing his face."

"What was wrong with him?"

"*Phthisis.* But I figured that before I even saw him."

"Whatever that is."

"The word means consumption. Hippocrates named it that because the patient wastes away. So, based on Erasmos's description—the cough, fever, and the wasting of the flesh—I knew. So, I filled my satchel with opium, barley water, fish, and fruit."

"How terrible!" Phoebe's voice thickened, but a moment later, it was as thin as a sheet of papyrus. "Uh-oh, look! The waiter is bringing our *dulce domestica.* Two platters! I didn't realize how big even a single order was going to be."

"Well, now you have your work cut out for you."

"I'll be able to eat more if you start your story about Yam from the beginning."

"Will do."

* * *

The rising sun warmed my back as Orestes and Solon carried me westward into the din of the city, its groaning millstones, clanging smithies, and clattering foundries. Once we passed the canal, the only people I saw were ragamuffins throwing stones in an alley, a circle of women nursing their babies in a listing doorway, and a couple of roustabouts picking their way through debris as they headed toward the docks.

My bearers dropped me off just beyond the Gate of the Moon so I could search for a sign of life in the abandoned tenements crouched near the harbor. But Yam was easy to find. I just wandered around till I heard his coughing fits rip through the air. Then, turning the corner into a sordid alley—actually more like a gutter—I was close enough to hear his recurrent wheeze coming from a darkly vacant building standing crippled in the weeds. When I saw the door was sealed with cobwebs, I shuddered as if I were about to walk into the World of the Dead.

I gagged upon entering the building. Tracking the stench of sickness, I found Yam lying on a pallet in a hallway nook framed by an alehouse bench and an immense, carved wooden chair, both probably left by previous occupants. The stink of his own excrement surrounded him like a lazy fly. But I detected other smells as well: a chocolate-like odor with a fishy edge that clung to his skin—no doubt from opium—and a hint in the air like myrrh, but sweeter, more delicate, and less astringent.

When he sat up to acknowledge my presence, he hawked a medallion of slime onto the floor.

"My name is Miriam, Miriam bat Isaac. I am a friend of Erasmos. He thought you might welcome a visitor."

"How's him doin'?" The words bubbled out with a sparkle of spit. His voice was hoarse but distant, as if blown in from the desert by our *Khamaseen* winds. I had to lean in to hear him.

"I brought you something from Erasmos." Okay, I fibbed, but I figured he'd be more likely to trust me if he thought I had a connection to his friend.

Uncorking the amphora of barley water, I dropped in a straw, bent down, and inserted it between his lips. His face felt like a burning kiln. He sipped slowly between labored breaths and rattling gasps, occasionally beating his fists against his chest. When he'd had enough, he handed it back to me, wiped his mouth with a corner of his bedsheet, and nodded. I moved the bench close to him, unpacked the opium, fish, and fruit, and set them out along with the rest of the barley water.

His eyes got a little bigger, but whether from drinking the barley water, seeing what else I brought, or just having a visitor I couldn't say.

"Who's you?" He managed to utter the question in its entirety before hacking up a clot of phlegm.

"Miriam. Erasmos told me where I could find you. He told me you weren't feeling well. In addition to bringing you these things, I wanted to ask you about a woman you once knew, Korinna. He told me she was once an important part of your life. Maybe you could tell me about her."

He swallowed hard and stared into the distance, his eyes fixed on a stain on the wall as if searching there for a memory. Then he lay back on his pallet and slipped into a dreamlike state as his breath softened to a rhythmic snore. How long he drifted, I can't say, but as the heat of the day bore down, I knew the morning had edged into the afternoon.

With a blast from the horn of an arriving ship, he rubbed his eyes, pulled himself up, and blinked his way back to reality.

"Maybe you could tell me about Korinna." I spoke in a phony singsong to hide my flagging patience.

He coughed to loosen a lung-full of phlegm and settled his back against the wall. At length, he summoned the strength to speak.

"Her father in the Lady Luck. Everybody there from the docks. Ophelos, with the muscles of an honest laborer. Woodworker. Shipbuilder. Brags about his daughter, Korinna this, Korinna that, like she was a goddess. Brings me home to meet her. What a beauty. Those lips. He asks me to court her. I'm on top of the world. But her mother—a viper with the eyes of a rabid dog."

He winced, drifting off again, this time for a minute or two, and then shook his head back to the present. "Ends suddenly. Then my love burnin' into this fever."

"So, how did you manage to recover, not from just that first stab of pain but the ache of losing her?" I was looking for that simmering motive.

"Ophelos, him tells me 'leave on this expedition—the *Oceanus*—'"

* * *

"Stop a minute, Miriam. Can you help me with this food?"

"Oh Pheeb, you've done so well! You've already finished the first platter."

"I just need to rest for a while, maybe take off my *calcei*."

"Your ankle straps too tight?"

"I don't know, but my feet are killing me. Besides, I have another problem."

"Oh?"

"Yeah. You're telling me his story, but I'm having trouble following it. I know he must have had to pause to catch his breath and—"

"You're right. I'm reporting what he said, but it took me hours of probing to get anything coherent. And don't forget, I'm leaving out all the coughing, hawking, and wheezing, the rambling false starts, the disjointed garbles, and the confusing dead ends. And all the while, he was entangled in the world of his fever."

"Well, could you just digest it a little so I can understand what he—"

"Sure. Yam told me Ophelos advised him to join the expedition on the *Oceanus*, that the sea would fill his loneliness—"

"No, that's not what I mean. Just tell it as if Yam were speaking directly to me."

"Okay."

* * *

"And so aboard ship, with many a curse and quite a few blows, I learned the skills of a sailor whether furling a sail, splicing a rope, or reading our course in the night sky. But all the sea did for me was harden my grief and whet my longing for the drink.

"When the ship moored for some maintenance—she tied up in a fishing village somewhere on the west coast of southern Africa— I took my shore leave and got so drunk I missed the call for her to set sail. No matter, I figured. All I had to do was find my way to the western branch of the Nile to get back to Alexandria. Ha!"

"So, I thought to head northeast across the continent, a hopeless venture, no map, no idea of the distance, the desert, mountains, and forests, only a rudimentary knowledge of the constellations I'd learned at sea. Instead, I soon succumbed to the scorching sun and surely would have died had it not been for these two little brown savages who adopted me, a man and a woman. They had this loose wrinkled skin, especially on their knees and elbows, small pointed ears, and gray woolly tufts of hair twisted into tight little buds. As I gained some understanding of their language, a combination of tongue clicks and a flutter and flick of their fingers, I came to learn they were the only survivors of a fever that had swept through their camp."

Chapter 9

"So, how was that, Pheeb?"

Phoebe sucked a tooth and nodded.

"Are we ready to leave?"

"Oh, let's have some tea so I can hear the rest of his story."

"Okay, and I'll help you out with the *dulce domestica*. Just order the tea while I go to the latrine, and then I'll continue where I left off."

"It was when the two rescued him. They were the only survivors—."

"Right."

* * *

And so, back from the latrine, I continued:

"I was valuable to them because of my sailor's knife and the coil of rope that hung from my waist, things they'd never seen but figured would be useful in their nomadic wandering and hunting. And, of course, they marveled at my size. But as it turned out, they had more strength and stamina than I, certainly as they found me, thirsty, starving, and covered with sun blisters.

"The old woman carried a digging stick weighted with a stone; slung a rawhide bag over her shoulder; and wore a beaded headband, a short leather skirt, and a rawhide girdle from which she hung containers made from gourds, buckhorns, even the shell of an ostrich egg. When she first approached me, she took out the ostrich egg, removed the wooden stopper, and fed me its precious water from her own mouth.

"Her mate also wore a beaded headband, but his interested me more. It held about a dozen arrows made from river reeds and eagles' feathers, each with a head of carved bone coated with a dry brownish paste. That paste fascinated me. Could it bring me that longed-for relief from my bitterness?

"Among the many skills I learned from my guides was hunting. And so, one evening, they told me it was time for me to kill my first antelope. Was I ready? I didn't know, but every hair on my body tingled.

"The trees were well behind us before the half-light of the next dawn dissolved the darkness. Trekking eastward ahead of the sunrise, we noticed the spectacular horns of a herd of antelope. The dominant bull stretched out his muzzle when he spotted me, but with the breeze whiffling past me, he couldn't get my scent. That's when, in response to my wave, he moved closer. Once he was in range, I took a deep breath, drew back my bow, and let the arrow sail through the air. When it fixed on his cheek just above his jaw, he reared back and took off running as he tried to shake it loose. The herd followed in a plume of dust.

"We tracked the bull into a copse of balsam trees. When we came upon him, he was teetering in agony. With his head matted with blood and his eyes turning cold, he toppled to the ground.

"His legs kicking madly at the air.

"A spasm of pain contorting his face.

"His head rolling back.

"His mouth gasping for breath.

"His lips twisting in a snarl that bared his teeth.

"That's when the self-pity in my heart hardened to hatred and revenge. I vowed to make that poison myself so if I ever got back to Alexandria, I would kill Korinna's mother and reclaim my sweetheart."

* * *

"The tea? Pheeb?"

Phoebe craned her neck to pitch her gaze over my shoulder. "It's on the way. I see the waiter. And look," she said, as she returned her gaze to me, "There's my snooty neighbor, Arria, in a cheap blonde wig strutting like she's Poppaea Sabina. Don't you think that paste she calls make-up is on too thick? It's caked into every wrinkle of her crooked face."

"Well, that reminds me. Did you want to hear about the paste Yam's guides made for their arrows?"

"Their poison, right?"

I nodded. "Yam told me he watched them make it many times before he trusted blending his own. They started out with ground-up beetle larvae."

"What? You must be kidding!"

"No, they use the larvae of these colorful leaf beetles. Every day they'd look for the plant that hosts the beetle, dig around it, sift out the cocoons from the sand with their fingers, and fill the shell of an ostrich egg with them—"

"Oh, Miriam. This is too much after all that *dulce domestica*."

"It's okay. I'm almost done."

A yellow sheen coated Phoebe's face.

"They break open each cocoon, tap out the larva, and smash it against the knucklebone of a giraffe—"

"Nooo—"

"Then they chew on the bark of this thorny shrub, spit their saliva into the

63

ground-up larvae, and apply it with a stick to the shaft of the arrow—not to the tip, of course. They don't want to poison themselves accidentally. Finally, they dry the arrows over hot coals. Knowing it could be years before he returned to Alexandria, Yam added the juice of an African snake plant to boost the potency of his paste, saved it in the shell of his own ostrich egg, and tied it to his waist."

Chapter 10

"So, I guess that's it. Yam's story: his voyage on the *Oceanus* and his return with a poison no one could identi—"

"Not by a long shot, Pheeb. He still had to confront a dark but unexpected turn of events."

"Tell me all about it."

* * *

"At first, I believed the bush was a barren wasteland, but as my skills improved, I learned it was a world of abundant food whether in the kelp beds, underwater reefs, and tidal pools, or on the savannas, rock islands, and shifting sands of the beaches and dunes. Once I learned how to keep alive and felt myself getting stronger, I was ready to head northeast where the dunes no longer dominated the landscape, where scraggy shrubs gradually replaced the thin desert grasses, and where mountains outlined the sky.

"And so, we traveled from dusk to sunrise to escape the scorching heat. Guided by the moon's milky light, erecting rudimentary shelters along the way so we could sleep during the day, we came to the fringe of their territory, to the verge of a misty, rain-shrouded forest. There, in a flurry of tongue clicks, finger flicks, and dancing, they gave me gifts of water, food, and a fishing net. Never could I have thanked them enough for their generosity or admired them more for living free, untouched by time, and in perfect harmony with their surroundings. And so, I entered the forest alone.

"I headed higher; where the humidity weighed on me like a wet blanket;

where the thorns grabbed me; where the gnats hummed, the mosquitoes whined, and the flies buzzed around me in a soot-like cloud; where the underbrush grew so dense that it took me hours to cut a path I covered in a few minutes; and where the canopy of trees left me in a shadowy world of wet leaves, rotting logs, and crawling termites. I fed on snails and a snake until I learned to catch some fish with the net, and all the while, inch-long leeches were everywhere, working their way under my clothes to leave me streaming with blood when I removed them.

"I can't tell how long I trudged. I soon lost track of how many times I'd hacked away at leaves and branches to make a bed for the night, and the soaring hardwoods obscured any reckoning by the moon. Continuing through light drizzles and torrential rains, safeguarding my ostrich egg as if it were a rare jewel, I followed brooks as they flowed into streams and streams as they flowed into tributaries and then rivers. By that time, I'd made a raft. True, I had to drag it for hours when I hit rapids, but soon enough, I found myself drifting northward on a wide, chocolate-brown river. And here and there, I was picked up by a boat until I reached the Delta and was spitting distance from home."

* * *

"You know, Pheeb, the only thing that got him through those grueling days was his determination to kill Tania. Imagine how he felt when he learned she died shortly before his return."

"Angry enough to kill somebody else, I guess."

"And that was Rufinus. Still, I wondered how he delivered the poison. But I'd find that out soon enough, just not the way I expected."

Chapter 11

"How soon did you go back to the tenement to see Yam?"

"The very next morning, Pheeb. When I saw him that first day, the blood tinging his phlegm was already black. So, I knew his time was nearing an end."

"But I don't understand. Why didn't he approach Korinna right after Rufinus died? Didn't he kill Rufinus to have a chance to win her over? Why did he wait until Dion had begun to court her?"

"He told me Korinna took up with Dion almost immediately. Don't forget Dion already knew her, had met her at Rufinus's banquet a year or two before. What's more, Yam was already feeling ill. He didn't know it was *phthisis*, of course. So, he waited, hoping to gain his strength, maybe even to save some money for their future, but by then she'd become engaged to Dion. And how could he compete against someone like Dion?"

"Okay. So, you were going to tell me how he delivered the poison."

I let the silence stretch while I worked out how to tell her the shocker that was yet to come.

* * *

Fortunately, I knew how to find him because this time, the abandoned tenements provided no clue. No wheezing, no hawking, no coughing fits ripped the air, only the mournful cry of a distant buoy and the savage howl of a stray dog. With the alley also quiet, I figured the opium I brought must have eased his breathing.

To enter his building, I had to step over a drunk slouching in the doorway and beg permission from the pigeons roosting on the lintel, but as I listened to the *clop* of my advancing boots, I recognized the same scent of sweet myrrh I'd detected the day before. In fact, it was so pronounced, I could identify it with certainty.

Covered by his throw, Yam lay on his pallet.

I moved everything off the bench—the fish and fruit, the rest of the barley water and the opium—all untouched—and pushed it out of the way, but gently so as not to wake him.

Heavier than I expected, it keened against the splintery floor.

But he didn't stir.

Not at all.

I froze
And stifled a scream.
I called to him.
That's when I noticed the green bottle flies.

* * *

"Oh, no! For the love of Isis, what did you do?"

"Of course, I could do nothing for Yam. And it was too early to find his friend at the Lady Luck. So, since I was there to learn how Yam injected the poison, I went ahead and searched his nook.

"Nothing. Not on the bench or stuck to its underside. Nothing on, under, or around the chair. The walls. That left his pallet, his clothing, his bedlinen, his chamber pot.

"Of course, all the while, I'd assumed he died of *phthisis*. But not after I took a good look at him. His head had rolled back. His limbs were swollen. His lips were pulled back. And his face wore a mask of cold, savage fury.

"Oh, yes, and one more thing. When I slapped away the flies, I saw the puncture on his neck."

Chapter 12

"What happened? Had he killed himself? Being he was so sick—"

"Well, I looked around once more for something he could have used to make the puncture. Again, nothing. Of course, he might have had time to throw away whatever it was, but why would he do that?"

"Oh, dear Isis!" Another yellow sheen coated Phoebe's face.

* * *

Of course, by that time, I knew who'd killed Yam and had a pretty good idea of why. I just had to clear up the details for my sake as well as Giovi's. He was after all my client and entitled to all the facts surrounding the death of his son.

So, I had one more place to go.

I got there around noon.

A pair of watery eyes answered the door.

"I just came from Yam's."

"I knew you'd come after you found him."

"I want to know why you killed him." *And how you delivered the poison.* "Can I come in?"

That same pinched frown and then a slow nod.

"You know he ruined my life. I finally figured out when Dion died that Yam must have killed them both, him and Rufinus. He was always so jealous of anyone who looked at me. Afterward everyone said I was cursed, that any other suitor would die like the two of them. And they all laughed at my misfortune! So, my mother and me, we moved out here. It took but a month to kill her, and it's doing the same to me.

"Sometime after Dion died, I went to the docks to see Erasmos. I knew he'd tell me where Yam lived—if you call that living. I told the old guy I missed my sweetheart, which was a lie, of course. I really didn't, but I told him I did, and he believed me."

I nodded.

"I'd fix myself up with a little perfume and what was left of my decent clothes—I still had a proper tunic—and I'd torment him, saying that he was too poor and too sick, that I had someone else.

"Well, yesterday when I visited him, he was so weak from that cough. Or maybe he was in an opium stupor. That's when I looked around and found a poison needle ring. That and the paste inside it would be enough to get him crucified. But in the end, I thought why bother to notify the authorities? So, I used the ring on him instead and then took it home. Wanna see it?"

I shook my head. I'd noticed it as soon as I came in, on her washstand near the vial of opopanax, the scent I'd detected in Yam's hallway. It was the kind of ring soldiers buy to escape torture in case they're taken prisoner.

I felt a wave of revulsion.

"Look, I know I did something wrong. That's why I sit here and cry. He was the only one in this whole world who still cared about me."

* * *

"So, what ever happened to her? Did you contact the authorities?"

"No, Pheeb, I didn't. When I went to see Giovi the next afternoon to give him my report, he told me the latest gossip, that some old guy had gone out there to see her and found her with her head rolled back, her limbs swollen, and her face twisted into an expression of utter horror."

"That just shows you. Korinna's mother was right. You can never tell the future."

"*Shsh*, Pheeb. The blare of the trumpet is announcing the departure of the *Oceanus*!"

The Fire

Alexandria *ad Aegyptum*
Toward Sunrise, The Nones of July, 52 CE (Friday, July 21)

On the upstairs landing of her Alexandria townhouse, twenty-eight-year-old Lucia Antonina tripped on the hem of her floaty *peplos*, a draped, ankle-length tubular garment open on one side. She plummeted down the sweeping staircase, past the walls veneered in red marble, the copiously gilded, carved balustrades smelling of fresh polish, and the marble pedestals supporting busts of the Greek poets. Her Herodian oil lamp, casting an apron of light that hardly scratched the darkness, escaped from her hand. Careening down the stairs, she heard it shatter against the lip of the bottom step. Its fragments soared through the air before the flame ignited the oil-soaked oriental rug at the base of the staircase.

Moments later, the flames were hissing like serpents. Soon they were crackling around her as she lay on the atrium floor. Her skirt fanned about her curvaceous legs, now contorted in a grotesque angle. Still, her long, Corinthian copper braids stayed in place with the hundreds of pearl-tipped pins her Egyptian maid had painstakingly arranged.

Had an onlooker been so pitiless as to stand there and watch this calamity through the grid of iron bars that crisscrossed the window in the thick, metal-studded entryway door, the eyes would have seen the snakes of fire slither toward Lucia, their viperous tongues licking at her face and wreathing her head in a coil of yellowish smoke. The ears would have heard her curses and cries before the growl of the fire smothered them, but the afterimage, like the reddish-orange flare of a setting sun, would continue to burn in the onlooker's memory.

Chapter 1
Shabbat, 5 days before the Ides, June, 62 CE (Saturday, June 5)

"So, tell me again, Miriam, why you went to—what's her name—the house you went to yesterday." Phoebe took a sip of wine and then licked her top lip.

"Abigail bat Levi's, the old woman from the synagogue."

Phoebe nodded. "I don't remember your ever mentioning her."

As usual on Shabbat, Phoebe was to have lunch with me under the linen canopy of my family's third-floor Egyptian-style roof garden. On this sunbaked Shabbat, the air was a mixture of heat, dust, and the breath of the sea as we sat around a marble table on teak benches banked with cushions of cerulean and turquoise silk.

"Well, like I said, she was an elderly member of our synagogue. I'd sit next to her on the Holy Days when we'd drowse in the heat and sway to the drone of the sermons."

"But what was she like?" Phoebe stared at me until the silence roared in my ears. "Come on, Miriam. If you're going to mention her, I have to be able to picture her."

"Well, I hardly knew her, but truthfully, she was a busybody of sorts, eyes constantly moving, spindly with twitchy hands and fetid breath—"

"So, why the visit?"

"Well, she died in her bed about three weeks ago, so I wanted to pay my respects to her son, who'd just arrived from Jerusalem. Abigail was so proud of him. He's a Torah scholar and scribe near the Temple Mount. But I had another reason too. Ten years ago, Abigail had asked me to look into the death of a wealthy Roman woman, Lucia Antonina, the young wife of Tittius Publius Melitius. That case lingered in my memory for many years clamoring for an answer as to how she died. I guess I just wanted to reflect on the closure I'd recently gotten."

"Tit-ti-us Pu-bli-us Me-li-ti-us," said Phoebe spacing out each syllable. "*Hmm.* Oh, the pear-shaped cheese merchant with the bald head. The one with a townhouse near Bion and me."

"Right. Do you remember when their house caught fire?"

"Not exactly."

"Well, his wife, Lucia Antonina—she was Publius's second wife. Wait, let me get my facts straight." My tongue waited until I could grab the thread of that memory. "Okay. His first wife and their adopted son were crushed by rolling barrels of henket when an overloaded wagon upended near the agora. Bystanders reported that the driver lost control—said he got distracted by a drove of pigs, something like that, and when he realized he'd killed a mother and her son—patricians no less—the boy was wearing a toga—he fled past the warehouses and into a maze of side streets in the *Rhakotis* quarter and was never found."

"Of course not! Those folks in the *Rhakotis* quarter know better than to wag their tongues unless they want to be bludgeoned to death in a squalid alley and dumped into that scummy canal to putrefy under the next day's sun—"

"Oh, Phoebe, please," I said in response to a stream of bile that shot up my gorge.

"Well, it's true."

"Okay, okay," I said as I patted down the air with my open palms.

"So, what about this Lucia, Publius's second wife? How in Hades was Abigail connected to her?"

"I'll tell you all about it, but let's have some lunch first. The cook saved us some of her grilled lamb and mint-flavored rice balls from last night."

* * *

"This is good, Miriam, the mint sauce especially." Phoebe chewed slowly while nodding at me. "So, what about your friend's connection to Lucia?"

"Yes, Lucia Antonina. The cause of her death was settled years ago. So, with Abigail's passing, I guess I can tell you about it now. She came to me a day or so after Lucia died."

Phoebe's eyebrows rose a little. "I don't understand. Did she even know, this Lucia?"

"No, certainly not, but her brother Jacob did, the glassblower—"

"Him? That guy with the pointy face? The one who owns that trendy shop?"

I nodded.

"What a phony! Full of himself and pulsing with social ambition." Phoebe sank back against the cushions, took a deep breath, and let out an extravagant sigh. "I'll bet he scents even the soles of his feet with that labdanum oil. And he must spend a fortune on his *tonsor* to wax, tweeze, and shave his face and body. I'm not even going to mention the face-whitening makeup he wears."

"Yes, that's her younger brother all right, but she was more like a mother to him. Now, of course, he's a husband, father, and artisan—"

"Who's prospered making those decorative flasks and bottles. Bion and I have some, you know. Very expensive. Shaped like fruits and—"

"But ten years ago, he was what? Only twenty or so, just starting out, single, and having a rather public affair with Publius's young wife."

"Lucia?" Phoebe shook her head in disbelief.

I nodded.

Phoebe's whole body wriggled with excitement. Then she put down her goblet and leaned over the table. The passing years hadn't dulled her taste for a juicy story.

"Anyway," I continued, "Abigail told me she was afraid Jacob killed her—"

"Oh, Isis!" Phoebe grasped the amber beads at her throat.

"Or at least could be implicated in her death. We're talking about a wealthy Roman woman. Abigail wanted me to find out how Lucia died so if there was any chance her brother could be blamed, rather than watch him be thrown to the lions, she'd send him out of the Empire, perhaps to Mosylon—"

Phoebe took a sip of wine and then, with a puckered brow, eyed me over the lip of her goblet. "Where?"

"That trading post along the Red Sea that imports Egyptian glassware."

"Oh, so he could make a living there."

"Exactly."

"So why did she suspect her brother?"

"Well, needless to say Abigail had long been pleading with him to end the affair. In the beginning, her brother found Lucia's flaunting vulgarity amusing and her impulsive extravagances exciting. But he eventually soured of her. According to Abigail, he'd spit curses like a pirate about her demands, her fits of temper, and her possessiveness, which he likened to a spoiled child's, until he got so dizzy he'd have to grab a wall for support."

Phoebe wrapped her arms around her chest as if a cold wind had swept through the roof garden.

"Thankfully, he became interested in Eve bat David, the daughter of an upstanding shipbuilder in our synagogue. In contrast to Lucia's jealous rages, Eve, with those angelic wings of blonde hair framing her comely face, offered a levelheadedness he was ready to appreciate. Clearly, she adored him. And so, her father pressed to announce their engagement on the condition, of course, that Jacob reform and sanitize his reputation."

"Okay," said Phoebe, rubbing her palms together. "So, he had a motive. He wanted to end the affair, but he was afraid Lucia would broadcast their liaison with every sordid detail, real or imagined, anything to arouse the contempt of decent people. And he was especially afraid Eve and her father would run from him like long-necked chickens. I understand that, but did he have the means and opportunity to kill her?"

"Oh, Phoebe, that was my question too. As soon as Abigail told me about her brother's dread of Lucia, I had to find out how that woman died."

"And let's face it, Miriam. You're like a dog with a bone."

"Of course, some questions weren't answered at the time, but let me clear the table, refill our goblets, and serve the dessert. Then I'll tell you all about it."

With a queenly swish of silk, Phoebe reached down to loosen the straps on her *calcei* and waggle her toes. Then she sat up, inched to the edge of her bench, planted her elbows on the table, and cocked her head to listen.

* * *

"I got the initial facts from Abigail, who read to me from the public record of Publius's statement. I think I can recite some passages verbatim: 'Lucia Antonina, wife of T. Publius Melitius, was home alone—'"

"Aha! Right there it sounds suspiciou—"

"Phoebe, they were childless, so the only other member of their household was their Egyptian maid, who was in the *Rhakotis* quarter assisting in the birth of her grandchild. Their other slaves lived in the outbuildings. Anyway, Publius had been aboard the *Eirene* making his way from Macedonia to Alexandria—"

"Again, I find that suspicious. How long was the voyage?"

"It took five days from Macedonia to Crete—"

"Really? Why so long? The winds would have been strong."

"Because of all the islands in the Aegean. But then add two days in Crete for exchanging cargo and passengers and then a little over three more to get to Alexandria. So, altogether the *Eirene* took ten and a half days to get to Alexandria. That means Lucia died when Publius was still aboard the *Eirene*."

"And his presence was confirmed by passengers?"

"Absolutely, by passengers and the captain."

"Okay. Go on."

"No interruptions?"

"Not if you serve the dessert. What are we having anyway?"

"*Dulcia domestica.* The cook pitted the dates and soaked them in wine, but she stuffed them with only the dried fruits, cake crumbs, and spices. She left the nuts in a pyramid on the side, just the way you like it."

"Oh, Miriam, you're the greatest." Phoebe's smile rivaled moonlight on the Nile as she watched me dish out a generous portion.

"But that means no interruptions," I said, reminding her with a pointed index finger.

Her stomach gurgled, and then with a regal nod that gave her bejeweled earrings a broad swing, she picked up her spoon.

* * *

Clearing my throat like a street philosopher about to address his curbside audience, I started anew, surprised that I remembered as much as I did:

"The morning after his wife died, T. Publius Melitius, an importer of select manouri cheeses, returned from Macedonia, unlocked the door to their main entrance, and found his wife's blackened remains at the bottom of the staircase that connected the atrium to their private quarters. He told the authorities that his dear Lucia must have died from the fall and its aftermath.

"'Something evidently disturbed her in the middle of the night,' he said, 'because she was carrying the oil lamp from her nightstand, which likely set the fire.'

"Thus T. Publius Melitius found his wife's charred body in the ashes of an oriental rug surrounded by fragments of her shattered oil lamp. The oil had likely drenched the rug and stoked the fire. Claiming all the doors had been locked with only himself, his wife, and their faithful maid each having a key, T. Publius Melitius was unable to offer the magistrates an alternate hypothesis to accidental death by fire."

"That's it?" Phoebe turned out her palms and wrinkled her nose as if she'd smelled something bad.

"Well, like I said, those were the initial facts, but Abigail was hardly relieved. In fact, she looked like she'd witnessed the death herself. You see, she knew the investigation was just beginning. What's more, her son was not only desperate to end the affair, but in contrast to his usual habits, was out late that very night."

"So, what happened next?" Phoebe rolled her hand in a gesture of impatience.

"A day or two later, Abigail got a copy of the autopsy report from the Public Records Office."

Phoebe shivered as if another cold wind had swept through the roof garden. Then she wiped the corners of her mouth and tucked her napkin under her plate.

* * *

"When I read the autopsy report, a shiver spasmed through my body too. The physician who performed the autopsy was Professor Jason from the medical sch—"

"Oh, I remember him. He's the one you told me about a few months ago when we were in the Flamingo's Tongue celebrating the Vernal Equin—"

"Yes—"

"The one who helped you solve the case involving the deaths of those two cousins."

"Except they weren't cousins, were they?"

"Well, you know what I mean."

"Yes, that very same soldierly old physician, scorned by his colleagues for his unorthodox conclusions, once again questioned the magistrates' finding of accidental death."

"Whaat?" My friend, her face flattened in disbelief, blinked slowly. "You must be kidding."

"He noted that Lucia had a broken leg and cuts in the soft tissue beneath the charred skin of her palms. Neither of those findings was significant to him. He concluded she likely broke her leg in the fall and cut her hands on the shards of the lamp when she struggled to get up. One observation, however, did bother him. He questioned why she was still dressed. She'd been wearing a *peplos* instead a sleeping chemise, and she hadn't brushed out her hair."

"Uh-oh!"

"Exactly."

"So, what did you do?"

"I went to see Jacob the very next day."

Chapter 2
The Calends, August, 52 CE (Tuesday, August 1)

Jacob's shop was outside the agora on the Street of the Soma a few blocks south of Phoebe and Bion's townhouse. I figured I'd have the best chance of questioning him if I arrived just before the mid-afternoon drowse, heralded by shutters rattling closed and grilles clanging shut against the pitiless heat. Already the pavement was baking through the soles of my *calcei*.

I entered on a spike of sunlight that illuminated the shelves at the back of his shop. They were so crammed with everyday glassware that if I exhaled extravagantly, I was sure all the pieces would topple over and smash to smithereens. But the vitrines in the front housed his treasures: the cups, vases, bowls, and goblets with custom designs in gold leaf; the decorative panels of colorful mosaics; and the novel flasks he'd fashioned with the latest glassblowing techniques he'd been perfecting.

"Jacob ben Levi?"

He was facing the entrance, seated on a high stool, arched over his workbench, intent on wrapping a set of mosaic tiles. When he looked up, I saw a young man's sharp-chinned face caked with a thick layer of makeup that outlined a pair of deep-set, haughty eyes and a grimly set, thin-lipped mouth. As he stood to greet me, I watched the folds of his blue silk tunic swish as they spilled over his muscled thighs and bathed his knees in little blue waves.

"Can I help you?"

"I've heard so much about your bottles and flasks, how unique they are—my friend has several—magnificent, irreplaceable —" My voice was ill controlled, my words rushing out too fast, and I was having trouble getting to the point. But after a deep breath, I took on a crisp steady tone that was both friendly and commanding. "Your sister is concerned about the death of Lucia Antonina and asked me to stop by and listen to what you have to say about that night."

A blue vein at his temple throbbed like a leech after feeding.

With a flick of his thumb and index finger, he dislodged a speck of sand on the skirt of his tunic. Next, he took a deep breath and let it out slowly in scarcely disguised exasperation. "Just like Abigail to interfere," he muttered. "She's not happy unless she's worrying about something," he added, leaning forward as if we were old friends sharing a confidence."

I gave him a nod as though in agreement.

"But let me lock up. Then we can sit behind that scrim." He turned his head and pointed with his chin toward the back. "I have a little office there."

He proceeded to the back of the shop. Reaching behind the scrim, he returned with a wooden key about the size of a table knife. After locking the grille, he closed the shutters against the blazing light.

The colors around me disappeared.

* * *

I followed him into a cave-like room, dim, low-raftered, and with a faint fecal odor I traced to a chamber pot. A sputtering oil lamp atop an iron stand spread a yellowish skin on two low stools, their seats stained with grease, and a narrow wooden table, its surface splintered and darkened with age. Floor-to-ceiling cubbyholes mounted on the back wall held the usual items: scrolls, oil lamps, an abacus, and writing supplies.

With a sweeping arm gesture, he directed me to the far seat. "So, what do you want to know?"

"Your sister asked me to investigate. So, what can you tell me about that night? I know Lucia was dressed to receive a guest and you were out late."

His lips pursed in annoyance before he spoke: "Yes, Lucia was expecting me. I'm not proud of it, but my sister—and others—knew that Lucia and I were having an affair." A red splotch of embarrassment formed on each cheekbone. "I know that sounds crude, but our relationship grew out of a deep friendship and mutual interest in the art of glassmaking. Moreover—"

"In fact, hadn't she been sponsoring your work?"

Jacob dipped his head in a barely perceptible nod. "Moreover, her husband had long since deserted their marriage bed, blaming her for their childlessness. So, with her husband visiting sheep farms in Macedonia and her maid away as well, we planned to spend the night together.

"But I had second thoughts. You see, I was trying to end that relationship. As amusing as it was, its termination was a necessary condition for my courting Eve bat David, something her father and my sister were pressing me to do. Still, I am sorry she's gone." His thin lips tightened as he shut his eyes momentarily. "I keep thinking if only I'd passed her house a little later,

I might have been able to prevent the tragedy."

He blinked away the film of moisture coating his eyes. Then, locking his arms across his chest, he leaned back and continued. "So, I walked over to Hiram and Hillel's house instead. I'm sure you know them, the twins."

I nodded.

Trusted by the Romans as well as the Jews, the Ephraim twins together serve as the secretary to the Council of Elders, a lifetime appointment in honor of their grandfather's and father's contributions to maintaining our synagogue. One of the secretary's duties is to choose the Torah reader each week, a privilege they frequently granted my late father.

"So, you're saying you didn't go to Lucia's house?"

"Well, almost. I did go but not for what you think."

"So, tell me."

"Well, I was restless. So, the twins decided to indulge me in an evening at The Gladiator, the tavern next to Aphrodite's brothel. They could tell I was upset, and as long as we were going to pass Lucia's house and I knew she was alone, I asked them to stop the litter so I could check on whether she was okay."

"Did you go in?"

"No, I lost my nerve."

"Well, what happened then?"

"I could see the sickly light of a flickering lantern through the lace curtains of her bedroom window, so I knew she was waiting for me. But I really didn't want to start up with her. Instead, I just walked around the outside of the house and peeped through the window in the door. All was quiet, so I left."

"How long were you there?"

"A few minutes, just long enough to walk around and look in."

"Could the twins see you as you walked around?"

"No, a grove of flowering hibiscus screens the house from the street."

"And did anyone else see you?"

"Not that I know of."

"So, the only ones who can confirm your story are Hillel and Hiram."

For a moment, I saw a flash of annoyance in his eyes. Then he stared at the ceiling as though gathering his patience before answering with another barely perceptible nod.

Chapter 3
Shabbat, 5 days before the Ides, June, 62 CE (Saturday, June 5)

The sun had already dipped below the canopy, its long slants of afternoon light brushing a lemony glow on one side of Phoebe's face.

"So, you went to see Hillel and Hiram," she said as she shifted her bulk to serve us each a cup of chamomile tea.

And so, my memory drifted back to that evening when I called on the twins in their modest home just north of the Gymnasium. I recalled watching my shadow pull me up their pebbled walkway as I breathed in the scent of the peonies fringing the path and counted the torches flinging their sparks into the fading light.

"Having already been questioned by the magistrates, the twins were surprised to see me."

"What were they like?"

"That's just it, Phoebe, they were identical in every way, their faces fair, their eyelashes long, and their mouths small. Only their bullnecks, broad shoulders, and massive chests kept them from looking feminine."

"So, how did you tell them apart?"

"Hillel would rub the back of his neck as if it were stiff whenever he said anything. But otherwise, they were like a performing duo. They confirmed Jacob's story. They'd stopped at Lucia's for a few minutes, and after that, they headed for The Gladiator. There, until the half-light of dawn edged the walls, they drank *posca* with the Roman soldiers and watched the mimes perform lewd sketches about adulterous wives and truant schoolboys."

Phoebe listened while aimlessly stirring her tea. "So, what was the problem? You could tell Abigail that Jacob was in the clear, that the twins had given him a solid alibi."

"Well, before I left, I asked them whether they noticed anything unusual about Jacob that night."

"And?" asked Phoebe, her eyes widening.

I took a sip of tea, but it was already tepid. "They said a couple of things. Hillel spoke first. 'Jacob didn't just ask us to stop at her house, Miss bat Isaac'—By the way, that was the first time I noticed him rubbing his neck—'he insisted. His words had that kind of intensity.' And Hiram agreed with his eyebrows before adding, 'His voice had an edge.'"

"And the other thing?"

"Wait, I'm not done with the first thing. Well, maybe there were three. They wondered that Jacob seemed to have a premonition about something terrible happening to her that night."

"And the third th—?"

"This time Hiram answered first. 'When Jacob came back, he slumped into the litter and pounded his cushion with a groan.' And, like an echo, Hillel with a deep sad breath replied, 'He looked the very image of a weary and remorseful man.'"

"So, you left without being sure whether Jacob was blameless in her death."

"That's why I said that even after all these years, the case still clamored for a solution, at least in my own mind. But the Romans regarded the twins as unimpeachable, and with Publius having been at sea, they closed the case as an accidental death by fire."

"You know, I was wondering why they didn't focus more on Publius," said Phoebe, lowering her voice to a conspiratorial whisper. "Then again, maybe I'm making too much of the death of his first wife. But listen: He could have hired someone, perhaps the wagon driver who killed his first wife. Didn't you say that Lucia was also childless? And surely, Publius was better off without the scandalmongers gossiping about her behind their curved palms."

"But let's not forget Lucia was dressed to receive someone. She certainly wouldn't have prepared herself to greet her husband or an assassin."

"So, you still thought Jacob was involved?"

"I wasn't sure. Suppose Lucia was listening for him. Upon hearing someone, she ran down the steps, tripped, broke her leg, and dropped the lamp so the rug caught fire. If Jacob was watching, he should have called for help from the twins and the slaves bearing their litter. The five of them might have been able to break in and rescue her. That's why I kept wondering: If he was there, could he have been so pitiless as to do nothing? And don't forget Jacob said he walked around the building, but the twins were in no position to corroborate that part—"

"Wait. I still have a question. After the twins dropped him off at home, couldn't Jacob have walked back to her house?"

"Great question, Phoebe! It was certainly an easy walk, hardly a mile between their houses. But it would've been morning by then, so Lucia wouldn't have been carrying the lamp."

"True. But something tells me your story isn't over."

* * *

"More *dulcia domestica*? There's still some left."

"No, I just want to listen." Phoebe reached down this time to unbuckle the straps on her *calcei* and kick them off. Then she sank back into the cushions and smoothed the wrinkles in her tunic.

"Well, the question of how Lucia died kept beating in my brain like a hammer all these years. Still, I was puzzled when, three weeks ago, Abigail's bearers called at my door to say she was asking for me. But as soon as I passed through her atrium and my nostrils caught the acrid breath of sickness, I knew why she sent for me.

"The stench of flatulence and soiled linens became more insistent with each tiptoe toward her room. There my former client lay on her sleeping couch, lodged between life and death, surrounded by Jacob, her physician, and a maid, who held a cup of honey-sweetened water to her mistress's lower lip. They in turn were surrounded by tables jammed with herbs and unguents, powders and lozenges, ligatures and sweat-drenched towels. Abigail looked thinner than ever, like a skin-draped broomstick with teeth too big for her face."

Phoebe lowered her eyes as she murmured, "Oh, Isis."

"As soon as Abigail's eyes flicked toward me, she sat up and pulled me toward her with convulsive strength. She leaned against the maid's shoulder while I tucked a cushion behind her back. Then she dismissed everyone else with a wave of her hand."

"'Thank you for coming, Miriam. I need to tell you about that night.' Her voice hadn't changed, but I could hear jagged rises in its pitch.

"Although her eyes were filmed with suffering, they lit with a sudden clarity as her mind floated back on a wave of memory. At times she paused to recall a detail. Occasionally she shuddered, but most of the time, the words gushed out like a raging sea.

"'It was I,' she said, shame coloring her voice, 'who watched the snakes of fire slither toward Lucia, and it was I who heard her cries before the growl of the fire smothered them. But the afterimage of that fire, like the reddish-orange flare of a setting sun, still burns in my eyes like a fever.'

"The sting of tears prickled behind my eyes. 'Why, Abigail, why did you go there?' For a moment, I wondered whether she heard me, but then she answered.

"'Oh, how that Siren tortured my poor brother's soul.'

"I lay my hand on her arm, but she held up hers to forestall any interruption.

"'Look,' she said, 'I admit it was madness, but I knew she was alone, that Jacob had changed his plans and gone to see the twins, and it might be my only chance to plead with her to let him go. So, I walked over there. She must have thought I was Jacob, the way she called to him as she rushed to the staircase. But when she heard my voice instead, she hurled curses at me in a rising howl, strings of them in a stream of vitriol until all I heard were clumps of sound.'"

Phoebe gnawed at her upper lip.

"'And then, in a rising gust of fury, glaring at me with the face of a demon, gesticulating, her fists pounding the air, she lost her balance. Lurching and catching her foot on the hem of her *peplos*, she fell, releasing the lamp as she pinwheeled down the steps. I watched, my heart palpitating in both relief and horror as the fire consumed her, and then I ran home praying I'd arrive before Jacob.

"'Then, when the authorities heard that my Jacob was at her house that very night, alarm bubbled through me. That's when I came to you. And once I had Professor Jason's report, terror lived in my bowels. I needed to know how the authorities were weighing his conclusions.'

"'And now?'

"Abigail answered in a sigh. 'I know my Maker is calling me, but I cannot face Him with the afterimage of that fire burning in my eyes. No one knows I was there, not even Jacob. So, I am confessing to you, hoping to ease this burden on my soul.'

"Those were her last words, Phoebe. Then her face lost its color, her eyelids lowered, and her jaw relaxed. I waited a few more minutes for that final breath. It came as a labored rasp followed by a profound stillness as she slipped into that eternity where all paths meet."

Phoebe waggled her head. "That poor woman, but she was lucky too. Why do you think the authorities ignored the professor's findings?"

"He was an ongoing embarrassment, the way he so often contradicted their conclusions, and all the more so because he was usually right."

"And so were you. It wasn't Jacob."

"But I was also wrong. I let Abigail use me to find out what the authorities knew, and I was naive to the end."

"So, to what extent was Abigail responsible for Lucia's death? And does Jacob share in that guilt?"

"Ah, we'll have to take up that question next Shabbat. The sun is already sinking into the trees."

The Guest

The Eighth Year of the Reign of Nero Claudius Caesar Augustus
Germanicus [Nero]
A day in late June, 62 CE, Alexandria *ad Aegyptum*

"Please madam, could you just blink your eyes or—I don't know—do something to show me you're alive?"

The stranger's imploring voice invaded my stupor while a tsunami of pain crashed inside my head forcing me to blunder back to consciousness. Groaning, rolling onto my side, I opened my reluctant lids and dragged my senses back to life. And that's when the details of my situation trickled back to me. I was lying in the alley next to our Alexandrian branch of the Bank of Gabinius, the stink of the sewer burning my nose, blood oozing from my right temple, my himation smeared with muck. And looming over me, eclipsing the late morning sun, was a man in a short-sleeved, bluish-purple tunic, dyed with that fabulously expensive extract from the glands of sea snails.

When I found the strength to look up and speak, my voice came out as thin and dry as a sheet of papyrus. "Oooh, you were in the bank. Who are you, and what happened to me?"

"You fell," he answered quickly.

Too quickly.

"Tell me more."

"My name is Titus. I was right behind you at the bank. You fell in this alley, landed on that boulder, and hit the right side of your head, but—"

"How could that be? I never go into this—"

"Well, actually, you fainted, you know, when I pulled you—"

"You pulled me? You mean you followed me and assaulted me!" I thundered, while fumbling for the fibula that pinned to the right shoulder of my himation proved my status as a Roman citizen. It had last belonged to my mother, a wedding present from my father, and before that, to his mother and grandmother. Thrusting my keepsake in his face, I said, "My name is Miriam bat Isaac, and I can report you to the magistrates!"

And then, absorbing his gentle manner, rose-scented pomade, and perfect Latin albeit spoken with the backcountry drawl of a Caesarean, I asked in a more controlled voice, "Why on Earth did you assault me?"

* * *

How did I end up at the Bank of Gabinius in the first place? My husband, Judah, does all our banking now. And then, closing my eyes, I remembered.

Early that morning, Gershon ben Israel, the keeper of the sacred objects in our synagogue, had come to ask my advice. Wearing the engraved face of an old man, the yellow-stained eyes that shroud his vision, and a crimson silk himation over an emerald linen tunic, he lumbered through my atrium and into my study with the forward stoop and wobbly knees that long ago replaced his loose-limbed grace. Then he perched on the edge of the stool in front of the massive ebony desk that had belonged to my father.

The rising sun was leaking color into my study and warming my back as it cast a milky sheen on Gershon's amethyst seal ring. Arranging his limbs, he adjusted the folds of his himation, which, like the *calcei* on his feet, were studded with garnets, and gripped the edge of my desk with his impossibly long fingers until his knuckles turned white.

He addressed me through quivering lips in the shrill voice I'd come to expect after the *Khamaseen* winds had burned out most of his hearing, but he still spoke with the unhurried speech and imperious tone of an aristocrat. "I have a guest now. Lucius. Perhaps you remember him from Caesarea."

"I remember the white stone houses near the harbor and our turning north onto the *Cardo Maximus* where he lived. And I remember marveling at his perfectly proportioned, marble mansion enclosed by that hedge of rosemary, but his hound-faced doorkeeper claimed you before I had a chance to see, let alone meet him."

"Oh my, that was more than twenty years ago."

"Fourteen to be exact."

"Yes, twenty. Well, he arrived yesterday—maybe the day before. He's my guest while his house is being renovated. Too drafty when the rains come. Chill makes his bones ache. They ache a lot, he says. But the noise and dust from the carpenters were making him—"

Already his voice was scraping my ears. "Maybe you could tell me just how I can help you."

"He went out yesterday, and when he returned, his face was white, white as bleached linen. I tell you, he was in the throes of panic, like a stretched spring about to snap. Said he'd been followed, that he needed a bodyguard. I knew your brother—" The glow of admiration warmed Gershon's features as he continued. "May he rest in peace—the most impressive gladiator in the Empire. So, I was wondering whether you might have a connection to any who retired."

Gershon was right. An aficionado of the games, he saw my brother when hardly more than a novice, slay Orcus, the highly favored and most popular gladiator in the Empire.

"So, you want to hire a bodyguar—"

"Kept asking myself how he could already need a bodyguard. He just got here!" Gershon shrieked. "Who could be threatening him? As his host, of course, I knew I was responsible for protecting him. But I was also afraid. My entire household might be in danger." The sweat beading on his forehead released a faint onion odor.

I took a deep breath to keep my own voice calm. "What do you know about this Lucius?"

"Met him years ago, when I was importing Palestinian wine. He and his brother maintained the warehouses—you remember the *horrei* along the harbor, those vaulted buildings lining the promenade? Stored my Palestinian wine there. He and his brother were partners until Lucius bought out his brother Paulus's share. Did I say that already? Lucius also said that despite his youth, Paulus had that loss of judgment that affects mostly the elderly. So, this Paulus joined a religious sect somewhere west of the Dead Sea."

"Does Lucius have any other family?"

"A son. An engineer in Caesarea who maintains the harbor's submarine foundation and breakwaters."

"Do you know where he—your guest, Lucius—went yesterday?"

"I didn't, but I asked my bearers."

Gershon's bearers were Nubians, identical twins, Wasi and Wedu. I can tell them apart only because one was disfigured by a rope-like scar that puckered his left cheek, but I still mix up their names.

"According to them, he went to the Bank of Gabinius to pay his carpenters through his home branch."

"*Hmm.* Well, before I try to find a bodyguard for him—my brother had an agent who might know someone—I need to find out what danger is threatening him."

* * *

Orestes, my lead bearer, helped me into my sedan chair, and then he and Solon, my other bearer, pushed westward through the bustle of shoppers, hordes of slaves, and knots of tourists that clogged the Canopic Way all the way to the Bank of Gabinius. My father bought them ages ago to transport him through the city in a style commensurate with his status as a promising young investment banker. Despite the passing years, both have remained strong, top-heavy men with huge, veiny hands and thick, corded necks. But of the two, I prefer the plucky Orestes to the phlegmatic Solon.

I shouldered past bankers and businessmen, civil servants and scribes, money changers and priests, all pressing to enter the bank's ornamental gate and immense bronze-paneled double doors. Once I crossed the freshly scrubbed marble threshold of its cavernous hall, I was deafened by the babble of commerce and blinded by the morning sun streaming through the arched clerestory windows.

I stood in the line for the frog-faced clerk, the one with the long earlobes, while I devised a cover story to find out whether Lucius had been here yesterday and if so, what his business had been.

"Good morning, Miss bat Isaac. It's been a long time. Your husband okay?" Frog Face had a retentive memory, a ready tongue, and an air of knowing something about everybody.

I nodded and returned his greeting. "I'm here to help an old friend of my father's, Lucius Didius Bassus, who's visiting from Caesarea. I'm afraid the stress of the trip has tangled his mind. He doesn't remember whether he asked someone yesterday to pay the carpenters working on his estate."

"Hold on. Let me check," he said before crossing the hall. And then, at the door of the head clerk's office, he asked in a voice that echoed through the hall, "Did you say Didius or Fabius?"

That was when I felt a spike in my gut and chastised myself for thinking I could keep my inquiry confidential. In the meantime, the minutes crawled by so slowly I had to dig my nails into my palms to squelch my churning innards.

"I couldn't hear whether you said Didius or Fabius," Frog Face repeated upon his return. "So, I looked them both up. Lucius Didius was here yesterday. I didn't serve him, but some time ago, he transferred his credit from our branch in Caesarea. That's all I'm allowed to tell you, nothing about any payment to his carpenters, only that he'd been with the branch in Caesarea for many years."

He rested his elbows on the sill separating us and leaned forward. "But being a valued client yourself, I guess I can tell you this."

I could have sworn his face sharpened. He swiveled his head left and right to check that no one was listening and lowered his voice to a confidential whisper. "Your father's friend has a credit of over 100,000 *drachmae*. Holy Isis, that's enough to buy an estate on Lake Mareotis and the dozens of slaves to run it! Imagine then his hearing he'd have to wait more than a month for the money to buy a loaf of bread. I tell you, he glared at the clerk like a demon."

His body bending over the sill, crow's-feet crinkling the corners of his eyes, Frog Face tipped back his head and erupted in a rollicking laugh. "Well, you should have seen what happened next. He stomped his feet like a madman, unleashing a string of curses, and flashing with rage, he raised his fists and struck the clerk."

His earlobes swung back and forth as he shook his head in disbelief.

Then, pointing with his forehead to the granite-faced soldiers poised at the entrance, he added in a voice vibrating with excitement, "Believe it or not, they had to carry your Lucius out!"

* * *

"Miss bat Isaac, could you please open your eyes, so I know you're still in this world!"

The flint in Titus's voice nudged me out of my recollections and back into the alley.

Squinting, I sat up with underwater slowness and lurched to my feet. After calming the wrinkles in my tunic and slapping the dust from my himation, I took a few uncertain steps, shifting side to side to ease the cramps in my legs. When my circulation returned, I plonked down on the boulder.

He took a few tentative steps toward me, almost hovering. "Are you all right? I really didn't mean to hurt you. I just wanted to ask you a few questions, you know, and you were walking away so quickly—"

"With good reason!"

Swallowing twice, he answered in a voice clotted with guilt: "I heard you making inquiry about a man named Lucius—"

Another spike in my gut, this time as if I'd been gored.

"Lucius who?" I asked.

"I don't know. Didius?"

"No, you must have misheard. I was inquiring about an Alexandrian shipbuilder named Lucius *Fabius*. My husband gave that thief a great deal of money to convert a warship into this huge grain ship"—I stretched out my arms as if they could span 180 feet— "one that could feed the entire city of

Athens for a year. His family owns and operates a fleet of freighters in the eastern Mediter—"

The lie slid out so easily I had to stop any more from growing in my mouth. "Besides," I said, pointing my accusing finger at his nose, "What business is it of yours?"

"None really," he said, staring for a moment and then lowering his eyes. "I paid an architect, another Lucius, a fortune to design a row of warehouses like those facing the harbor in Caesarea and then to build them along your smaller, western harbor, the uh..."

"The Eunostos—"

"Yes, the Eunostos, but the scoundrel absconded with my money. I just want it back. So, when I heard you mention his name—or I don't know, I thought I did—I figured you were his accomplice. And I'm so sorry I hurt you. See, I thought if I could put pressure on him through his bank..." He poured out these words, his brow puckering with distress. "Anyway, I hope you can forgive me. I'd consider it a favor if you'd let me make it up to—"

I was a little skeptical of his story. After all, shouldn't he have known the name of our smaller harbor? But he claimed to be familiar with the warehouses in Caesarea. So, maybe he'd know something about Gershon's guest. And, given the report of Lucius's temper and penchant for violence, I was afraid for Gershon and eager to invite a pair of fists to accompany me to his house.

"Well, yes, there is something you can do for me. My friend has a guest I'm curious about. I wonder whether you'd accompany me to—"

"Miss bat Isaac, I'd be delighted."

* * *

An Interruption in Miriam's Story

I better tell you right now my name is not Titus. In fact, most of what I told Miss bat Isaac was a lie. My name is Hostus. Yes, I'm from Caesarea, sailed here on a military patrol vessel since I didn't have time to apply for a civilian travel pass. I arrived just three weeks after finding my father, Lucius, under a droning mass of green bottle flies. Brutally murdered, his eyes staring into eternity, his fingers and toes had been hacked off, probably one at a time and scattered like scraps, each soaking in a soup of blood.

But sadly, there was more. His loyal servant must have died trying to defend him. The doorkeeper's torso was mottled with eggplant bruises, his mouth contorted in a fierce grimace, and the floor around his crushed skull spattered with a fine crimson rain. Judging by the stillness, everyone else, the dozens of other servants, must have fled for their lives.

I live in an apartment on the street that runs tangent to the southeast corner of the Temple of Augustus and Roma, an easy walk from my father's. But I confess to having been negligent in visiting him regularly, not out of indifference mind you, but as a new engineer eager to make his mark in the job my father's fortune secured for me. Still, as the manager of my father's affairs, when I received notice from the bank that he'd transferred most of his assets to Alexandria, I knew which duty came first. So, I hurried to his estate as if chased by a growling tiger.

In the unnatural quiet, I stood like a statue over my father's dismembered corpse, seesawing between terror and fury. It was only through the rod of discipline acquired during my professional studies that I managed to stiffen my spine and break through the paralysis. Accordingly, I was able to muddle through my father's funeral, terminate his affairs, and sail here.

And now, with my nerves at their highest pitch, I doggedly pursue any stranger. If any man so much as emerges from an inn, gazes like a tourist, or stops to ask directions, I regard him as the thief who stole my father's identity and his life. That's why, aside from my wish to make amends to Miss bat Isaac, I seized the opportunity to meet this guest of her friend.

* * *

Orestes and Solon were waiting in a sliver of shade near the front of the bank. I introduced them to my new friend, and squeezing into the chair, we headed back toward Gershon's limestone mansion, an architectural hodgepodge of arches, columns, and balconies on a cobbled lane near the Gymnasium complex. When stalled behind a groaning oxcart or a rumbling dray, a platoon of soldiers or a caravan of camels, Titus and I exchanged pieces of polite conversation while the sun licked our backs with tongues of fire.

Although by the time we reached Gershon's house the light had shifted, the slant of the afternoon sun on the garden pool gave no indication of anything amiss. After that, though, as in any crisis, the events unfolded with appalling swiftness.

The rhythm of time changed the moment I passed under the ivy-covered pergola and saw the entry doors ajar. Crossing the threshold into Gershon's atrium, I didn't have the breath to shout, "Where is everybody?" Instead, I retched from the smell, everywhere the stink of blood, the stench of fear, and the reek of sour breath.

Turning toward a low guttural moan, I saw Gershon crumpled on the floor in a blue silk robe, doubled over on his side, his eyes glazed with pain, his brow creased in bewilderment. When he whined, "Why, Miriam, why?" the emptiness in his voice was so defenseless, worse than any tears.

I called to Titus to bring in a stool and position it next to Gershon to see whether my old friend could pull himself up. He finally lifted his shoulders and gripped the leg with one hand. Then, leaning forward, his lips tightening in a grimace, he staggered to his feet. Titus was there to grab him by the elbows and lower him onto the seat cushion. Trying to hide the tremor in his legs, Gershon gripped his thighs with his long fingers. I automatically straightened my own back as if to straighten his, but he stayed hunched over, tense and tired.

"You're bleeding from the nose, Gershon. Let me call a physician."

"What?" The shrillness in his voice was like a siren in my ears.

"A physician."

"Who?"

"The one with the triangular face. The one adept with ligatures. To staunch the bleeding." Then, pointing to my own nose to prompt him, I asked, "What happened?"

He shrugged with open palms. And then, after a heavy pause, he mumbled, "My guest."

"Titus, go to the outbuilding—the one on the northside of the house—and call in his bearers, Wasi and Wedu. And hurry. We're dealing with Lucius, and maybe they know where he is."

* * *

I sent Wasi—I think it was he—to bring the physician. "But," I warned, "under no conditions is the physician to let Gershon's blood. He's already lost too much. Instead, have him tie ligatures to trap the blood in Gershon's limbs and keep it from flooding his head and chest."

Then I asked the other one, the twin with the scar, to give Gershon some garlic to ease his breathing and put him to bed.

While Titus and I waited on a bench in the atrium for Wedu to come back from the bedroom, I passed the time by mashing the draw-string purse tied to my belt.

"I don't know, but I think we should search for this guest, the one you call Lucius," Titus said, wringing his hands. "We might be able to find—"

I raised a hand to silence him just as Wedu joined us. "How is he?" I asked, as I stood and turned toward the bearer.

"He's resting now, Miss bat Isaac. I gave him a measure of that chalky powder he keeps in the vial next to his sleeping couch." The scar pulled at the left corner of his mouth as he spoke.

"Good. Now tell me what you know."

"We were in the outbuilding waxing the supporting poles of the litter when Lucius dashed out of the house with his travel bag and demanded we take him to the harbor. Of course, we refused. We don't take orders from him. So, he ran into the street and hired a sedan chair. All that happened just a few minutes before you arrived."

"And tell us. What does the master's guest, this Lucius, look like?"

"About the same size as the master, as Mr. Gershon, but with an athletic build and broad shoulders. *Hmm.* The same complexion too, like the belly of a fish, if you don't mind my saying so. But his hair is dark, not white like the master's, and he's stronger, of course."

Then, in a thickened voice, standing slump-shouldered, he added, "Listen, we are so sorry. We had no idea he hurt the master."

A swift, unexpected prick of tears gathered behind my own eyes as he bowed and withdrew.

Titus stood and wheeled around to face me. "Quick. Which harbor?"

"Surely the Eunostos. Lucius must have anticipated trouble, applied for an exit visa, and booked passage on the first merchantman slated to depart. They dock in the Eunostos. The other harbor is for the imperial navy and the private crafts of Roman officials."

"Then let's go right away."

* * *

In the amber light of late afternoon, there was no litter to be found. All must have been engaged by theater-goers eager to marvel at Heron's latest inventions for staging *Antigone*. Eventually, we settled for what we could get, an open litter with tattered cushions. The lead bearer was a stoop-shouldered Egyptian, his wrinkled tunic stretched smooth over his bloated gut, and the other was a knock-kneed, hollow-chested youth with a tentative mustache. With the same pig-like eyes, they surely were father and son.

I counted out a few bronze coins from my purse and dropped them into the father's cupped palm. Then his son held the cushions in place while Titus and I seated ourselves.

The unlikely bearers joggled us around the corner of our most congested intersection, the junction of the Canopic Way and the Street of the Soma, while I tried to will away my queasiness and Titus kept slamming his fist into his open palm.

"For the love of Jupiter, can't they go any faster?"

Catching sight of the sun-bleached rooftops angling toward the harbor like a row of broken teeth, I smelled the charred flesh of the pre-sail sacrifice and watched its ribbon of smoke lean into the sea breeze. Rage clawed at my insides at the thought of this ruthless monster slipping through our fingers.

"Stop here," I called to the bearers as we approached the pier.

The mournful, human-like cries of a squadron of gulls soaring, wheeling, and swooping over the breakers dispirited me as we elbowed through the crowd while the kaleidoscope of colors flooding my eyes resolved themselves into a throng of passengers tramping toward the gangplank.

Then the blare of a trumpet. The shriek of a whistle. The groan of ropes. And the whine of hatches.

"The gods have failed us. We're too late! The scoundrel has escaped. And we don't even know who he is."

"No, Titus, look over there!"

"Where?"

"Over there." I pointed, standing on my toes to get a better view. "The man near the end of the boarding queue. The one with the travel bag."

"Everyone has a travel bag!"

"But this one's wearing Gershon's crimson himation studded with garnets. Can't you see the spikes of brilliance calling to us?"

And then, with his eyes narrowing in a spasm of pain, my companion howled, "Oh Jupiter, let me lose my mind and eyes! That man, he's my Uncle Paulus!"

* * *

"So, who are you really?" I asked turning to the man sitting next to me. We'd folded ourselves into a curtain-lined litter to head back to Gershon's. Once we'd turned onto the Canopic Way, our shadow crawled eastward with us until it mingled with the darkness.

"I think you know a lot, Miss bat Isaac, maybe everything but my name. I am Hostus, Lucius's only son. I came to Alexandria as soon as I could after finding my blessed father's lifeless, mutilated body. Since then, I have been desperate to find out what happened to him, recover whatever assets I could, and avenge his murder. I was sure his killer was here in Alexandria, that he'd be impersonating my father to claim—"

"Oh, dear Lord, I'm so sorry about your—"

"But I certainly had no idea the killer was my uncle. That he was staying with your friend and, you know, about to prey on him. For that I too am truly sorry."

"Poor, poor Gershon, so trusting but not so sharp anymore. And it had been almost fifteen years since he'd seen your father. But tell me, who is this uncle, the one you called Paulus?"

"Yes, Paulus, my father's younger brother. I don't know, but from what my father told me, since he bought out his brother from their warehouse partnership, my uncle had been living in a religious community near Bethlehem. But I was only a lad then, and neither I nor my father—as far as I know—saw or heard from him after that."

"Have you any idea why your uncle would do this?"

"I don't know, but his bitterness dates back many years, since they were children. My father used to tell me how he tried to befriend his brother, but Uncle Paulus was always so, you know, jealous. When my father won the marathon, my uncle's resentment hardened like the concrete in our harbor back home. Anyway, after that, Uncle Paulus refused to go to the gymnasium and brought only shame to our family. I know my father saved him from disgrace many times, but he thought all would be well once Uncle Paulus joined that religious community. I can assure you we never imagined he'd be capable of this."

Hostus shivered like the leaves of a plane tree catching a sudden breeze, and then asked, "What do you think will happen to him?"

"Well, the magistrates have him now. Rather than being summarily fed to the lions, as a Roman citizen he can petition the emperor for a trial. And if he does, you'll likely be called as a witness. Perhaps Gershon as well. If found guilty, your uncle will be given the favor of a presumed painless execution by beheading."

I felt a soreness along the base of my neck as I explained this fate to Hostus.

Then a stillness settled around us like two actors who'd forgotten their lines. Thoughts of Paulus may have hovered over our litter, but neither of us broke the silence with words. And so, we rode the last miles hearing only the clop of our bearers' boots and the plod of the torch lighters making their rounds. Only the occasional scamper of rats, the thrum of wings, and the howl of a feral pup punctuated the evening stink of spewed beer, fried grease, and rotting garbage.

"Well, we're here. Let's see how Gershon is doing."

* * *

With his lantern cutting through the inky darkness, Wasi greeted us at the entrance.

"How is he?" I asked as we followed the funnel of light into the atrium.

"Better," he reported with a bow. "The physician managed to stop the bleeding. The master will remain in bed for the rest of the evening, but he is awake and would welcome your presence."

Leaving Hostus on a bench in the atrium, I followed Wasi down a corridor lined with planters of clipped boxwood and cages of talking parrots until we reached Gershon's suite: his sitting room, sleeping chamber, and peristyle.

Amid the complex odors of an old man's room, he was sitting up on his sleeping couch staring at the walls frescoed with swirling vines and flowers. I searched his face to gauge his level of awareness, and then a small smile lit up his eyes.

"What happened to me, Miriam?"

I decided to save most of my explanation for a day when Gershon would be feeling better. So, I simply told him that the man staying with him was not his old friend after all. Instead he was some scoundrel who meant to do him harm.

"But," I explained, "in his place, Lucius's son will likely be staying in Alexandria for some business with the courts and would be grateful for a chance to stay with you."

Gershon nodded. Then closing his heavily lidded eyes, he slid under his coverlet, curled onto one side, and drifted into the arms of Morpheus.

The Mistress

The Eighth Year of the Reign of
Nero Claudius Caesar Augustus Germanicus [Nero]
Fall, 62 CE, Alexandria *ad Aegyptum*

Chapter 1
The day before the November Calends (October 31)

"...I'll kill her on the calends."

When the music stopped suddenly, those words spilled into the silence.

"Phoebe, did you hear what that man just said?"

Phoebe and I were having lunch at the Flamingo's Tongue with a view of the lighthouse and the hundreds of ships moored in the Great Harbor. To celebrate the start of the four-day festival dedicated to Isis, we were among the crush of celebrants watching the passion play depicting the death of Osiris and Isis's returning him to life. We were enjoying their signature dish, marinated flamingo tongues in a spicy pepper sauce, the luxury of a latrine on the premises, and plump dining couches in the front row of an improvised central stage.

"Which man are you talking about?" Phoebe whispered.

"Lying belly down on the couch at the next table, fiddling with his emerald ring—"

Phoebe swiveled her head, her earrings jingling as they swayed. "Wait. I can't see. That horsey matron just got in my way—"

"—Supporting his forearms on the green cushion while the guy next to

101

him is picking his teeth."

Phoebe turned to look again. "Him?" she asked pointing with a spoon and jabbing it in his direction behind her curved palm.

Her voice cut the silence like a saw.

"*Shsh*—"

"Okay, okay," said Phoebe as she patted down the air with her dumpling-like hands, the massive gems on her fingers catching the shimmer of the afternoon sun. After a thoughtful pause, my stubbornly girlish best friend continued in a voice reserved for secrets. "I heard him say something, but I didn't bother to listen. Anyway, I figured he was muttering about the waiter."

I sat up, jerking my head in the direction of a scuffle that rose above the snatches of speculation burgeoning about the room. "Phoebe, the musician. He's on the floor, and his nose is bleeding."

"Wait, I want to see!" Bracing her chubby arms on each edge of the couch, Phoebe lifted her torso, slid onto her knees, and sprang to her feet. Never mind cramming her feet back into her *calcei*. "*Ma Zeus*, you're right. I'll bet he's a drunk, too!" she said, her round, girlish face puckering in distaste.

"How can you tell?"

"His nose is blooming with a ruby flush, and his forehead is glassy with sweat. And he has these tufts of black hair curling out of his nostrils and an immense belly hanging over his hips."

"Still, that doesn't mean he's—"

"See for yourself, Miriam. He's vomiting." Phoebe's eyebrows knitted in disgust. Then she reached inside the bodice of her *stola*. "Quick," she said as she withdrew a lavender-scented sachet from her ample bosom. "Take this to neutralize the stale garlic, grilled fish, Egyptian beer, and whatever else he had for lunch."

Amid the voices of the chorus swirling upward, the thud of anxious foot-falls, and the shift of impatient revelers, the scrape of couches complained against the floor. Over each sound's moment of life, Phoebe shouted, "Let's get out of here."

"But Phoebe, that man said he's going to kill some woman on the calends."

"The calends? Holy Isis, that's tomorrow!"

* * *

With a throng of others, we herded out of the restaurant into a wall of dust, noise, and the smell of horse droppings. Phoebe, her eyes blinking against the afternoon sun, swept the street with a troubled gaze before peering into the alley like a cat waiting for a mouse. "Where's the litter, Miriam?"

"Uh-oh, I forgot," I said, tapping my forehead with an open palm. "I told Orestes and Solon we'd be staying until late afternoon. No doubt they're in some cookshop in the neighborhood. I could fetch them, or we could wait—"

Phoebe looked over her shoulder to make sure no one was listening. "You know, Miriam, I believe Isis meant us to overhear what that man said."

Part of me wanted to forget the whole thing, of course, to pretend I hadn't heard anything or attribute it to my second goblet of wine. But another part was thrilled with the prospect of a new case.

"Maybe you're right," I said, stroking my chin. "What do you think we should do?"

A grave intensity clouded Phoebe's childlike face. "I think you should ask the doorkeeper whether he knows that man. Maybe he's a regular."

"Me? Why me? It's your idea—"

"Oh, Miriam, you're so much better at—"

I feigned objection with my hand to my chest and an audible swallow—my friend was not the only one with theatrical talent—but I was pleased. "Okay, but first I'll peek in to see whether he's still there."

While rubbing her palms together with a conspiratorial glee, Phoebe trilled with delight.

* * *

I poked my head into the dining room. Either the man had left along with us, or he was in the latrine.

"What do you want?" Emerging from the shadows, the doorkeeper asked through a mouth stuffed with crooked teeth and in a twang that smacked of

103

the sea.

I shrank back as if I'd been struck by the cudgel tucked in his belt.

"What's the matter, Missy? I startle you?"

"I'm looking for someone who was here this afternoon, a man in his 30s, thick black hair precisely parted in the middle, a large, emerald seal ring—"

He flicked his tongue like a cobra.

A film of icy sweat pearled above my upper lip. But at the same time, folding my arms so that each hand grasped the opposite forearm, I managed to unhook the gold chain that encircled my left arm. "Here," I said, dangling my bracelet in front of his nose. "When he waved for his bearers, he dropped this chain. I'd like to return it to him. Can you tell me who he is?"

"*Hmm.*" He closed his eyes and pinched the bridge of his pulpy nose. "Ring. Seal ring. Large. Emerald." When he raised his lids, I searched his face for an answer. "Ah-ha! That must be Mr. Kosmos. My wife always asks about him, says he must be bald under that—"

"Well, do you know where I could find him?" I asked while, with some ceremony, I dug out a bronze coin from the drawstring purse tied to my sash.

"Under his wig, of course!" He burst into a rollicking peal of laughter that left threads of saliva clinging to his overhanging teeth.

Ignoring his paltry attempt at humor, I pressed the coin into his open palm, flashed him a fake smile before it could harden, and stepped into the street to see Phoebe exhale a sigh of relief.

"Let's meet early tomorrow to track down this Mr. Kosmos," I said. "And as long as I'm near Judah's shop, I may as well drop in to see whether I can find out anything about this man who wears such an extravagant ring."

I left Phoebe with the glitter of adventure in her widely spaced eyes.

* * *

Whenever I entered my husband's jewelry shop, my eyes eagerly sought the new pieces. This time, I saw he'd added a rosewood display case crammed with presentation pieces in silver, gold, brass, and bronze. And then I saw the familiar row of cases, the ones with the personal pieces he creates and arranges so artfully. Each signet ring, bejeweled chain, amulet, cuff bracelet, and pendant, whether in silver or gold, and each brooch with its complex mosaic design, expressed his taste and craftsmanship.

"I saw a gorgeous seal ring at the Flamingo's Tongue this afternoon and wondered if you made it."

"If it's gorgeous, I made it," said Judah, thrusting his chin forward.

"No, seriously."

"What is this? Now that I'm your husband, I'm no longer the world-famous jeweler you fell in love with?" A smile flickered on his lips. "I'll bet you don't even remember how you relentlessly pursued me till, in exhaustion, I was forced to surrender to your lust."

"Somehow I remember it the other way around."

Actually, Judah had no idea what I remembered. Nor did I intend to tell him.

"So, what about that ring? You know I'd gladly make one for you, but you haven't seemed interest—"

"It belongs to a man named Kosmos."

"Kosmos. Kosmos. Of course, the emerald. How could I forget? The Cleopatra mines kept me waiting a month for a quality stone that large."

He paused for a thoughtful moment and then began again. "You know, Miriam, I forbid you to have anything to do with that man." I was taken aback by how suddenly his smile turned into a scowl. "First, he's a womanizer. Oh, he's married to a wealthy patrician woman, but you'd never know it. His wife's been locked away in an *asclepeion*—I forget where—supposedly being treated for some kind of madness—that's the scuttlebutt anyway. In the meantime, he orders a lot of jewelry for a lot of women. I know because they come in to make their selections—"

I'd love to get a list of those women.

"—and charge the bill to him."

"And the second reason?" I asked, half expecting Judah to say "Oh, he's also a murderer."

"He's in a shady business. Sells these phony Etruscan vases—claims they're antiques—to tourists in a fancy shop near the Street of the Soma. That's why when I make anything for him, his payment has to come in a purse sealed with the mark of a moneychanger I trust." Judah nodded as if in agreement with his inner voice. "So, promise me you won't have anything to do with him."

"Promise," I said, pasting on a wifely smile. But I had no intention of complying.

Chapter 2
The Calends (November 1)

The rising sun warmed my back as my bearers sped me westward to the Street of the Soma past the Canopic Way's marble colonnades, stone sphinxes, and polished building facades. The only sounds were the mournful cries of the gulls and the beat of my bearers' boots against the pavement. By the time they stopped and lowered the litter in front of Phoebe and Bion's three-story limestone townhouse, prim, solid, and respectable, the dread of murder had claimed my bowels.

A maid was waiting by the door. As soon as I dismissed the litter, she ushered me into my friend's dressing room, its ceiling set with green marble and its frescoed walls lined with polished bronze mirrors. Swagged drapes with fringe concealed the entrances to her sitting room, bedchamber, and peristyle. After scooping up armfuls of tunics from her trunks and arranging her wigs by color on mannequin heads, we got busy trying on outfits to wear to Kosmos's shop. The sleek onyx-tiled floor, strewn with our rejects—tunics, wigs, sashes, belts, and purses—already looked like the aftermath of a cyclone.

"No, Miriam," she said with all the condescension of an older sister. "The wig. It's wrong, wrong, wrong. You look like a floozy."

"Well, aren't we trying to disguise ourselves so when we go to Kosmos's shop, he won't recognize us?"

"You want to look different, not cheap. His shop caters to rich tourists. Isn't that what you told me Judah said?"

I wasn't going to suggest to Phoebe that maybe she too looked like a floozy in that honey-blonde wig with those outrageous curls floating to her shoulders and that high fringe coiling at her temples. I wouldn't dare. Anyone else but not Phoebe. Since childhood she's been the self-appointed arbiter of my manners and dress, reproving me with unsolicited and unvarnished criticisms for breaching Roman fashion trends.

"Aren't you listening?" Phoebe shook her head. "Isn't that what Judah said?"

I grumbled something while assessing my image in a mirror. The wig didn't look so bad. Not bad at all. In fact, I thought it made me look taller and younger.

"Here, put on this black one, use this salve to rouge your lips, and then do what I do: Line your eyes with this." She poked me with a pot of kohl. "And while you're at it—you look a little sulky—paint your lids green with some of this powder."

I complied with an extravagant sigh.

"And hurry." Phoebe wagged a warning finger under my nose. "Don't forget: We're not here to play dress-up. We're here to stop a murder!"

I mumbled a half-hearted apology, but she'd already grabbed her purse and was striding toward the door.

* * *

"Are you sure this is his shop, Miriam?"

"Do you see any other Etruscan antiques around?"

"You're snapping at me. You're angry because I made you wear the black wig."

Phoebe lagged behind to straighten her wig in a passing window—she'd ultimately chosen the honey-blonde one for herself—while I mounted the low, long flat steps and crossed the threshold on an apron of light. The faintly sweet, earthy scent of myrrh greeted my nose as I entered the marbled interior. It displayed an orderly arrangement of vases, pitchers, statues, chalices, amphora, and amulets, each type in its own cluster of vitrines, each piece professing in calligraphy to be at least 500 years old.

I was standing in the center aisle crushed against a rainbow of silk, linen, and Indian cotton. Women clad in their native garb were chatting in a host of languages, bobbing their heads, and calling for a clerk, when Phoebe came up behind me.

"Do you see him?" she asked in a whisper fit for the stage.

"*Shsh—*" I said with a flick of my hand.

"What now, Miriam?" Phoebe turned up her palms. "You're not going to let me even speak—"

"Hello, ladies. My name is Nicholas. Can I interest you in an antique vessel today?" The intimate pitch of the clerk's voice licked at my ear. Thin as a blade with a face pitted by acne, he spoke barely above a whisper, his lips scarcely moving as his words oozed out in a well-rehearsed pretense of refinement.

"No, thank you," I said. "We're just—"

Spotting a group of Macedonians admiring a collection of chalices, he moved toward them with the agility and speed of a Nile crocodile.

Phoebe elbowed me as her eyes narrowed and her gaze followed him. "That's him, isn't it?"

"Yes, he was the one at the table with Kosmos."

"The one picking his teeth." She said with a giggle. "And did you hear that oily voice?" She scanned the shop and then snapped her eyes back to me. "And who's that, the redheaded rent-a-girl at the desk in the far corner? Did you see that ring? Another emerald! How can she even lift her left hand!" This time Phoebe erupted in a fit of hilarity. Then, looking around, surprised at the volume, she stifled it with a clamped palm against her mouth before adding, "Really Miriam, it must have cost—"

"I'll ask the clerk about her, but let's look around until he has a free moment."

Embraced by the shadows, the redhead was dressed entirely in green—an inner tunic with a rich flounce, a matching outer tunic, and a himation. She sat enthroned at a long narrow table, its tapered legs stabbing a Persian rug, its side table stacked with scrolls, an abacus, and a tray of reed pens with a sharpening knife. Moving closer, I could see she was young, with fair skin and a heart-shaped face. In addition to the ring—Phoebe was right; the vivid green, oval-cut, faceted stone was huge—she wore a gold Roman collar necklace with spearheads and a pair of matching earrings.

"Ladies, have you decided on a purchase?" That was Nicholas, licking my ear again.

I moved to the vitrine nearest the woman. "Yes," I said, touching a spot in the air with my forefinger. "I'm interested in that Etruscan amphora, the black-figured—"

"An excellent choice. One of our finest pieces, an incredible value, on sale today in honor of the festival—"

"But tell me first. I'm curious. That lovely woman at the desk. She looks so familiar to me—"

"She's not for sale," he said with a chortle and a spray of saliva through his chipped teeth.

I responded with a manufactured smile. "I just can't think of her name—"

"Amara. She's our incredible scribe—"

"Yes, that's it. Amara. I think I know her from a perfumery in the agora—but no, perhaps from Aspasia's apothecary. You know, the one just south of the Great Harbor, which reminds me, I—"

"Hold on. She's calling—"

"My pens!"

Calling? The whole city could have heard her. A stunned silence followed her shriek as if a door had slammed.

Then standing up with a rustle of fine fabric, folding her arms across her chest, Amara stamped her foot until a crippled slave boy with welts on his legs hobbled over. "Sharp reed pens. Now!" she ordered with a clap. "And more carbon black!" she added, spitting out each word with infinite scorn.

"Pardon me," said Nicholas, resuming our conversation with a greasy smile. "Amara comes to us from another shop." He stretched out his arm toward her in an imperious gesture. "An expert in calligraphy as well as bookkeeping." Then leaning toward me in a pretense of confidentiality, he added with a collusive wink, "Her other job is to keep an eye on anyone Mr. Kosmos suspects of stealing. Hasn't worked here long though, just a few months.

Can't remember when, but she came to us with impeccable references, an incredible stroke of luck for Mr. Kos—"

"*Ma Zeus!*" cursed Amara. More expletives tumbled out of her mouth in a high-pitched stream of bile. "And where's that wretch, that *koprophagos*? I'm bleeding all over, and that cripple is nowhere in sight."

When the boy hobbled over, she scorched him with enough profanity to parch the air. "You good-for-nothing idiot! See what you've done! I've cut my hand sharpening this stupid pen while waiting for the ones you should have brought. Now get me some honey. And don't forget the ox fat and lint for a bandage." He edged away with a slight bow while the blood dripping from her right palm painted a crimson stain on the Persian rug. Her voice, guttural with enough contempt to sear everyone in the shop, spewed out one more flame of rage along with a dribble of spit: "And make it snappy, or you'll feel Mr. Kosmos's wrath against your miserable legs again."

Pulling in a deep breath, Nicholas flattened his features into a mask before addressing me with a head-shaking dismissal and an apology muttered to his knees.

"And where did you say she lives?" I asked, as if he'd already told me.

"Yes, she lives near—"

I stared at him with an air of expectancy, but that was all I was going to get. Kosmos had just made his entrance in a cloud of lemon-scented verbena, his mouth pinched in distaste. Feeling a nudge from his boss, whose head was pointing to none other than a son of the Valerii family, Nicholas excused himself with a "Right away, sir."

A wave of frustration flooded my chest, but with nothing else to glean, I searched for Phoebe, who'd strayed toward a display of amphorae and was opening her purse. Grabbing her elbow, I pulled her out of the shop.

"What did you do that for? It was a real bargain—"

"They're fakes, Phoebe. Besides we have to stop Kosmos from killing Amara."

"Amara? But—"

I raised a hand to silence her. "I'm sure she's the intended victim. Look, she's wearing a ring no scribe could afford, and it matches the one Kosmos wears. Second, she hasn't worked for him long but is already charged with keeping an eye on the others. And third, other than his wife, what other woman would a man want to kill? His mistress, of course."

"And he's going to kill her today. I suspect he plans to kill her in the privacy of her home when the shop closes, either during the siesta this afternoon or tonight."

"Oh, Isis! We have no time to lose."

* * *

I told Phoebe to order lunch for us and wait for me in Zenon's café while I went to see whether Judah had an address for Amara. Like a cave dweller, I squinted in the noonday sun as it polished the stone steps to his row of shops. Upon entering Judah's, my knees turned to jelly at the thought of failing to locate Amara's house. So, I leaned against a showcase of artfully arranged signet rings, each piece the work of a master craftsman in his prime.

Facing the entrance, arched over his workbench, Judah was seated on a high stool in front of the scrim at the rear of his shop. Intent on his craft, his lips folded into his mouth, he was carving an inversely inscribed monogram onto an agate cabochon. I must have broken his concentration when I shifted my weight because he put down the water-filled glass globe that magnified the stone and raised his lids to greet me.

"To what do I owe this visit from my favorite wife?"

"I have a question."

"Just a question? No 'good morning' first?" Judah arched his eyebrows and pursed his lips in mock disappointment.

"It's afternoon."

"Ah, I'm getting closer to a civil greeting. So, let me hear your question, but don't make it too hard." A playful gleam danced in his luminous eyes.

"Did you make an emerald ring for a woman named Amara?"

"So, you'd like a ring like that after all. You've come to the right place."

"You remember her?" I asked.

"I couldn't forget her if I tried! Without a doubt, she was the most unreasonable and demanding customer I've ever had."

"Oh?" I said, feigning incredulity.

A vertical furrow cut into Judah's brow. "'Oh' is right! I told her when she placed the order that I'd try to have the ring for her on the ides, that I could get the stone but was waiting for the ingots from Spain, that their delivery was uncertain—no, my exact word was 'unpredictable'—what with pirates continuing to target gold shipments even when carried by military transport.

"Then, two months ago, three days before the ides, she flounced into the shop demanding the ring. You'd think Nero and Poppaea had invited her to their wedding. In a voice loud enough to wake the Pharaohs and with a froth gathering at the corners of her mouth, she accused me of delaying the order to extort more money from Kosmos. 'My fiancé will surely hear about this,' she barked, 'and I'll see to it that he reports you to the tax collector.' Finally, she called me a name I thought only sailors knew and stalked out in high dudgeon.

"But now I'm wondering whether Kosmos ever did challenge that bill." The faintest smile curved his lips. "I should have charged him double for her churlishness." The smile turned into a chuckle when he added, "But then again, he has to live with her; I don't."

My gaze followed Judah as he ducked behind the scrim. He returned with a ledger, and placing it on his workbench, he sat back on his stool. Standing beside him, I fixed my eyes on his calloused hands as they unrolled the scroll. And then on his forefinger as it slid down the panel and stopped at a name with Kosmos's in parentheses: Amara, from outside the Gate of the Moon near the main necropolis.

"No, he paid the full price. No arguments. No accusations. No tax collector." Judah unwrapped a triumphant grin but as an afterthought, added this warning: "I hope you're not going to butt into that woman's business. Take it from me, she's trouble. The worst kind."

"Oh, don't worry." I said with a dismissive wave. Then, flashing him another wifely smile, I was close enough to the door to pretend I didn't hear him say, "Hey, how about having lunch with me?"

* * *

Zenon's café seasoned the agora with the aroma of fresh cinnamon rolls and the spikey jabber of hungry laborers on their lunch break, their boastful voices and vulgar laughter sweeping through the café. Phoebe was sitting at the marble-topped counter behind two plates, a full order of *tiropita*, a multi-layered pastry of phyllo and feta cheese, and another with just a few morsels remaining. Pinching the stem of her goblet of pomegranate wine, twirling it slowly in her stubby fingers, she took a drink, licked her lips, and set the goblet down with a clatter. Then she sucked some cheese off her fingers, tapped her mouth with a napkin, and belched softly.

"Well, did you find out where she lives?" Phoebe asked while shaking crumbs off her *stola*.

"Just outside the Gate of the Moon near the necropolis."

"So, now what?"

I took a seat on the stool next to her, pulled over my plate of *tiropita*, and waved for the one-eyed counterman to bring me a goblet of the same wine as Phoebe's and some figs.

"Figs, Miriam?"

"They're for you so you don't ogle my *tiropita*."

"I never do that!"

"Because I always give you figs."

Phoebe looked at me with wounded eyes and let out a theatrical sigh.

I got even with a long silence while I rolled the ball of flakey dough and creamy cheese around on my tongue and let it slide down my throat. Just then, the counterman, jostling several plates, put the goblet and a basket of figs down on the sticky counter. I took a sip to refresh my parched palate. It tickled my throat like a thousand pinpricks.

"I think we should go to Amara's house to warn her," suggested Phoebe. "She probably won't be home from the shop, but we can wait for her."

I nodded. "Sounds like a plan."

Her bracelets chimed as she wriggled with anticipation.

We were about three miles from the necropolis and just as far from my house. So, rather than send a message for Orestes and Solon to come and take us through the Gate of the Moon, I figured we'd save time by hiring a litter. Besides, I didn't want Judah to hear from our bearers that we'd gone to Amara's house.

* * *

With the agora clotted with tourists in addition to the usual mix of peddlers, beggars, pickpockets, swindlers, and sailors, I ended up hiring a most unlikely pair of bearers: a set of sharp-chinned twins with tentative mustaches and buckteeth, identical save for the leader's prominent limp.

"Yikes! Is this the best you could find?" asked Phoebe, wrinkling her nose as if she smelled something bad.

"Get in. We're not heading for China on the Silk Road."

With a grunt and a groan from the bearers, we were soon aloft, gripping the sides of the litter to keep from falling out. The most impressive buildings shimmered in the afternoon warmth while they carried us south on the Street of the Soma and west on the Canopic Way, through the harangue of hawkers, the bickering of moneychangers, and the haggling of vendors until we were in front of the Palace of Justice.

"Stop!" I shouted.

"What is it, Miriam?"

"Look over there." I said, pointing with a trembling finger toward the textile shop across the Way."

"What am I supposed to see, other than your finger?"

"That couple admiring the hanging tapestries."

"Oh, Isis! That's Kosmos and Amara."

"But she's not wearing the ring."

"Maybe she's having the prongs tightened."

I didn't bother to mention that the ring was new, only two months old, and that Judah would never hand over a ring with a loose stone. "But look, her hand isn't bandaged, and it's curled into an odd-looking fist with the forefinger pressing down on her thumb."

"Oh, Miriam, you notice the weirdest things! Why would she go out with Kosmos wearing a bloody bandage? Surely the cut has begun to heal, and she keeps her hand closed to protect it from being jostled."

"And look how she holds her head when the breeze kicks—"

"Who knows? Maybe she has a headache." Phoebe continued with a shrug. "Well, there's no sense going to her house now. She and Kosmos are out for the afternoo—Hey, he just turned his head, probably wondering why we stopped. Uh-oh, don't look now, but he's staring right at us with viperish eyes.

"Can't wait all day, ladies," the lead bearer interjected with the whine of a pubescent boy. "Make up your minds. Get out, or I'm gonna have to move on."

"Okay. Okay," I said, twisting my neck. "Take us back to the agora."

Once the bearers turned the litter around, Phoebe asked, her eyebrows rising a little, "Why there?"

"Well, I can drop you off at your house, and then from the agora, I can send a ragamuffin to tell Orestes and Solon to pick me up there. Anyway, that's exactly where Judah would expect me to have been this afternoon."

"I have a better idea. Stop at my house, we can rest there, and then after the siesta, we can go to the shop to make sure Amara's okay. I can see you're still a little worried despite having just seen her with Kosmos."

Actually, a clutch of alarm was growing in my vitals, but I nodded anyway, as much in acknowledgment of my own feelings as in agreement with Phoebe's plan.

We were back on the Street of the Soma when Phoebe said in a voice flowing like honey, "Oh, Miriam, did you see the way Kosmos looked at her, caressing her with his gaze?" By now romance was dancing in Phoebe's imagination. "They were like sweethearts. Are you sure Kosmos said he was going to kill her?"

"Well, I did have that second goblet of wine."

That's what I told Phoebe anyway. It was useless to argue with her when her heart was spinning in a sentimental orbit. But I knew trouble was afoot.

* * *

We waited out the siesta at Phoebe's and then walked over to Kosmos's, our shadows stretched out in front of us like ghosts. I hoped to ease the dread that was prickling my skin like a million needles, but instead, upon crossing the threshold and gazing into the far corner, my worst fear materialized. I blinked and looked again, but Amara's desk was still deserted.

"Can I help you, ladies?" Nicholas greeted us again, but this time his eyes bored into mine like gimlets before narrowing with a sly intelligence.

I could barely breathe let alone piece together a sentence, but I forced myself to utter her name.

"Not here. Not back after the siesta." Now suspicion was constricting his response.

"Where can I find her?" I asked, challenging him with my own eyes, seeing that hidden well of violence within him.

"Failed to come to work once before. No message then either. When her mother took sick and died. Poor soul. Her only relative."

He closed his eyes with a sigh. I thought he was finished, but a few moments later, his eyes flew open to deliver a threat more venomous than the words he spoke, which in fact he dispensed in a tone so cool, so neutral, so hushed that my blood turned to ice. "You better take your prying eyes elsewhere, Miss Snoop, or believe me, Mr. Kosmos will remove them for you."

I stood there feeling as if I'd been struck by a rock. But why should I come back? She'd already been killed, and I'd done nothing to stop it.

* * *

This time it was Phoebe who whisked me out of the shop.

"Miriam, what's the matter with you? You're shaking like you caught a chill."

I managed to sputter something about Amara being dead, but that was all.

"There you go, jumping to conclusions again! Amara decided to go out with Kosmos and just forgot to notify Nicholas. And why should she? He's not her boss. Besides, you saw the way Kosmos looked at her during the siesta. They were inseparable. So, don't tell me he's a killer!"

That's when Phoebe insisted we meet for breakfast in the morning so she could make sure I hadn't caught a cold and prove to me that Amara was still alive. Rather than argue—I knew better—I consented.

Chapter 3
Six days before the Nones (November 2)

"Miriam, taste the muffins," coaxed Phoebe in a phony singsong. "They're flavored with coriander seeds, just like the ones we ate when we were kids. Remember how the cook would cradle them like babies in a basket for us? And here," she offered, "dip into these olives and candied chestnuts— No wait." Snatching the platter as abruptly as she'd passed it, she thrust a bowl of fruits and cheeses under my nose. "Try these first: African figs, Arabian dates, and Macedonia cheeses. The best."

She might as well have presented me with a tray of raw pork, laced with fat and gristle, dotted with maggots, and swarming with flies. With the death of Amara, that's how revolted I was at the prospect of eating.

We were at Zenon's again, sitting at a table in the back, the light from the rising sun spilling gold across the mudbrick floor. The scene was dominated now by produce venders still chalky from the dust they'd gathered leading their mule-drawn carts through the countryside to the Gate of the Sun. Meanwhile, astrologers, street philosophers, and soothsayers were vying for a location to set up their pushcarts, tables, awnings, and umbrellas in preparation for the river of tourists.

Phoebe paused to scoop up a wedge of Mariovo hard cheese. Then she leaned back, chewing slowly. "Come on. Don't tell me you're still upset about Amara. Look, as soon as the shop opens, we can walk over there. You don't even have to go inside. Just look in. I guarantee you'll see her, that is, if you don't hear her scolding that poor lad first. So, eat something. I ordered all this for you."

I shook my head like a recalcitrant child.

117

"Well, I'll send the food over to Judah then. He at least will appreciate it." She stretched out the word *he* and emphasized it with a crisp dip of her head. "You know," she continued, "maybe instead of waiting for the shop to open—it's going to be a couple of hours—we should just go to Amara's house. Not because I think anything's wrong, but you're still shaking like a frightened horse."

And so, she tipped the one-eyed counterman to wrap up the food and call for a ragamuffin to take it to Judah while I found us another litter for hire.

* * *

The glare from the young sun set the treetops ablaze and sifted through the litter's curtain to sting my eyes. But I could rely on the expanding noise of the city—the clamor of commerce, the clang of metalworkers, and the throb of legionnaires' hobnailed boots—to track our progress. And my nose told me, as we sped along the Canopic Way, whenever we were sailing past a splendid building radiating the scent of warm stone or a graffiti-scarred tenement tainted with the tang of stale urine and putrefying garbage.

Once we passed through the Gate of the Moon, we were near the necropolis, where Alexandrians have been burying their dead for more than a century. It was easy to spot Amara's hamlet at the end of a gritty access road. On the brow of a hill, a few ugly cottages were threaded together by a dusty path fringed by a riot of untended brambles and a few stunted plane trees infested with wasps and gasping for water. No wonder so few lived beyond the Gate. My own nostrils were smarting from the putrid stink of rotting flesh, the pickle-like stench of the embalming workshops, and the cloying reek of funereal oils.

The bearers laid us down on a wiry clump of prickly weeds at the hamlet's dismal gate. Swinging with one post listing, the bottom rail scraped up plumes of dust with the breath of every breeze while its rusty hinges shrieked in protest. Only a second bronze coin in the leader's hand could persuade the pair to wait until we were ready to leave.

"So, which one, Miriam? They all look like boxes of misery, if you ask

118

me. Any one of them could be a fitting scene for tragedy. Which reminds me, wasn't it here last year that a madman butchered a woman and left her bleeding corpse to rot in the sun? As I recall, two beggars witnessed the event. One had his tongue cut out so he couldn't tattle to the authorities and the other had his manhood cut off so he wouldn't have the courage."

"Well, perhaps that explains why only two houses are occupied: The hovel with a woman's garments hanging from that drooping clothesline—"

"Where?" asked Phoebe, twisting her neck and squinting.

I pointed to a thorny hedge scrabbling for life. "Crouched behind there."

"And the other?"

"Straight ahead. Where the pigeons are squirting excrement on its cracked lintels."

"But how do you know that one is occupied?"

"See the light leaking out of its grimy window?"

"Oh, yeah."

"Let's try that one. At least we know someone's awake."

We crossed the yard, sunbaked into ruts and fissures and studded with dog scats, to knock on the door. Three times. At last, my plaintive "Hello, anybody home?" was answered by a clang of pots and pans, the *thwack* of sandals drawing near, and a redhaired woman wearing a green tunic and a thunderous frown.

Her hair was elaborately dressed in a tall style of multilayered curls, the tiniest ones coiling across her smooth, child-like forehead. Every feature was amplified with makeup: red ochre to tint her lips and cheeks, kohl to line her eyes, malachite powder to add shadow to them, and ashes to darken her eyebrows and lashes and paint a smudged mole on her left cheek. But no amount of Arabian perfume could mask the smell of the white lead paste that clung to every crease and pucker in her face. What's more, the shade of her foundation, too chalky for her honey-colored skin, coated her face with a pallid look.

Her jaw set and her eyes narrowed, the woman acknowledged us with a combative look. I thought she was going to breathe fire on us, but instead she asked in a harsh whisper, pointing to her throat to hint she had laryngitis,

"What do you want?"

I turned cold with horror when I saw the emerald ring on her left hand. And yet it was her right hand that attracted my attention. Not that it was curled into that same awkward fist, but as soon as she saw us, she tucked it under the sash of her robe. Just not before I got a close look at what she was hiding.

"Uh-oh," I said with a staged slap of my forehead. "We have the wrong house. Excuse us."

We turned and left quickly, hearing only an exasperated breath, not even looking at the door as it slammed behind us.

"What was that all about, our leaving so abruptly?" asked Phoebe with bemused disapproval when we were back on the path. "We at least could have wished her a good day."

"Take it from me," I said, "she's not going to have one."

* * *

"Well, you could've been a little friendlier. But at least you saw she's alive! Maybe next time you'll believe me without having to drag me all over the city."

Wasn't coming here her idea? Still, I said nothing.

"Anyway, you must be feeling better, so we may as well go back. By then, it'll be time for lunch."

I suppose I'd been staring, but I have no idea where my eyes were reaching.

"Miriam, what now? That look of yours is scaring me."

"What look?"

"You know, when you draw down your eyebrows."

"I want to see who lives in that other house."

"Aw, come on! Any minute, the bearers are going to leave us stranded."

"It won't take long."

Phoebe trailed behind me like a shadow, a few sour words escaping from deep in her throat and a gasp when she tripped over a spiny-tailed lizard. Wading through knee-high weeds, grasshoppers leaping in protest, we crossed the yard to the door. With the paint peeling like dead skin, the patches of wood had long since been silvered by the wind and sun.

Before I could knock, an elderly woman, her eyes yellowish and her face faded, greeted us with a dowager's hump and a nearsighted squint. "Need some help?" she asked through a drawstring mouth, her few remaining teeth brown to the gumline. "Not many folks pass this way, 'course, unless they're going to a funeral." She spoke gently, like a woman who's breathed pain and endured loss.

"We're friends of Amara's." I said as if that answered her question. As a woman who, judging by the garments flapping and snapping on her clothesline, lived alone, I hoped she'd be willing to pass the time with two strangers. "It was quite an effort to get here, but we are charmed by the peace and quiet here," I fibbed in a voice that could rival birdsong.

"Oh, I've lived here many years. Stayed even after the mister died. Only one I see 'round now, 'course, is Amara. Unless there's a funeral. The professional mourners, weeping, wailing, scratching their faces, ripping out their hair, worse, 'course, when it's someone wealthy or famous. And the flute dirges, had enough of them too. Told the mister, none of that for us. He objected, 'course, but when the time came, he had nothing to stay." A look of triumph played on her face.

"Wanna rest awhile?" she asked.

Phoebe poked me in the back. Her finger felt like a fishhook, but I said, "Just a few minutes. We have to get back to town. My name is Miriam, and this is my friend, Phoebe."

"I'm Lydia. Can't offer much, 'course. Ain't got much, but come sit in the back. At least there's some shade."

She led us to the crumbling stoop of a dingy hut strangled by foliage, its battered door enveloped in cobwebs, its frowning walls gray with dust. One corner of its sagging roof was propped up with a stack of lichen-blotched rocks. I felt like I was walking into the Land of the Dead. Inside, the air buzzed with insistent flies diving in wide arcs. When Lydia pointed to a row of splintery stools along the wall and dragged one to the center of the earthen floor, Phoebe and I did the same.

I shifted my legs, so my knees pointed in Lydia's direction. "So, you see Amara now and then."

"Used to see more of her."

When Phoebe pulled in a breath to speak, I flashed her a thin-lipped warning.

Lydia continued. "She works long hours. Ambitious. That's why she minds her appearance, 'course. Beautiful clothes. And does she love that jewelry! But she's keeps to herself. No visitors. Oh, except this man. Can't tell you what he looks like, 'course—I don't see so well—but I sure can smell him when he comes up the path. Like we don't have enough to smell around here! Verbena. He must buy it by the shipload. I'd give the rest of my teeth to find out how much he pays—" Exploding in a guffaw, her mouth morphed into a black hole.

She calmed herself with a long breath, and then, with a lopsided smile, asked, "So, where was I?"

"The man." I said, leaning toward her with an encouraging nod.

But Lydia started her narrative all over again: about Amara's ambitiousness, her jewelry, her visitor, his verbena. Along the way, through many gasps and pauses, her mind darted from one tangent to another. I even had to listen to her contrasting Amara with her lazy cousin Cora, who lives near the hippodrome and whose boyfriend, without a *drachma* to his name, smells like sour onions.

Phoebe, who long ago mastered the art of expressing impatience, folded her arms across her bosom and threw me a steady look of angry suffering.

"Anyway, he's got the voice of a patrician, 'course. Kind of comical the way they speak in their throats and scrape the words against the roof of their mouth. And rich too, not like Cora's boyfriend whose talk fouls the air. I can tell Amara's boyfriend is rich because he speaks slow, like a man who's used to keeping others wait—"

Phoebe made a sound halfway between a throat-clearing cough and the gag of a dying woman.

"But no, Amara, ain't been living here long. Hard to remember—*hmm*—well, maybe less than a year. Let's see. Another young woman before her—*hmm*—but she didn't live here long either—"

"Another?"

"Also, with red hair. Just disappeared, never even said good-bye, even though I thought we was friends. *Hmm.* Wait. I remember something else. A dog."

"A dog?"

By now, Phoebe was pacing the floor. When she circled behind me, I thought she might kick me.

"A stray, brown and white with a whiny bark. Mangy, 'course, but still playful despite life's disappointments. It would come around, mincing and scraping at Amara's doorway, and 'course, she'd feed it. And then it would sit up on its haunches, look up at her, and wiggle its stubby tail. Oh, it would sniff me and accept a scratch behind the ear now and then, but it was Amara's dog all right."

Even the flies seemed to be listening now.

"But it hasn't come around, not since yesterday evening. I heard the poor thing whimper, so 'course, I came out. And there was Amara with a broom in her hands thrashing that scrawny mutt. Said it was rabid. Why she'd hurt her faithful little friend is more than I can say. So, me and the dog have been staying away. I didn't even greet her this morning."

* * *

In the buttery noonday light, the bearers carried us to my house in the Jewish quarter, where Phoebe and I could have lunch as we waited out the afternoon. While the cook prepared some sesame cakes, smoked sardines, and a salad of rosemary flowers, I positioned two of the three dining couches across from each other, each with a view of the courtyard, the low ivory table in between.

"Miriam, could you shift my couch over a little? When the sun inches down, it's going to jab me right in the eye."

"How's this?"

Phoebe answered by bellying down on her couch and propping up her

123

torso and elbows with a cushion. "By the way, I hope you're going to have something to eat with me. You know how I hate to eat alone, and I can smell the sesame cakes warming."

Minta, with her usual whirl of energy and lightness of foot, set the table with an Indian cotton cloth and napkins, followed by our red-gloss pottery, crystal goblets, and silver flatware. A moment later she was back with a crater of wine mixed with honey-sweetened water and a ladle for serving it into our goblets. When Minta asked in her high warble whether we were ready for the food, Phoebe, before I could say a word, gave her a succession of eager nods accompanied by the tinkling of her earrings.

"Not so much," Phoebe said as she offered me her goblet.

But I filled it anyway and watched her hold it up to the light flooding in from the courtyard. After examining its color, she took a gulp, smacked her lips, and downed the rest in a single draft as if it were medicine. When she offered me her goblet again, I refilled it, but this time she took a small sip and savored it before swallowing.

"You know, the aroma of the sesame cakes reminds me of something," Phoebe said as she rearranged her cutlery. "Remember when you risked your life to track down those stolen alchemical documents? I told you not to, but I still packed you a bundle of those very same cakes to bring along."

"Yes, you were my guardian angel that night. I even remember when you reached behind your back and pulled out that silver-handled carving knife, saying 'Tuck this under your belt, just in case.'"

When Minta brought in the food, Phoebe grabbed one of the cakes, broke off a wedge, and chewed it slowly. After swallowing, she stared into space as if deciding whether to take another piece. Instead, she fished a flower out of the salad and tasted it while she served herself a hefty portion of each dish.

"Oh, Miriam, you don't know what you're missing." And then, while rearranging the food on her plate, she continued her recollection. "You came home smeared with filth and without the knife." Phoebe squared her shoulders, her face opening with pride. "I'm still your guardian angel, you know. That's why I want you to eat something. No need to fret anymore. We've seen Amara—though I still can't believe how abrupt you were with her. Just because she has to work—"

I knew she'd been leading up to something. "Listen, Pheeb, I want to talk to you about that."

"What's there to say? You were rude. Just admit it."

"Rude to Amara?"

"Who do you think I'm talking about?"

"Phoebe, Amara wasn't in that house." I spoke slowly, trying to keep my voice calm and uninflected so she'd believe me.

"Whaaat?" she said, her voice shrill with incredulity, her eyes narrowed to slits. "What are you saying?"

I'd hoped the wine would have softened the blow, but it didn't. "Amara is dead. That woman you saw is an imposter."

"You must be kidding. She looked just like her. And who says so anyway?"

"The dog knew. That's why it got beaten."

"Oh, Isis." Phoebe rubbed the back of her neck until a flicker of understanding brightened her eyes. Then, with all the strength leached from her voice, she asked in a tone that was more a sigh than a whisper, "What should we do?"

"We must get proof—"

"How?"

"We must find out how Kosmos disposed of the body."

"Oh, no, Miriam. I don't know if I can do—" The corners of her mouth turned down, as if the very thought tasted foul.

"Kosmos is a killer, Phoebe. If we don't stop him, he'll kill again. Besides, I have a hunch he also killed the red-haired woman before Amara, the one Lydia said just disappeared."

* * *

The autumn sun was well into its descent when a new pair of bearers, a father and son with ears that stuck out like pot handles, took Phoebe and me westward toward the Gate of the Moon. We sat in silence as I watched the long slants of light infuse my friend's ashen face with an amber wash.

As soon as we reached the hamlet, the gate still shrieking in rhythm with the breeze, we headed directly down the path to Amara's house.

"Look, Miriam. That same dog is sniffing around her house."

With its right foreleg dangling and patches of its fur stiff with blood, the poor mutt hopped toward us announcing its presence with a series of high-pitched yelps and a stink that could fell an enemy from a hundred cubits. Then jittering around, looking up, its eyes hot with excitement, it let out one long, low mournful howl.

That's when I figured out what the dog was trying to tell us, that its friend was gone but so was its abuser. So, instead of knocking on the door, I swung it right open. Phoebe followed at my heels.

The house exhaled a complex of odors that assaulted my nose and clawed at my throat. The mustiness of underventilation clung to my lips, while the tang of old food, soiled bedding, and a ripe chamber pot sunk into my clothes. We split up to search for any clue as to what could have happened to Amara. Entering through its low door, Phoebe took the tiny room in the back while I examined the front room with a kitchenette in its corner. The walls were splotched with deep stains as if they carried an ancient disease. The sun had inched down enough to struggle through the west-facing window, slant across the sagging floorboards, and outline the clumps of porridge, smithereens of pottery, and sundry tableware strewn across the floor.

Another shaft of light spilling into the corner fell across a meat cleaver on the cooking surface of the charcoal-burning furnace. When I picked it up by the merest corner of its handle, the blade glinted with menace, but the smudge along its edge was too scant for me to infer its most recent use. Nevertheless, my ears imagined the grunts of a scuffle and the smack of fists. Amid the toppling of kitchenware, I heard the trill of a blade slashing flesh and severing bone along with screams so shrill they could have come only from the Pit of Tartarus. And then a silence gathered as if a toxic gas had invaded the house.

"Miriam, did you hear that?"

"Hear what?"

"That noise."

"All old houses make noise."

"No, this is different. Someone is scratching. I can hear her scraping the floor with her fingernails. I can tell she's signaling us, trying to get out."

"Where is sh—?"

"*Shsh*. I hear some movement. Very faint."

"I'll be right there."

"She's under the bed. Hurry. I can't bring myself to look."

Was our pathetic search over?

Here in the back of the house, the dearth of light and the grimy walls painted the air black. I had to stretch open my eyes and hold out my hands to feel my way.

But then I felt the doorway. *Bang!* "Ouch!"

"Miriam, what was that noise?"

"Nothing. Just my head."

"Are you all right?"

"Never mind. Where are you? Wait. I can see you now."

"Hurry."

"Move over so I can get in there." I heard her silk hem brush over the floor as I knelt to look under the cot. I felt as if I were gazing into the mouth of a tomb. But then I heard movement. When my eyes adjusted, I thought I was looking at a snake, but it was just a tail. Still, when it turned and flashed its teeth, I shivered in horror.

"Who is she, Miriam?"

I rose to my feet feeling the stiffness in my muscles. "She's a mother rat building a nest to welcome her litter." I said, gripping the corner of the cot to stand up.

Phoebe waggled her head. "I'm so sorry I made you bang your head and for nothing." Then, after a sigh, she spread out her hands to say, "Now what?"

I slapped the dust off my skirt and calmed the wrinkles. "We'll keep on looking. But we don't have much time. The afternoon light is fadin—"

"Look, the dog. I must have left the door open. Maybe it's looking for something."

"No, it's yelping and hopping toward the courtyard. It wants to show us something."

Following its twitching stub of a tail, we pushed through another low door in the back room—this time Phoebe reminded me to duck—and found ourselves in a weed-blanketed, cobbled courtyard with a washtub in the center. The far side of the tub was a riot of thorny brambles; otherwise, it was surrounded by rusty poles supporting a tangle of clotheslines.

"Why are the cobbles around the tub caked with mud?" asked Phoebe, kicking a clod with the toe of her *calceus*. "The last time it rained was eight months ago, the very day I had that party to surprise Bion. Remember? I got him that Chinese silk *synthesis*, the fancy kind Romans wear at their own dinner parties, and I got myself that crimson *tunica interior* with the wide embroidered flounce. So, at the last minute I had to change the venue fr—"

"Phoebe, do you smell anything funny? It gets stronger around the tub?"

"You mean like Fulvius' s Butcher Shop?"

"Exactly. A sweet coppery smell, almost like rust. I can taste it on my lips. No wonder Amara's imposter hated that dog. She was afraid of what it could smell. And look, the poor thing is lying by the tub and crying."

"Crying for Amara."

"Yes, Phoebe, her little four-legged friend knows Amara was killed yesterday, probably in the afternoon, and butchered in the tub last night. And no one else, not Lydia nor the drudges in the embalming workshops, would notice the stench. Not in this neighborhood. We certainly know, but we have no way to prove it."

A feeling of impotence hung over me like a swag of brooding clouds.

"Can't we look a little longer?"

"No, the sun is already sinking into the trees."

"Oh, Miriam, how can we let someone get away with murder like that!" Threads of frustration burning in her eyes, Phoebe clenched her fists and then closed her eyes wearily.

"Well, at least we can take the dog back outside."

"Where'd it go?"

"Oh, no. It's hiding in the brambles!"

"I'll get the poor thing," offered Phoebe.

"No, you'll ruin your *stola*. Let me. You go fetch the bearers."

Accompanied by the drone of wasps, I waded through some knee-high, thickly overgrown scrub to find the dog crouching along the base of the tub.

"Here, little friend," I cooed. "Come to Miriam. Come on now. You're not going to make me crawl through that prickly brush, are you?"

Just as I paddled through the thorns,

The barbs scratching my arms, drawing blood,

The foliage closed in behind me.

That's when I saw on the side of the tub the proof I needed.

But that's also when I felt the breath of yesterday's whiskey on the back of my neck.

A pair of muscular forearms grabbed my shoulders, turned me around, and two thick-palmed hands with long, blunt, hairy fingers encircled my throat.

* * *

"If you make a sound, I'll kill you right here and now—"

His first punch was a left hook that drilled into my shoulder. It felt like a brick jarring the bones in my neck, traveling up, and rattling my teeth.

But he didn't know my late brother had been a gladiator who'd taught me to watch my opponent's feet and measure his reach.

I moved in quick, sidestepped a second punch, and slugged him in the mouth with a right before twisting to drive my left elbow into his face. He responded with a feeble left, but I'd leaned away.

This was a fight where only one of us was going to be left alive.

His hand folding into a meaty fist, he rocked me with a left to my jaw. I tasted blood in my mouth and heard a ringing in my ear. But with a lot of shoulder behind it, I sent him a hook that broke his nose.

Then a butt to the head knocked the wind out of him, and a thread of blood trickled out of the angry hole that was his mouth. His breath came in a series of labored whistles as he pinwheeled backwards into the tub. When he cracked his head on the bottom, the whistling stopped, and a puddle of urine stained the front of his tunic.

* * *

"What's Nicholas doing in the tub?" asked Phoebe, a pucker settling on her brow, the bearers in tow.

"What took you so long? For all you know, he could have killed me."

"What is it, Miriam? Your face is bruised, and look, your arms are all scratched—"

"Never mind that. Look under the brush at the side of the tub."

"What am I supposed to see—Oh, Isis! Not this! It's a bloody print of—It looks something like a hand."

"Yes, it was probably too dark or screened by the brambles when Nicholas, Kosmos, and his latest mistress cleaned up after their butchery."

"But what is it?"

"You were right, Phoebe. It's a handprint, a woman's right hand, and fortunately for us, a remarkable one. The owner has more than five fingers on that hand. And in her case, even more unusual, her two thumbs are fully formed."

"But how will we ever find that woman?"

"We already have."

Chapter 4
Three days before the Nones (November 5)

The next morning, Phoebe and I went to the Palace of Justice and reported Amara's disappearance, our findings at her house, especially the handprint on the washtub, and my struggle with Nicholas. The magistrate agreed to send an *immune*, a legionnaire trained as an investigator, to the hamlet and asked me to meet the soldier there in the early afternoon. This time I went without Phoebe, who'd promised to help Bion in the bookshop for the last day of the festival. With no threat of danger, I confessed my exploits to Judah. Mocking me with a sigh of infinite patience, he admitted he'd already figured that I'd gone in a hired litter to the hamlet beyond the Gate of the Moon. So, with a clear conscience, I had Orestes and Solon carry me westward in the sedan chair.

I caught up with Phoebe two days later. She was waiting for me at what we'd begun to call "our table" at Zenon's, the one in the back, but this time it was well past the dinner hour. The tinkle of glass, the rattle of tableware, and the tuneless clatter of a dropped plate reminded us that the counterman was preparing to close for the night. With the meager light bleeding in from a torch in the plaza and a feeble yellow circle from the table lantern, I could see from the pouches under my friend's eyes that she had been working long hours serving Bion's customers and re-shelving the stock.

"So, what happened with the *immune*?" asked Phoebe.

"Well, it was what happened before he arrived that was so interesting."

"Oh, good. I can't wait to hear." Phoebe folded her hands on the table and leaned forward.

"I arrived early to verify the location of the handprint in the full light of day. Orestes and Solon dropped me off right at Amara's door. Oh, and Amara's dog was there to amuse them. Its eyes hinting at playfulness, its tail wagging, it wobbled over to Orestes, sat on its haunches, and when Orestes laughed, it leaped onto his lap."

"Is that the interesting thing you wanted to tell me?"

Did I hear a hint of sarcasm in Phoebe's tone?

"Gee, Pheeb, give me a chance." I thought she was going to sit back and fiddle with her cameo ring, but she just sat back.

"I heard noises in the house, the slap of bare feet and the whoosh of fabric, so angling my shoulder as if against the wind, I barged in and saw Amara's imposter—Her name is Dido, by the way, and she's from Carthage—I saw her packing her few things— a jeweled comb, a tiny scroll, and a miniature of the lighthouse. You know, I couldn't resist staring at her right hand. I'd learned about that kind of variation—it's a familial trait—but I'd never seen it before. Anyway, I warned her that an *immune* was coming to arrest her for murdering Amara and that she'd fare better if she told the truth.

"She blamed it on Kosmos. Claimed it was all his idea, that she went along only because she was afraid if she didn't, he'd kill her too, like he killed the redhead who lived there before Amara. She said his motive to kill that first one—she thinks it was his first one—and then Amara was because they found out he'd been unfaithful to them and threatened to tell his wife. Besides, she said, he got tired of Amara. He complained she had a nasty temper and kept wanting more and more jewelry, so much so that she cost him more than she was worth."

"And Nicholas?"

"Dido said Nicholas and Kosmos's partnership went way back. Kosmos found him when Nicholas was a boy living on the streets. Nicholas's parents had been about to sell him into slavery to pay his father's poll tax, but the kid ran away. The result was that the tax collector and his soldiers tortured and killed his parents in the agora as an appalling lesson to others. Kosmos happened to witness the spectacle and swore he'd get even with the tax collector by saving their son. So, he found the boy, took him in, bought a tutor for him, and then gave him the store to manage.

"Anyway, Nicholas had gone to the property to remove whatever was left of value before burning the house down and destroying any other evidence that might have been left behind."

"Like the tub."

"Yes, Phoebe, like the tub."

"Do you think Dido is as innocent as she claims?"

"That will be for the magistrate to determine. She did say though that in the beginning, before he became 'a coldblooded monster'—her exact words—Kosmos would make her wear the wig but wouldn't tell her why except that he loved red hair, that his mother had red hair. So, she thought it was just a harmless obsession and went along with it."

"Well, I guess Lydia will take the dog."

"No. I saw Lydia as I was leaving. With the entire hamlet deserted now, she's decided to move in with her cousin Cora near the Hippodrome."

"Oh, that poor thing."

"Lydia?"

"No, Miriam, the dog."

"Oh, don't worry about the dog. Orestes and Solon fell in love with it. When it was time to go, it lay at Orestes's feet, its head on its paws and couldn't be coaxed to move. You should've seen it snuggling in my lap all the way back to the Jewish quarter. Believe me, it's going to be well taken care of."

The Recollection

The Eighth Year of the Reign of
Nero Claudius Caesar Augustus Germanicus [Nero]
An autumn day, 62 CE, Alexandria *ad Aegyptum*

He didn't feel the warmth of the afternoon sun. Nor did he see the sapphire sky arching high above him, its pieces changing shape between the waving treetops. He didn't even hear the shrill voice of the woman leaning over him.

"Oh, for the love of Jupiter," she shrieked.

"Do you know this man?" the other woman asked.

"Kind man. Would help me up the stairs." She took a deep breath and swallowed. "Is he dead?"

"Yes, I'm sorry, but he is. He's been stabbed in the chest with a short blade."

Chapter 1
Morning

The kind man's head reeled as if the rubble under him was rolling in waves, and a fishy reflux shot up his gorge and coated the back of his throat.

He swallowed down the bitterness.

Groaning, rolling onto his side, sitting up, opening his gummed eyelids, squinting against the morning sun, he took a greedy gulp of air. Colors spun as he tried to focus on his whereabouts.

Questions stirred in him: *Who am I? Where am I? How did I get here?*

Tapping his lips with his first two fingers, he groped in the far corners of his mind, coaxing a memory to trickle back to him.

Nothing. Not a clue. Not even about the blood staining the chest of his tunic.

He folded his legs under his haunches and leaning forward, his palms pressing against the unidentifiable ground cover, he lurched to his feet, his joints stiff, his muscles cramped. He winced as a flare of pain burned through his left hip. He uttered a low growl and shifted his weight. Then he rubbed the hip with the heel of his hand.

Well, now I know who I am, he thought as the corner of his purplish lips twitched into a lopsided smirk. *The man with arthritis.* Thoughts furrowed his brow. *Maybe I better work on where I am first.*

He inhaled the tang of brine and the stench of decaying fish and rotting seaweed. A squadron of gulls, blue and gray, lifted into the wind. As their wings spread, they wheeled overhead, swooping low, soaring, and diving. He watched them inscribe arcs over the buildings and then plane off, flapping toward the sea and disappearing into the sky.

So, I'm near the harbor.

Blinking away the gauze that veiled his eyes, he swept his gaze toward the plaza in front of him, its cobbles scratched with graffiti and its public fountain splattered with pigeon droppings. Women in a huddle against a background of screaming children nursed their babies in the doorway of one of the tenements jammed around the plaza.

The tenements. A shred of memory spooled toward the front of his brain. *Those flat roofs look familiar.* He waddled over to the bench on the other side of the fountain and sat down. *I must be in one of those rutted lanes next to the Palace of Justice. That's where I used to visit my Sophia. I can still picture her, innocent of makeup with her alabaster face and cheeks like blushing roses, her hair like skeins of sunshine held back from her face with cheap copper pins.*

He closed his eyes and drew in a breath to nourish that memory.

Maybe, if I find her, she can tell me who I am.

So, he walked toward the agora in search of her.

135

Chapter 2

He felt a stab in his left hip with every step, but as he rode the pain, its edge dulled. He walked a mile, maybe a little more, east to the Street of the Soma and then north toward the agora. He recalled the sun-bleached rooftops in the distance angling toward the agora and how they used to remind him of a row of broken teeth.

Passing through the West Gate of the agora, he watched with fresh eyes the clamorous throngs, the swaggering soldiers, and the haranguing soothsayers eager to predict a miracle for a price.

A river of humanity. How will I ever find her?

He paused at a wig shop and elbowed through the crush of Chinese silks and jewel-threaded hairstyles to catch his image in one of the polished bronze mirrors positioned beside the wigs, each an imitation of Empress Messalina's layered curls. He was pleasantly surprised to see he had a still-young face, almost handsome, with a strong square jawline and deeply sculpted cheeks. Only a nose a little too crooked kept him from looking rugged. He flashed a wide smile into the mirror to see that despite his overlapping, slightly protruding teeth and the creases bracketing the corners of his mouth, his full lips gave him a sensitive look.

Another sliver of memory came back when, passing a jeweler's barrow, he spotted a gold snake ring. Wound into a three-coil spiral, the tail curled back sharply while the lithe reptile's neck and head formed a graceful curve. He remembered buying a ring like that to protect her until they could marry.

She worked for a fuller, sorting, soaking, and stirring laundry in a tub of stale urine before the slaves stomped on the garments. Perhaps I should look for the earthenware bowls at every fuller's gate that collect the urine of men passing by.

As he passed a moneychanger's table, a sausage stand, and a peddler of honey-sweetened water crouching in a polygon of shade, he dreamed backward in time, resurrecting images—

Wait! Is that my Sophia lined up at the baker's stall?

He rubbed his eyes with his fingertips.

Perhaps it was her height or stance, the straightness of her back, or the tilt of her head, but just a distant glimpse of her and he had to grab the column of a portico until his trembling subsided. He waggled his head as if to declutter his mind.

I wish she'd turn around. I need to see more than those luxuriant coils of blonde hair cascading down her back. I need to see my Sophia's pure oval face with its small, pointed features and slightly flared nostrils. Oh, please, please beautiful woman, turn around so I can reclaim my identity and love you again!

Chapter 3
Early Afternoon

"Miriam, I have been waiting for you!" Phoebe was drumming the bejeweled fingers of her dumpling-like hands on the sticky surface of the back table of Zenon's café. The pitch of her wounded voice circled around the banter and rollicking guffaws of tradesmen, produce vendors, and laborers before floating up to the rafters.

"I knew you'd be displeased, but I couldn't get here sooner." I replied. "The traffic on the Canopic Way—"

"Oh, the Way is choked every afternoon. If it isn't those nagging beggars and gawking tourists, it's those ranting street philosophers. Admit it. You didn't allow enough time. Unless you really don't want to go with me."

"Come on, Phoebe. I told you yesterday I'd go, didn't I? Besides, you're my best friend. I just forget why you asked me to go."

"Well, you didn't forget. I just didn't tell you. I need to deliver an emergency supply of papyrus scrolls to the clerks in the morgue. I should have sent the order with Bion's helpers a week ago, but I kept procrastinating."

Phoebe's husband, Bion, owns the most prosperous bookshop in the agora. But his liveliest trade is in writing supplies, especially the sheets and scrolls of papyrus and parchment for the myriad of scribes, students, and scholars who populate our city.

"That's so unlike you, Pheeb, to procrastinate."

"I was afraid Bion's helpers would bring the god of death back with them. You know, Thanatos. And he'd carry one of us off to the Underworld. But now the clerks are flat out of scrolls, and the shop is too busy to send anyone else."

Phoebe sighed and then continued. "Anyway, Bion told me how the morgue reeked, that a fit of retching ripped through him when he went there to identify that tenant of ours, and how, if it hadn't been for you going with him, he wouldn't have been able to do it at all."

"Yes, I remember the stench, how it engulfed us as we made our way down that dark and narrow flight of steps."

"So, you'll go with me?"

I nodded.

"Good. So, dismiss your bearers, and let's have lunch now because neither of us is going to feel like eating afterward."

Chapter 4

His memory of Sophia, having blurred into a haunting dream, came back when the woman turned around and he saw she was wearing the ring he gave her. He called to her and felt the pleasure of saying her name.

"Sophia, is that you? I've been looking all over for you."

Her face opened with delight. "Silly, you know I love to shop. Where else would I be?" Her body angled toward his just like it used to.

He felt a thrill as if he'd inhaled the juice of the poppy. And so, he took the risk of asking her to spend some time with him.

"Would you like some *tiropita*? There's a café over there. Zenon's."

"*Tiropita*? He makes the best!" Her heavily lashed, sometimes green, sometimes blue eyes widened under her arched eyebrows.

Swinging his arm, he said, "Here, let me carry your purchases," as he picked up her satchel with lighthearted ease.

"Gladly! You know I always buy too much." Her lips curved before unwrapping a life-loving smile that, behind her parted lips, revealed two even rows of pearly white teeth. Wiping her raw chapped hands on the skirt of her unadorned linen tunic, she grasped his ink-stained hand as if he were her sweetheart and pulled him across the agora to the café.

* * *

Zenon's one-eyed counterman shouldered their order to a table tucked in the back: two goblets of pomegranate wine, plates of *tiropita*, and clutches of cutlery wrapped in cotton napkins. Then he maneuvered through the maze of tables to wait on others.

After arranging her tableware, Sophia tried a dainty morsel from the corner of her triangle of pie. She rolled the flakey dough and creamy cheese around on her tongue and let it slide down her throat. Then she let out a breath that faded into a small sigh.

"So, how is it?" he asked, his heart fluttering, his pulse hammering in his ears.

"*Hmm.* Those undercurrents of mint."

He could not get enough of her, looking into her eyes, hearing her voice, and sensing her presence.

They lapsed into a comfortable silence relieved by only the clink of their spoons against their plates and the sounds of their chewing, sipping, and swallowing. His eyes clung to every part of her but remained on alert to shift their gaze if she looked up. He thought of things to say, but did not speak them. Still the question of who he was lodged on his tongue, but not wanting to break into her enjoyment, he allowed the general cacophony of the café to fill the space between them.

Watching the slow rise and fall of her breasts and enjoying the trills of pleasure bubbling from her throat, he hoped he could accompany her home. Suddenly, she'd become the focus of his most private fantasies. He knew he'd go mad without her, the rhythm of her breath, the movement of her hands, and the lilt of her voice.

"Can I carry your packages home for you?" he asked, unable to hide the tremble in his voice.

Her head pivoted upward. She flipped back a wing of hair from her right eye and, cocking her head like a sparrow, scrutinized his face. With a dreamy look drifting across her face, she dipped her head in an almost imperceptible nod and blushed.

Chapter 5
Mid-Afternoon

"Here, Pheeb. Put some of the scrolls in my satchel."

"No, never mind. Couldn't be more than a mile. But what I really want to know," she said as she threw her forefinger at me, "is what took you so long this afternoon."

"Well, just as my sedan chair was rounding the corner onto the Street of the Soma, we encountered a parade of sorts, a procession of the crippled and the sick hobbling toward the Temple of Isis on Pharos Island. I'd forgotten the sanctuary would be open for private prayer and meditation this afterno—"

"See, that's what I mean. You never allow for the ordinary—"

"But it was far from ordinary. Along that very same stretch of the Way, we had to zigzag around a drove of pigs, elude a caravan of camels, and sidestep a cohort of legionnaires headed for the armory."

"Oh."

I think I convinced her to forgive me.

We trooped along the Great Harbor past the clamor of warehouses, the shriek of foundries, the din of factories, and the squawks of pigeons fluttering around the grain bins. Beyond a row of vendors in shabby stalls hawking olives, boiled elephant beans, and honey-sweetened water, we entered a knot of narrow lanes. The shoulder-to-shoulder tenements fringing them were close enough to the saloons, restaurants, and inns to be fouled by their heaps of stagnant garbage.

"You know what, Miriam? You were right. My satchel is getting too heavy." Phoebe extended her arm to point to a waist-high spot in the air. "I see a couple of benches by the fountain in the—"

"But we're almost there. Look, we could switch bags. Let me carry—"

"No, no, no. I need to rest now."

"Okay. Just watch for the pigeon droppings."

Phoebe dropped her satchel on the graffiti-scarred cobbles with a sigh of relief, plopped down on the bench, and loosened the straps on her *calcei*. "Whew! I'm tired. I'm going to have to wait for my feet to stop throbbing."

I perched on the edge of the seat next to her. "It's those shoes, Phoebe."

"I, at least, wear what's fashionable."

Did I hear an edge in my best friend's voice?

After a few deep breaths, Phoebe leaned forward and cocked her head to listen. "Don't turn around now, Miriam, but the women on the bench behind us are gossiping. The one talking now has this sharp staccato voice that's piercing my ear like an icepick."

"Do you want to move?" I asked.

"*Shsh!* No, I want to listen."

"Who?" asked the other one, not Icepick but the one who had a gravelly voice as if she'd swallowed a mouthful of pebbles.

Icepick answered: "The one who owns the herb stall by the lumberyard. You know, with the face of a tired dog and the breath of a gravedigger. And those gross swags of fat spilling over his belt."

"His belt? I never noticed he wore a belt."

"Of course, you didn't. It's hidden under that immense belly of his. Where else do you think he keeps the tools to cut and chop his herbs?"

"Ooh, you must mean Greg—"

"Gregor!" The whole city must have flinched when she squealed his name. "Yeah, that's it. I just couldn't think of—"

"So, what about him?"

"Well, he was only screaming at her early this morning. That's all."

"What could she have done? So beautiful, like a goddess that one."

"She wants to enroll their son in a school, but he said no way was he gonna spend the money on a kid that don't even look like him. Then I heard a gasp followed by a grunt and a scuffle, the smack of a fist, the clunk of his boots, and the slam of their door. After that, I could make out her whimpering, but only with my ear pressed to the wall."

"And I'll bet he's got the money, all right," said Gravel Voice. "I just knew—Uh-oh. My twins are fighting again. Gotta go."

When it was safe to turn around, I watched the tall one leap from the bench and mutter "*Ma Zeus*" as she clipped her knee on a splintery edge. My guess that she was Gravel Voice was confirmed when I heard her call over her shoulder, "I'll be back later." But Icepick, shaking her head, rolled to her feet and waddled away in the other direction.

"Oh, that poor mother," said Phoebe, sagging back into the bench, emotion filling her eyes and clogging her throat.

"You mean the one with the twins?"

"No, the one married to Gregor." As a follower of Isis, Phoebe was especially sensitive to the plight of battered women.

Chapter 6

Although the man was careful not to touch Sophia or even graze her arm, an onlooker might have thought they were lovers looking for a deserted beach as they sauntered along the harbor. Perhaps it was in their stolen glances, the synchrony of their steps, or the enchantment in their faces. Or perhaps it was only in the way the sea breeze so reluctantly whiffled between them. Passing warehouses and foundries, the man felt the whirr of their machines, the clanks and clatters, like music warming his veins. Otherwise, he heard only the quiet *woosh* of her tunic as if she were floating just above the pavement.

As they approached her tenement, the melody changed to the warbling of the fountain, the whisper of a broom against the cobbles, and the carefree banter of impossibly skinny, walnut-colored boys bouncing past them. And all the while, with each thump of her satchel against his thigh, he was reminded of his good fortune.

"Will I intrude on your landlady if I carry your satchel inside for you?" Again, his voice trembled.

"No, she's visiting her children in Cyprus."

* * *

The stairs creaked in protest as he shifted his weight to ease the pain in his hip. Then with the screech of the turning key, the click of the lifting latch, and the moan of the swinging door, he experienced that old rush of both rapture and terror. Once again walking into his dreams, she stirred him to life with an unbearable longing but burdened his heart with the renewed dread of losing her.

Her room was as narrow as a coffin with a low-raftered ceiling and a small, uncovered window above eye level. Not even the afternoon sun could find the opening, only the smoke from fish roasting in the courtyard. It was sparsely furnished with a *lectus* draped in a light woolen blanket over a mattress of straw, a washstand and basin, and a rough-hewn table and chair. Two raw pine shelves held the rest of her needs and attached to the lower shelf were several hooks with another tunic, a pair of boots, and two amphorae joined by a knotted rope for hauling water from the fountain. But to the man, the room could have been a villa with soaring, thickly draped, arched windows overlooking a garden of palms and pomegranate trees.

In the warm stillness, aching to wrap himself around her, he saw a matching ardor in her own widening eyes. Reaching around to put her satchel on the table, he embraced her. As he leaned in to bury his face in her hair, he removed the pins that held the golden locks back from her face and let them spill into his hands.

It had been so long since he'd loosened her hair.

* * *

On her bed, their clothes a tangled heap on the floor, time trembled to a halt.

Clinging to him, her skin as smooth as silk, she arched up and opened wide to receive him.

He plunged into her warmth.

She enclosed him and found his rhythm as he moved inside her.

Her hips rising, his thrusts deepening, they drowned in each other's waves of ecstasy as they journeyed toward fulfillment.

And then, for the duration of a few heartbeats, they shuddered and melted in each other's arms.

Lying between the rumpled sheets, his arm around her shoulders, her lips against his skin, he declared, "I want to marry you, Sophia. To have you for

143

my own."

"Yes, Basil, yes."

How sweet it was to hear her speak his name.

Chapter 7
Late Afternoon

"Pheeb?" I asked with a tug on her forearm.

"*Hmm*," she groaned as she spiraled out of a thin sleep.

"Are you ready to go yet?"

"Okay, okay. Just let me get my *calcei* back on."

That's when an explosive howl split the drowsy air.

"Holy Isis, what is that?" asked Phoebe, pressing her palms against her ears.

"Hurry!" I said, pointing to one of the rutted lanes next to the Palace of Justice.

I left Phoebe to squeeze her swollen feet into her *calcei* while I bolted toward the location of the howl and saw a hefty matron on the edge of hysteria bent over a body in a yard of prickly weeds.

The chest of his tunic was stained with blood.

Next to him lay a cane and the body of a pig-faced older man, his belly layered in curtains of fat from his armpits to his hips.

"Oh, for the love of Jupiter," she cried, rocking back and forth wringing her hands as she fought back the tears.

Kneeling beside her, I patted her arm with a touch as light as the breath of dawn.

She gripped my arm, her hand twitching like a branch in the wind. Then, turning to face me, she grasped my hands and rose with me as I stood.

"Do you know this man?" I asked.

Covering her mouth with both hands, she nodded with a bowed head. "Kind man." Her words choked in rhythm with her sobs. "Would help me up the stairs."

She took a deep breath and then swallowed.

"Is he dead?" She spoke in a grief-clotted voice, but great sighs had replaced her sobs.

I kneeled beside the man she called Basil. He had a strong square jawline, deeply sculpted cheeks, and protruding front teeth. "Yes, I'm sorry, but he is. He's been stabbed in the chest with a short blade. Was the blood still flowing when you found him?"

"No. It had already dried on the front of his tunic, Basil's tunic, I mean."

"And do you know the other man?"

"Gregor, the herb vendor."

Kneeling beside the vendor, his monstrous belly pointing skyward, one leg contorted at a grotesque angle, I saw he'd been struck on the side of his head. A ribbon of red still oozed from his left temple. "This one is still alive," I said, raising my head to report to Icepick.

That's when the edge of my mind heard a low dragging shuffle approach from the distance.

"Oh, Isis! What's this?" asked Phoebe. She arrived gasping, her breath jagged as if she'd run the whole way.

"Phoebe, can you go to the morgue? Drop off your scrolls, and then fetch a soldier to take this body back with him." I pointed with my chin to Basil still sprawled in the prickly weeds with his cane beside him. "I'll join you later to identify him."

"And you." I said, turning to Icepick—I still didn't know her name. "Can you get a doctor and bring him here for the other one?"

It was too late to do anything for Basil, of course, but I tore off the tail of my himation to administer to Gregor. Lifting his head and resting it in the crook of my elbow, I put pressure on his left temple to stop the bleeding, and then I used that piece of my himation to soak up water from the fountain and wash his face.

Icepick was right. He had the breath of a gravedigger.

"Can you tell me what happened, Gregor?"

"I stomped out a' our apartment early this morning, me and my wife's, for some air. Angry I was at her. Her tricks, you know. Always asking for money for the kid. I know, you all do it. So, I was walking past this here yard when I saw Basil—heard him first, the tap a' his cane—it was him all right—and noticed, this time with a certainty, how my son looks just like him." Gregor's voice cracked as the emotion ripped through him. "Oh, he's still a boy, but no mistaking the resemblance. The wife, she keeps asking me to send that bastard to school. But I'm no fool, see?

"Look, I figure my wife was pregnant when I married her, probably married me 'cause she was pregnant. See, I got this here business. Big deal. She must 'a' figured I'd take care a' her and the kid. Anyways, I was in love with her, so beautiful with that golden hair, and at first, I thought she loved me too, foolish as that sounds, till I heard her calling for him in her dreams.

"So, I charged out a' the apartment only to bump into this Basil, the fuller's slave. Works there as his scribe. I saw only the same square jawline and protruding teeth as my son's, and in my madness, I lunged at him with this here blade on my belt." He tapped his belly. "Got him right in the chest. He felled me with his cane, but I knew he was as good as dead when I heard him hit the ground."

"Listen, Gregor, can you wait here a while?"

"Don't leave me," he groaned, his mouth tightening into a grimace as he tried to shift his weight. "Must 'a' broken this here leg when I fell."

"I'll stay with you till the doctor comes. He'll help you back to your apartment and take care of you, but then you'll have to tell your story to the magistrate."

He closed his eyes to wait.

Chapter 8
Early Evening

"What do you think will happen to Gregor?" asked Phoebe.

She was sitting at Zenon's back table while I wiped the *tiropita* crumbs off with the rest of my himation.

"He may be arrested, but then again, he killed only a slave, and if he can compensate the fuller for the loss, then it's just a civil matter between them."

"And Sophia?"

"No telling," I replied. "She and her son may be the ones to suffer. Gregor may blame her for the cost of replacing the scribe. On the other hand, I'm wondering how Gregor could be so sure Basil was the boy's father."

"What do you mean?"

"Well, can you picture Gregor without all that fat? Not so much in his belly but his face? Melt it away, and you can see that he too once had a square jaw, maybe even well-defined cheekbones. Even if his wife was pregnant when he married her—and I'm not saying she was—that still doesn't mean the baby was Basil's. It still could have been his."

"Oh, Miriam, that would mean he killed Basil for nothing!"

"We can only hope that as the boy grows older, he will come to resemble Gregor more and more. Gregor might then embrace the boy as his own and make amends with Sophia. Who knows? And maybe with Basil out of the picture, Gregor will make his peace with her."

After an extravagant sigh, Phoebe asked, "So, what are you going to have for supper?"

"The *tiropita* looks good. That and a glass of pomegranate wine should do it for me."

"Make that two."

The Dagger

The Ninth Year of the Reign of
Nero Claudius Caesar Augustus Germanicus [Nero]
March, 63 CE, Alexandria *ad Aegyptum*

Achilles's Story

I spotted Ursus in the agora. Figured he'd be in one of those greasy cookshops. You know the kind. They stink up the neighborhood with their rotting garbage and the dirty feet of their regulars. Too early for the saloons and much too early for the whorehouses. So, where else would an old gladiator hang out in the middle of the day when the ports were closed?

You could say I'd been hunting him down for years, starting at his home in Capua and then riding a hired mule from one grubby inn to the next along the *Via Appia*. And that was just to get to Rome. From the port of Ostia, I sailed to Athens and trekked to Ephesus, Tarsus, and a million other fleapits along the way before catching this glimpse of him in Alexandria. But, you know, all I really wanted was to have a friendly chat with him. Just me and him. About his wife. After all, wasn't I his old pal, Achilles? Weren't we members of the same savage brotherhood, professionals in the arena rather than the scum the Empire was eager to exterminate?

We'd bunked in the same cell at the *ludus* in Capua. In case you're lucky enough not to know what I'm talking about, that's the most famous gladiator school in the Empire. As the property of that *ludus*, we trained there and belonged to that gladiatorial family. Remo, the manager who owned us during each of our two five-year stints, put us together because we both were hired volunteers. We trained side-by-side to become a *retiarius*, the gladiator who fights with just a net and trident—oh yeah, and a dagger to cut the poor bastard's throat so the crowd doesn't feel cheated. Since a *retiarius* only fights the gladiator who wears heavy armor, we'd never be matched to fight each other.

Once in a while, I'd eye the sharp edge of sunlight as it advanced along the cookshop's mudbrick floor and glazed the grizzled hairs curling off the back of Ursus's bull neck. There the slob sat, right behind the charcoal-burning furnace recessed into the street-front, marble-topped counter. Sure enough, his burly back toward me, his colossal thighs spilling over his stool, his eyes were riveted on the backwall frescoes of men manning the seats in a latrine. Of course, I could read the captions—I'd had a tutor until my father was forced to sell our farm to pay the Roman's damn taxes—but believe me, the images and the graffiti left nothing to the imagination.

Anyways, cramming that last slab of *tiropita* into his mouth, Ursus chewed the pastry open-mouthed as was his habit with his teeth clacking together—I should say what was left of them. You know, I could've predicted what my old mate would do next. He sucked the crumbs off his fingers and threw back the rest of his drink like a desert nomad. Then, smacking his lips before lurching to his feet, he exploded with a fart that sounded like a groan from deep inside the earth. After tugging his tunic over his sagging front porch, he snatched a few apricot tarts from a passing tray and stuffed them into his mouth. That's when I slipped behind the corner of the building ready to resume tailing him with the energy of a hunter on the heels of his quarry.

He led me along the harbor past drinking dens and gaming houses seedy enough for the likes of smugglers, swindlers, and sailors. Inhaling the salty tang of the sea, I paused to watch a gull dive under a whitecap and return with a silvery fish. That prize reminded me of when I signed the *sacramentum gladiatorium*, that binding and solemn oath to suffer the worst humiliation and torture the arena could inflict, including the surrender of my very life. By doing so, I saved my father from that *kaka* tax collector, who would've had him thrown to the lions for failing to fork over the rest of the poll tax. *Ma Zeus*! My fish for diving into the brutal world of the barracks was clearing that debt. And so, taking that oath was a matter of honor for me. At least I had hopes of surviving whereas my father would've had none.

Sons of the wealthy and privileged risked their neck for the thrill of being a gladiator, but the rest of us signed on to get our debts forgiven. So it was with Ursus as well, who'd run up such a tab from whoring, drinking, and gambling that the Ferryman of Hades was rumored to be on the way to carry his body across the River Styx.

My recollections were interrupted by the stench of the canal. By now, we were well into the *Rhakotis* quarter, a haven for predators if there ever was one, its canal being the perfect place to ditch the proof of their crimes. A warren of pocked streets and rutted alleys, the quarter's ramshackle houses were slathered with graffiti and jammed together like spectators in the arena. Old whores, naked children, and idle drunks held court in its rubble-strewn lots. And the reek of poverty, a mix of fried grease, cheap wine, piss, and desolation, leeched out of the shadows to grab me by the throat.

But it was a mangy dog, an ugly lop-eared creature resting in a shady pothole, its eyes convex with hunger and despair, that proved how dangerous, even evil, that buddy of mine had become. Diverted by the critter's thumping tail, Ursus lowered his chin and addressed it with enough profanity to scald the air. With no response from the pooch, he narrowed his eyes and gave it a sharp kick to the belly, booting it straight into the air so it landed once again in the hole but on its back. Doubling over, he whooped with a laughter so maniacal I had to cover my ears. Mounting a feeble challenge in response, the brave little mutt, teeth bared, hackles up, and with a low growl of warning, crouched, ready to spring.

That's when Ursus's laughter froze. His mouth twisting into a grin of rage, his hand flew to the sheath on his belt. He pulled out his dagger. I recognized it. I got the same kind, a souvenir we each managed to pinch from the *ludus*. Its blade can split the skin with the touch of a feather. Anyways, he cut the dog down with a single slice across its throat, and then, like it was nothing, he shoved the bloody dagger back into its sheath. That poor pup's torso turned a slaughterous red as its lifeless head tilted to one side, and a crimson froth sprayed out of its muzzle like a fine rain. I'll never forget that look in its sightless eyes as Ursus shoved its pathetic ass into the gutter and spat a glob of phlegm at its face.

I bit my underlip so hard it bled.

* * *

Ursus led me along the western harbor to The Pegasus, a waterfront inn indicated by a sign depicting the white, winged stallion as he sprung from Medusa's womb. The façade of the inn itself, set back from the waterfront, was decorated with a mural of Bellerophon on his divine mount. I took cover behind a plane tree at the foot of the well-worn path to observe my target's next move. Watching him swagger in through the scarred oak door that cut through one of the stallion's wings, I figured he must be lodging there.

Minutes later, I ducked through that same doorway accompanied by a sliver of early afternoon light. With no hostess at the reception desk, I had to find my own way. The Public Room was empty save for the ferocious flies. Wooden tables and benches strewn about the earthen floor were lit by a dying ring of oil lamps suspended from the stained ceiling. They spat out a greasy smoke that spiraled to the ceiling like a nest of vipers and left a curtain of soot so thick I had to swallow back a coughing fit.

Anyways, passing through that shadowy gloom, I wandered past the kitchen down a hallway to the only door with a ribbon of light along its threshold. And knocked.

Ursus answered all right, looking like he could be anywhere from twenty-five to fifty-five. He slapped me on the shoulder with the hand that had been hovering over the hilt of his dagger. "Well, I'll eat shit! Look what the rats dragged in! How the fuck are you?"

"Okay, okay. Doing goo—"

"Don't jus' stand there, cocksucker, c'mon in!" Stepping aside from the doorframe, he grabbed me by the wrist and pulled me in behind him. His bulging arms arced out like an ape's as he led me into a low-raftered, cage-like room that exhaled a mixture of fusty clothing, his own animal stink, and a ripe chamber pot. The other smell, of tallow grease, came from a candle burning in the stone holder next to his cot.

He took a seat on the edge of the cot, its boggy mattress splotched with dried blood, stale sweat, and fermented semen. The chamber pot claimed a spot on the splintered floor beneath the bedframe. A washstand with a jug and basin, a rickety bench, and a battered seaman's trunk swallowed the space against the wall across from him and completed the room's sad furnishings. The other walls were paneled in a dark wood that sucked up the afternoon light as it zigzagged through the shrubbery and into the lone, waist-high window.

He patted down the air with his palms, his signal for me to sit on the bench. It creaked in protest.

"Easy, chum. You break that shit, you own it." Another burst of laughter, more hysterical than joyous, more savage than hearty. "Looks like these shit-smeared years been easy on you."

I nodded. I suppose he said that because having kept to the routine of an athlete, I was still trim. Upon discharge from the *ludus*, we'd both stayed in Capua, but I hadn't seen much of him. We went our separate ways, especially after he married Thea. He still lived there but spent lots of time away.

"What the fuck you been doin'?"

"Keeping busy. Working as a bodyguard for the Horatius family and a trainer for the new hires at the *ludus*—"

"No shit! For that same prick—what's his name?"

"You mean Remo?"

"Yeah. You still workin' for that old motherfucker."

I nodded and raised my chin to toss the question back at him. "You?"

"Same old shit. Whorin', drinkin' and gamblin' where the action is. Right now, that's here in Alexandria."

A wary silence stretched between us. I could hear the tallow drip from the candle.

"Look," he said, stabbing the air with his forefinger. "I know you followed me here. No fuckin' way you jus' happened by. What's up?"

A sea breeze sifted through the foliage, and finding the open window, it flattened the candle flame and licked the sweat greasing my body. I shivered. It was time for the conversation I both longed for and dreaded, but the words just piled up on my tongue.

I opened my palms, you know, in a gesture of frankness, but he brushed away my unspoken words as if I were a pesky fly. "No, let me guess. It's about Thea. You think I don't know you been nailin' her? And why not? As long as you close your eyes. She looks like shit, but she knows how to give—"

I raised a hand to silence him. That he should speak like that of the woman I love, so tiny and birdlike, yielding and fragile. Not pretty but her features, gentle and mobile, bloom with an inner glow. Only the fear of that brute dimmed her spark of life.

"Ursus, I want to marry her."

He erupted in a fresh gale of laughter, this one pierced with contempt. "Look, shithead, I don't give an ass kisser's damn what you wanna do with her. You can fuck her till your dick falls off, but don't think I'd ever give up my meal ticket—"

I felt a tightening in my chest. "Ursus, be reasonable. We can work out a deal." I could hear the resentment rising in my voice.

"Listen," he said in a tone so cold, so flat that it made me afraid. "So, I'm a shitty husband with a pair a' knuckles to match, but if you're thinkin' a' disappearin' with her, forget it. I'll hunt your asses down from Rome to Antioch, Carthage to Britannia. I jus' ain't sure which one a' yous—you or the bitch—I'd kill first. But it ain't gonna be fast, and it ain't gonna be easy."

A fury was burning through my soul, beginning as a smolder and then bursting into flames.

The bench creaked as I stood.

Then I was crushing my fist into his jaw. It was the roundhouse I'd worked on with him years ago. It sounded like two stones colliding. I felt the jolt through my arm all the way to my teeth.

He retched, his mouth an angry hole, blood spouting onto his lips. But I knew what was coming next, that like intimate lovers, his hands would wrap around my neck.

"You fucker!" he shrieked, charging as he spit out a tooth.

I reached for my dagger.

The hilt felt cool in my palm.

I gripped it so hard my hand hurt.

Then I firmed my right thigh, bent my left knee, and lunged.

I heard the familiar sound of metal splitting flesh.

I made a clean slash, slicing through not just the soft tissue but the bone beneath.

The blade hummed and left a gaping red slit across his throat.

I heard a gurgle as his eyes rolled up, his last breath like a foul gust of wind.

He toppled to the floor, upturning the washstand, his belly skyward, his arms flung out, his lifeless head tilting as if on a hinge.

I had to keep blinking to make the room stop spinning.

Blood, feces, and urine everywhere.

* * *

Ma Zeus! What have I done?

I stood there. I hadn't meant to hurt him, certainly not to kill him. I just wanted to talk to him, reason with him, make him listen. He didn't love her; she was simply a piece of property to him. So, I would've paid him. Whatever it cost. He always needed money, didn't he?

And I had to save my Thea, didn't I? That goddess in the soup kitchen who so many years ago gave my mother food when that spittle-licking tax collector extorted my father's last *drachma*. I knew her, you know, when we were kids. She used to tease me, saying I chopped my vowels like a bumpkin and ate porridge for supper, all because my father grew spelt. Her father owned a foundry famous for its bronze dinnerware. Anyways, I liked her even then. She was like a wounded small child, rawboned and gaunt with hair whitened by the sun. I remember we'd fly home-made kites in a yard near the amphitheater when my father brought his spelt to the market.

Sure, I can look back now and say I wished I'd've courted her then, but I was a triangular-faced, wide-mouthed farmer's kid, and she was a rich man's daughter. But I can guess how Ursus came to court her.

All the young women in Capua, intoxicated by their own erotic fantasies, would moon over the well-oiled bodies of us gladiators as we marched through the streets on the mornings of the games. Perhaps Thea, bewitched by the spectacle, caught Ursus's eye with a thrown kiss or lewd gesture. Anyways, for a little money, our trainer knew when to unlock the gate so an eager virgin could wait for one of us inside the exercise grounds. And Ursus, of course, keen for the smell of money, knew how to play up to the rich ones. So, I can imagine how she happened to marry the brute, but she's suffered plenty for her folly, she of all people, all devotion and submissive tenderness.

Ma Zeus! The pool of his stink is widening. What am I going to do?

My first impulse was to run out of the inn and then keep on running. But no one saw me in The Pegasus. No one saw me following Ursus either, and even if they did, we were just two ordinary scoundrels among the drunkards, pickpockets, and derelicts who frequent the harbor when the ports are closed. And who in Alexandria even knew of the issue between us? Still, I knew to slip out of the inn fast. Someone must've heard the thud and clatter of the washstand before the noise melted into the walls.

It wasn't until I set my eyes on the window that my legs stopped trembling.

I took back my dagger, now as loathsome as a serpent, slid it into my sheath, and wiped my hands inside the skirt of my tunic. My eyes darted left and right. Nothing. No other evidence of my presence. So, I climbed onto that old trunk and straddled the windowsill. Looking back to make sure I hadn't scraped the pigeon shit, dead flies, and dust caked on the windowsill, I paddled through the foliage. Quickly I sprang to the ground with only one thought, to get rid of the only remaining proof of my crime. So, I let my nose lead me back to that putrid the canal.

The skin of the canal was blistered with debris and blotched with oily stains. What if the dagger just floated on the scum? Icy sweat drilled down my spine. I paused for a group of walnut-colored ragamuffins to scamper by, and then holding my breath, I hurled it into the filth.

And waited.

It lay there on an island of froth.

Ma Zeus! *Why won't it sink?*

Crossing the lane, a pair of potato-faced men, probably brothers the way their ears stuck out like pot handles, strolled toward me along the canal. As they drew near and the slaps and echoes of their steps swelled in my ears, my own fear swelled until I saw only two smudges walking toward me.

Keep going! I screamed but only to myself.

I gnawed on a cuticle until I tasted blood.

They were hardly a foot away when the dagger cleared the grease with a soft plop.

My bowels turned to water.

* * *

I traipsed around the twisting lanes and weed-choked lots of the neighborhood, watching the shadows lengthen in the fading light, wishing like a child I could undo what I'd done. No luck, the weight of that guilt was going to stay with me. Nevertheless, as I wandered through those byways, I worked out a plan. See, I hadn't noticed anyone other than Ursus at the inn, but what if the hostess had noticed *me*? What if she'd been in the kitchen and seen me walk by? In other words, I might need an alibi. So once again, I approached the door with Bellerophon on his divine stallion.

The hostess was at the reception desk, her huge hand buried in a bowl of boiled elephant beans. Scooping up a fistful, she popped them into her mouth one-by-one. Then licking the salt off her fingers, she wiped them on the bodice of her shabby tunic and said, "Whatcha want?"

"Room."

"Gonna have to wait for the maid to make it up for ya," she said, spitting through a gap in her teeth and trailing the thread of saliva.

I asked her to bring me some *posca*, that cheap watered-down wine popular with soldiers—unless she had something stronger—and then settled on a bench in a dimly lit corner of the Public Room to dodge the frenzied arcs of the buzzing flies. I tipped her well, so she'd remember me, and to my disgust, she joined me on the bench with a drink of her own.

"So, what brings ya' to this here cesspool, a good-looking fella like ya'?" She asked, shifting over so our thighs touched, her stink closing in on me like a fog. Her fetid breath fouled my mouth, and the reek of yesterday's *posca* stung my nose.

I swilled my drink to buy some time before responding. Then I took a mouthful and let the warmth spread though my chest. "You been here long?" I asked, ignoring her question. *With that flabby jawline and sagging breasts, she looks like she's been here forever*, I thought as I chewed the inside of my cheek to stifle a rising guffaw. She startled me though when she said, "Seems like forever," like she'd been reading my mind.

She took a few gulps as if she were drinking water and then smacked her lip. "Yup, seems like forever," she repeated, "working my ass off for that cheap bastard. Konstantine. Know 'im?" She quaffed the rest of her drink and then with the back of her hand, wiped away the rill trickling down her chin.

I shook my head.

"Owns this here dump. Threatens to fire me. Says I'm der-ee-lict, like I'm supposed to know what that means!" She erupted in a bark of laughter so bitter it made me shudder.

"Okay, okay," I said with a downward gesture of my palm. "What's it mean?"

"He says I break the rules, that I leave the desk unattended, which is a bloody lie. I only go out when business is slow and only then to the agora. Unless, of course, someone asks for me." Her bloodshot eye shot me a conspiratorial wink. "And he says I drink and socialize with the tenants. So, don't tell 'im I'm having this here itty-bitty chat wi'cha." She was speaking now through the *posca*, with a throaty, lazy timbre.

She'd put her hand on my knee when she said "socialize with the tenants," but by the time she came out with "this here itty-bitty chat," her hand had slid all the way up to my fork.

Pushing her hand away and downing the rest of my drink, I stood abruptly, saying "Hey, gotta get some stuff. Back in a while, when the room's ready."

This time I left through the door, my arms swinging with ease, knowing she hadn't seen me either entering or leaving the inn earlier that afternoon and that soon I'd be with my Thea. Anyways, for that moment, nothing existed but the thought of my beloved and her cinnamon breath warming my skin as I wrapped my arms around her.

* * *

With the seasonal reopening of the commercial ports, I figured I could book passage on the first cargo ship headed for Rome. So, against a legion of blood-sucking flies, I set out along the western harbor to see whether departure schedules had been posted in the waterfront saloons.

I entered The Lizard's Tail, a dive most likely named for the mean-faced reptile that struck my bare ankle with its spiny-spiked tail. The darkness had only begun to press on the windowpanes, so it wasn't yet busy. Still the voices were boisterous, and the talk was virile. The row of wall-mounted oil lamps threw my shadows past shelves crammed with amphorae, crockery, and glassware and into the tang of boiled cabbage and smoked fish. With the eyes of the few scrotes boring into me, I felt edgy, like I had to keep looking over my shoulder.

There in the gloom, mounted on the rear wall, I found some faded nautical maps, their brittle edges curling, and next to them, a crude sketch of each vessel with its latest sailing schedule. Grabbing a candle from a back table and crouching under the cobwebbed eaves, I saw the first departure for Rome would be on the *Soteria*. What could be better than a ship named for the goddess of safety and deliverance?

Despite my sore ankle, I glided out of the saloon into the greater darkness, relief surging through my veins as if I'd been inhaling the smoke of the mandrake. The trainers, you know, would ease the pain of our injuries by burning that magical root for us in censers. Still, I vowed to stay alert. I had yet to book passage with the master of the ships, buy enough supplies to get me at least to Cypress, store my provisions in a waterfront inn, apply for an exit visa, present it with the fee to the port official, and wait for the herald's trumpet to announce the ship's departure.

Of course, I couldn't go back to The Pegasus, so I spent those last days in another pigsty-of-a-joint near the *Kibotos* cooped up in a cramped windowless garret. The management was too cheap to supply candles or prostitutes, but the neighborhood abounded with brothels, restaurants, bathhouses, and small shops. Even so, I rarely went out, imagining that every face was intent on arresting me. Besides, I was saving my money for an engagement ring.

I recall so clearly that morning when the ship set sail. Along with the bray of the herald's trumpet, a spike of sunlight squeezed through a gap in the roof and poked my eyelids. I put on my clothes in that feeble light, even remembering to tie a pouch with some coins around my neck so in case of a storm at sea, someone finding my corpse would have the money to bury me. Then I slung my travel bag over my shoulder and made my way eastward in the crisp briny air toward the forehead of the sun and the activity of the harbor. Smelling the charred flesh of the pre-sail sacrifice and watching its pigtails of smoke merge with the sea breeze, I heard the shriek of a whistle, the groan of the ropes, and the whine of the hatches. And then, as a team of bare-chested stevedores finished loading the sacks of grain, the queue of passengers tramped toward the gangplank.

But as I elbowed through the throng, I felt something. Was it the sigh of a breeze that happened to find the dampness at the nape of my neck or the chilly breath of some goon committed to arresting me?

Phoebe's Story

I was visiting Miriam that afternoon hardly expecting to start my own career as a sleuth before the day was over. What's more, I certainly didn't foresee dealing with a grizzle-haired, almost headless corpse swaged in fat. The most experience I'd had was as Miriam's faithful scout and hardly much of that except in Caesarea. There, when tracking a secret that could have rocked the Empire, I shadowed a Parthian merchant with the blessings of Isis and a few stones in my satchel to defend myself.

It was really too early in the spring for us to be sitting out under the canopy of her third-floor, Egyptian-style roof garden. The ports had yet to reopen, but we were eager to stretch our eyes beyond the sprawl of the city, its balconies and tile roofs, beyond even the lighthouse, to where the sea's deep blue line meets the horizon.

We sat across the table from each other on teak benches banked with cushions of cerulean and turquoise silk. The lunch we were about to enjoy was spread out before us: grilled fish livers seasoned with garum; barley cakes; and a salad of lettuce, beets, onions, and cucumbers. Just as Miriam was ladling the wine into our goblets—a grape wine from a vineyard in the Delta—we turned like a dancing duo toward the bells frantically ringing in the street.

"Are you expecting anyone?" I asked.

"No, but that sounds like Gershon's litter, Gershon ben Israel. You remember him, my father's elderly friend, the one who imports Palestinian wine?"

I shrugged. I remembered Miriam's mentioning his impossibly long fingers and his luxuriant silver hair but not much more.

"I don't hear Gershon though," my best friend added, "just his—"

A moment later, his bearers were ascending the stairs with swift light steps as if on the edge of a blustery wind. Immediately behind them, Miriam's energetic housemaid, Minta, stood nibbling on her upper lip.

"I'm so sorry, Miss Miriam. They charged right in, even when I told them you were lunching with Miss Phoebe—"

"It's all right, Minta."

My friend dismissed her with a thank you, but she had already gone, the patter of her feet drawing whispers on the marble steps.

Before us stood Wasi and Wedu, Gershon's bearers, matching Nubian giants resplendent in their white linen tunics and pigskin boots. The only difference between the twins is that one—Wedu, I think—is disfigured by a ropelike scar on the right side of his face that stretches when he smiles.

Wedu turned to Miriam and bowed. "I'm so sorry to intrude, Miss Miriam." And then he took a deep sad breath. "But our master is very ill and asking for you. Please come. There's not a moment to lose."

Her face slack with dread, Miriam turned and without saying a word, held me in a short embrace. Then, with a *swoosh* of her tunic, she was gone. My own hands lifted to my mouth as I heard the bells of their litter ring through streets.

Working my feet into my *calcei*, I didn't get much chance to gather the lunch dishes before Minta was back with a tray.

"Miss Phoebe," she said in her fast, high-pitched warble, "there's someone else here to see Miss Miriam, a Professor Jason."

"Well, you must have told him she's gone for the day."

"I did, but he says it's urgent and asked whether anyone else could help him."

Help him? The physician at the medical school who investigates the deaths that baffle the authorities? The one they and his colleagues mock for his unorthodox findings? Miriam says he's an ongoing embarrassment to them, the way he so often contradicts their conclusions, and all the more so because he's usually right.

"I can't think of anyone here who could help him," I said, shrugging with open palms. "Unless he'd like to speak to me. Strictly as a courtesy, of course. He's helped out Miss Miriam more than once. So, yes, Minta, on second thought, tell him I'll be right down."

With her milk-white face poised to please, she mumbled a "Right away, miss" and turned to leave with me following her down the steps, watching her coarse woolen tunic nip at her ankles.

* * *

Minutes later, wrapped in the odor of warm leather and the shimmer of the late afternoon sun, I was flying westward high above the mica-flecked pavement in the official litter of the soldierly built, thin-lipped professor at my side. The bodyguards ran ahead to secure our safety and clear the way. With their long bamboo canes, they pressed past hawkers and hucksters, priests and astrologers, magicians and swindlers, as well as the usual gawkers and gossipers, vendors and tinkers.

How could I have turned down this chance to be a sleuth like Miriam, who, by using her common sense, had solved a host of cases and saved the lives of countless innocents? On the other hand, I didn't tell the professor the whole story when he asked whether I'd worked with Miss bat Isaac on her cases. See, when I told him I was her duly appointed official deputy assistant, he was in such a hurry I didn't get the chance to say I was really more her sounding board than her partner. But the task seemed easy enough.

All he wanted, he said, was someone to view the crime scene with him before he granted permission for the body to be moved to the morgue, where, if warranted, he'd perform an autopsy. He confided that lately the authorities had been questioning his judgment, but with an experienced detective and trusted citizen like Miss bat Isaac—or in this case, her very own deputy—he felt his opinion would be accepted without the threat of sniggers and sneers.

Surely, I could do that, right?

So, now we were on the way to examine the body of a one-time gladiator who'd bled out in a sleazy inn, and all I could feel were waves of fear and revulsion accompanied by a sour taste rising from my empty innards.

I clung to Wedu for support. My knees were about to give way as he guided me out of the litter and up the path to The Pegasus. Then, passing under the stallion's wing, I took a few deep breaths to quell my queasiness. Having committed myself to the cause of justice, what else could I do?

* * *

"This here's The Pegasus, folks. Who are ya's and whatchas looking for?" asked the ferret-faced hostess probably in response to our mismatch with the surroundings. Squinting her eyes, she greeted us behind a sputter of elephant beans and a postmenopausal mustache.

The professor answered in a voice accustomed to echoing through the hallowed halls of the medical school. "We're here, Madame, to investigate the death that occurred here this afterno—"

"Oh, the gladiator from Capua, that fella Ursus," she said, clucking her tongue with a series of *tsks*.

A *hmm* and a barely perceptible nod from the professor.

"His room's that way." She touched a spot in the air with the tip of her stubby forefinger.

"No, Madame, we'd like to speak with you first. My name is Jason, Professor Jason, and this is my assistant, Miss Phoebe. Please take us to where we can—"

"Sorry, Mr. Prof'ser. Can't leave the reception area,'cept to go to the latrine. My boss, Mr. Konsta—"

The professor folded his arms across his chest. "We're here, Madame, by orders of the magistrate." His imperious tone cut through the air like a blade.

"Oh," she said, standing taller as if her shoulders had been lifted by a pulley. Then she smoothed out the folds in her tunic. "My name's Selene. That's *Miss* Selene. We can sit in the Public Room but not for long. We're gonna serve dinner soon."

So, that's the smell. I was afraid I'd stepped in something on the path and ruined my new pigskin calcei.

Selene pointed with her chin to the table nearest the entrance so the maid could set up the rest of the room. I was grateful to escape the carnivorous flies and the blanketing soot, but when she plonked down next to me, the stench of the lead paste foundation she wore to mask the crimson capillaries on her pulpy nose brought back my queasiness.

The professor looked around, took a seat, and crossed one leg over the other. "I need to know, Miss Selene, who entered or left the inn this afternoon."

"Why no one, sir. Only Ursus. Came in shortly after the noon hour."

The professor bowed his head for a moment, leaned in, and then asked with flint in his tone. "*Hmm*, are you absolutely sure?"

Her head jerked back as if he'd slapped her. "Of course, I am!" Spittle sprayed from her mouth. "Mr. Konstantine don't permit me to leave my station. Much later, a man—a good looker, too"—she added licking her lips—"came in asking for a room—must've been late this afternoon—but left right away." She shook her head. "Never went beyond my station. 'Gainst the rules." She shook her head again, faster this time, as if in agreement with herself.

Like an actor with no lines, I shook mine as well to contribute to the conversation. Then a silence stretched into such a stillness that until the professor spoke again, the only sound was the buzz of the flies.

"So, you're telling me that other than this man, no one entered the inn after the gladiator, and no one left."

"Yes, sir! I swear by Zeus and Mr. Konstantine, the kindest boss ever lived. And I never left my station neither, not even to go to the latrine."

"And there're no other entrances?"

"None."

Another *hmm* from the professor while he gathered his thoughts, uncrossed his legs, and then recrossed them the other way. "Well, let me ask you a different question. How was the body discovered?"

Selene had half risen from the bench but sat down again.

"The maid, she discovered it. Said she was going to the kitchen when she smelled that awful stink. 'Attacked by the smell of… well… like a chamber pot only worse,' she said. So, she knocked on the door, Ursus's. Only room occupied. The door was unlocked so she opened it and seen it for herself. That's when she came running, squealing like a pig at the slaughterhouse. Churned my blood, it did."

Selene shifted on the bench and crossed her ankles.

"I called for our slave boy and sent 'im to fetch a soldier. As soon as the soldier opened Ursus's door—told ya' it was unlocked, didn't I? —he looked in but knew not to enter. Said, 'Case of foul play. Need permission from the magistrate.' Then he left. That fast," Selene added with a snap of her fingers.

"Madame, was it the habit of your tenants to keep their doors unlocked?"

"Don't know. Never left my station. Told ya', not allowed. Ya' thinking he could've been expecting someone? A man that big don't need to worry 'bout no lock."

The professor shook his head, slapped the table, and was about to get to his feet when his eyes lit up with another question. "Who else works here?"

"This here's offseason. Ports won't open for another few days. So, we have only the one maid and the boy to fetch. Cook comes in the morning for a couple hours, and the maid serves the food in the evening. In season, it's differ—"

"And the other tenants?"

"Getting a few tomorrow. Only Ursus right now and the regulars who come by for dinner."

With that answer, the professor rose, taking a few fluid strides toward the hall before looking back to make sure I was following him.

"Soldier left a lantern on the floor by the door for ya's," she called as we passed the kitchen.

* * *

"Well, what do you think, Professor?" I asked as I caught up with him.

"*Hmm. We still have to examine the body.*"

Does he actually expect me to look at the body? I felt another wave of queasiness as if I'd stepped into a boat. This time, I clung to the wall for support while wishing I could redo that piece of time when I'd offered to accompany him.

The hallway reeked of feces and urine. So, covering my nose with the lavender-scented sachet I keep in my bosom, I followed the funnel of light the soldier's lantern had painted on the pitted floorboards. When the professor pushed open the door and picked up the lantern, its light rushed in and painted Ursus's room with a sickly yellow skin. With the whiff of death brushing my face, I saw that a mass of blow flies in their metallic green armor was feasting on the gash that severed Ursus's throat.

I choked back the impulse to gag, figuring any real deputy would be too seasoned to do that, but it didn't matter anyway. The professor was already engrossed, crouching over the body, smelling the skin, sticking his fingers and then his hand deep into the wound, and pressing his lips from the abdomen to the inside of the gladiator's wrists and back again. I stayed a few paces away to take note of the corpse in case I had to vouch for its appearance, but in simple terms, it looked like a walrus stuffed with sawdust.

"Well?" I asked when the professor stood. Whether it was the presence of death or the meager light, I spoke in the hushed tone that matched my somber spirit.

Wiping his bloody hands on his tunic, he answered, "It's a puzzle all right. The gladiator died this afternoon, no more than a few hours ago. I know because his body has lost only a little heat. And my nose tells me he was hardly intoxicated. It looks like murder—clearest case I've ever seen—but no one came in or out of the inn, and even together, the maid, boy, and Miss Selene couldn't have overpowered a man this big.

"And something else: His throat was slit with a *pugio*, the long straight-bladed dagger a *retiarius* uses to slit his opponent's throat. Such a dagger, along with all the other weaponry a gladiator uses, would be the property of his *ludus*. Quite unusual to find it anywhere else. So, we'll have to look further. You check the window, and I'll see whether I can find the weapon."

"What should I check for? The window looks ordinary enough."

"Look for smudges, especially on the sill. The window is rather high, so someone climbing in or out could have left a mark. As for the bushes outside, look for broken branches or torn leaves. Unfortunately, the ground is too dusty for any prints."

Though too ashamed to admit it, I was relieved. I couldn't examine a dead body, especially under siege by an army of flies, but I could certainly check out a window. So, I edged toward the window, my eyes on alert as I cast them downward to spot any fresh scars on the floor. Then, as I'd seen Miriam do, I sank down on my haunches to examine the wall below the window. Finally, standing so abruptly I almost knocked over the chest, I checked the window, the sill, and the bushes outside for any sign of disturbance.

Shaking out my legs to revive my circulation, I saw the professor pacing the length of the room, his hands clasped behind his back.

"Nothing's been disturbed. Not the floor or the wall under the window, the window itself, the sill, or the shrubbery outside. What about you?" I asked.

A momentary pucker settled on his brow. "*Humm*. I did find something, something so peculiar I want you to see it. When I rolled Ursus's body onto its side to see whether he'd sustained other injuries, look what I found."

My eyes opened wider, and my mouth hinged open. "Oh Isis, no! The dagger!"

"And it's his. It bears the insignia of his *ludus* in Capua. Here, see for yourself," said the professor as he held it up.

"No, that's okay." I didn't have to touch it. Just looking at the blood and bits of flesh caked onto the blade made the room sway. But then it was as if a bolt of lightning illuminated the room. "Now we know how Ursus died!"

"We do?" His voice raised in disbelief, he stared at me with startled eyes.

"The dagger."

"Of course, bu—"

"Suicide! Ursus killed himself and then crashed into the washstand as he fell to the floor and landed on top of the dagger!"

"I just can't picture—"

"It's easy," I said. "I'll show you: He slits his throat." I slid my forefinger across my neck and continued the demonstration as I explained. "He might have momentarily clutched his throat as his breathing stopped, but then his arms dropped, the fist holding the dagger opened, and the dagger fell. A moment later, he collapsed on top of it."

He watched me and then nodded reflectively while gnawing on the corner of his upper lip. "Well, I have to admit it makes some sense. It certainly explains why there's no evidence of anyone else being here. But why would he do such a thing?"

"Oh, that's easy. He must have been so lonely for his wife that he killed himself rather than have to wait any longer for the port to open."

"You, Miss Phoebe, are indeed Miss bat Isaac's most valuable asset." And then he gave me a smile like a beam of light that took over his entire face.

* * *

"So, how was Gershon?"

Miriam and I were once again sitting out under the canopy of her roof garden. Having started on a barley cake, I looked forward to the lunch we'd missed yesterday.

"Oh, you know Gershon. All he needed was a little garlic to ease his breathing and some willow bark to reduce his aches. By the time I left last evening, he was resting comfortably." Miriam reached into the salad and fished out a stray slice of cucumber. Then she continued after a long silence of chewing. "But Minta tells me you helped Professor Jason, something about your figuring out how some gladiator in The Pegasus died."

"Well, I have to tell you this straight out. I know you have a lot of respect for the professor, but he really did very little. He examined the body, of course, but he couldn't put the facts together. He kept thinking it had to be murder even though no one could have done it."

"And then I have to say, Miriam, I just don't know how you do it."

"What do you mean?"

"Well, take this case. It's so sad. I keep thinking what if Ursus has a wife, how she must be anticipating a romantic reunion with him, and then after all that wait for the ports to reopen, he never comes home. All she gets is a message from some courier that he died in a sleazy waterfront inn waiting for a ship to bring him home."

"Yes, that poor woman, but think of the good you've done. And now Professor Jason is praising you to the sky. I am so proud of you. I'll just have to make you my permanent number one deputy."

A rush of well-being flooded my veins like warm honey.

The Missing Widow

Monday
Noon

I knew the day would be charged with trouble the minute I had to wait for Demetra at the entrance to the Flamingo's Tongue. Why was she late, especially when she had something so important to discuss with me?

She'd asked me yesterday to meet her at noon. "Phoebe, I need some advice about Helios," she said, her face deathly pale and her nervous hands clenched in a tight fist.

"Who?"

"You know, my new tenant, the sea captain from Ephesus." Her red-rimmed, watery eyes flared out from their swollen lids with what I thought was impatience. Only later did I realize it was fear.

Lowering her voice to a whisper, she pivoted her head left and right as if someone might overhear us. "The one who's been rooming with me until the ports re-open. He takes his meals at Cato's but otherwise has access to my entire house."

I took in a quick breath. "So?"

"He hasn't paid his rent for December. It was due on the calends, already four days ago."

"Well, why don't you ask him for it? Maybe he just forgot."

"That's just it. I'm afraid."

"You're afraid?"

She nodded before I even finished asking.

My next-door neighbor is the last person to be late for a lunch at the Flamingo's Tongue. Not just to see and be seen decked out in her prized pieces of custom-made jewelry, but to indulge in its signature dish, marinated flamingo tongues in a spicy pepper sauce.

Demetra is also the last one to be afraid. A widow for many years, she's become accustomed to living alone. But last month, she decided to rent out her upstairs rooms because her townhouse, with its years of exposure to sun and brine, needed extensive repairs. Least among them, she wanted the latest Roman steel-spring lock to replace the wood pin-tumbler lock that's rotting on the gate to her yard.

So last month, right before the ports closed for the season, she posted a notice in the agora. When Helios responded, she was quite taken by this jaw-jutting man who reeked of the sea. "Built thick, like a tree," she said, "with the muscles of stevedore and a face of rawhide."

But she came to regret her decision.

"It's his look," she said. "It's hard to explain." She took a hard swallow as if to gather her thoughts. "He flashes me this smile, but it turns into a sneer, and all the while he's leering at me, flashing his sharp teeth—the teeth of a wolf, all yellow and curved—and he's nibbling with them on the scales of his chapped lips. That's when the fear of him makes my heart pound." Dropping her head, her palm flew to her chest.

So, my next-door neighbor asked me to meet her. But I'm not talking about just any next-door neighbor. We look out for each other. Our relationship began a few years ago when I encountered her in the agora and she admired my hammered gold, medallion pendant. When she recognized the symbol on the disc was more than six hundred years old, I knew she was an enthusiast of the antique jewelry I collect. So, we began borrowing favorite pieces from each other's collection.

The few years she has on me show in the fans at the corners of her eyes, but she shimmers with energy. This very morning when I was cutting sprigs of rosemary for a salad, I saw her loose-limbed, long-legged stride heading toward the agora, her satchel slicing the air with every swing of her arms. Anyway, we adopted each other. She became the big sister I never had, and I became the little squirt she longed to protect.

I waited for Demetra as I watched the indigo shadows swallow up the pavement. By then it was late afternoon, time for me check out the agora in case she'd gotten waylaid there. *Who knows?* I thought. *Maybe she chanced upon Helios at Cato's, and they settled the problem.*

But a moment later, I imagined something horrible had happened to her, that she'd been hacked to death, lying in a widening pool of blood, her face smashed to a pulp. When an acidic tang shot up my gorge, I had to give myself the usual pep-talk: *Stop thinking like a thin-skinned, fraidy-cat. You always worry yourself sick. Maybe she just forgot.*

So, I nursed an ember of anger instead to keep away my fears as I charged over to the agora, hoping to encounter her there. And when I couldn't find her there, I stormed over to her house, all the while rehearsing how I'd scold her for making me lurk like a mugger in the dark and then hunt for her like a hound on a leash. But when I knocked on her thick, bronze-studded door, I got no response, only stillness. So, I knocked again and again, first calling, then shouting, and finally screaming her name. Nothing, until the silence became unbearable. That's when I had my bearers rush me to Miriam's.

Monday
Late Afternoon

My bearers ferried me past a drove of pigs only to get stalled behind a cohort of soldiers, their pack animals, and wagons. When I wasn't twisting my intaglio gold ring, the one with a bird engraved on a carnelian, or fingering the Roman glass beads on my necklace, I was gnawing on my lips until they bled.

Her energetic maid must have heard the frenetic clang of the bells on my litter when I finally reached Miriam's side street because I barely had a chance to dismiss my bearers before she pulled me in as if the air outside were poisonous. Breathing like a bellows, I rushed into the mosaic-floored atrium. Then, passing the sunken marble pool, I paused to catch my breath as I approached the great mahogany doors to the small square room that was both her study and laboratory.

An oil lamp was throwing an apron of flickering light onto my best friend's tall, fragile-looking frame as she turned from her furnace to greet me with a life-loving smile. I was familiar enough with her work to recognize the smell of camel dung and know from the chemical tang that she was roasting crystals of cinnabar to extract the mercury that would impart a silvery color to her metals. Otherwise, the room was as it had always been. The massive, ebony desk that had belonged to her father still dominated the room as did the purple, tied-back drapes that skirted the floor and separated her room from the peristyle.

I explained the events of my morning to just the accomplished sleuth I needed on such a distressing day. Miriam's main pursuit, however, is still alchemy, which, given the risk of being accused of and executed for conspiring to devalue the emperor's currency, she keeps as a well-guarded secret.

Folding her brow in concentration, she pointed her chin toward a curule chair, her signal for me to sit down. Then, drawing in a quick breath, she said, "I'll be right back with a crater of honey-sweetened pomegranate wine."

Just what I needed.

Miriam was gone long enough for the shadows in the peristyle to inch into the twilight. Carrying a tray with a basket of warm caraway muffins, a crater of wine, ladle, goblets, and napkins, she placed our refreshments on the marble desktop.

"Here, Phoebe, we can think better with some wine," she said as she filled the goblets and took a seat in the armchair behind the desk.

As soon as she handed me my glass, I downed the wine like a desert nomad, welcoming its warmth as it spread through my chest.

Miriam pinched the stem of her goblet with her thumb and forefinger, raised it to her lips, and took a dainty sip. The goblet made a little ping when she placed it back on the desk. She then passed me the basket of muffins. I grabbed two and wolfed them down like a beast in the arena. After a long chewy silence, I whisked the crumbs off my bosom, curled my fingers around my goblet, and continued my account.

"I want to find out what happened to Demetra—Oh, could I have a little more please? Just a drop. Oh, that's too much—but I'm so upset—and afraid—that I don't know what to do."

"Of course, you are. Anyone would be, but you've already proved your mettle. Remember in Caesarea when you followed that Parthian merchant to Vesta's Teahouse? At the risk of your very life, you eavesdropped on his meeting with those thick-faced men."

I closed my eyes and nodded, my elbow on the desk, my chin cupped in my palm. "Little did he know I was protecting a secret that could have rocked the Empire." Pride flowed through me like a tide and washed away my doubts, but only temporarily.

"And don't forget when you figured out how that gladiator was killed in the Pega—"

"Well," I said rubbing my jaw. "This is different. I *know* Demetra."

"Every case is different. The point is you've done it, and you can do it again."

"But where do I start?"

"You suspect her tenant is involved in her disappearance, but it's way too early to go to the magistrate. We have no proof a crime was committed. But one thing we can do—and I'll go with you—we can wait at Cato's for—what did you say his name was?"

"Heli—".

"Yes, Helios. We can wait for him at the cookshop tomorrow, and once he's there, we can search Demetra's house."

"And you'll come with me?"

"Of course."

When I stood to leave, I felt a wave of sweet relief relax my shoulders, but I also knew deep down that the trouble ahead would be far worse than anything in Caesarea or at The Pegasus.

Tuesday
Noon

The air of Cato's dining room was seasoned with the aroma of grilled sausages; the spiky consonants of Anatolian tourists; and the ribald talk of merchants and moneychangers, soldiers and stevedores, masons and mule drivers. Cato, a swollen man, all gut and jowls with purple threads wriggling up his hatchet-shaped nose, dried his hands on the skirt of his apron and led us to a sticky table in the back. I took the opportunity in the watery light to scan the crowd before sitting down in a sliver of light below a grimy slot-like window.

"What does this Helios look like?" whispered Miriam behind a cupped palm.

"I never saw him, but Demetra says he's muscular. 'Built like a tree,' she said, 'with a face baked by the sun.' Something like that."

Miriam rolled her eyes and wagged her head, "Phoebe, that could describe most of the men here."

"So, what should we do?"

"Look, Cato must know him. Just ask him which one is Helios."

"You know, I'm scared to."

"A perfect time to draw on your courage."

So I did, and by the time Cato lumbered back to our table, I'd pasted on a greasy smile and prepared a phony story. At first, I had to force my mouth to move, but as I spoke, my voice gathered strength until my words came out with ease. In conclusion, I said, "We're here to see Helios, but the crowd's so thick we can't seem to spot him."

"Don't know 'im." Cato sucked in his upper lip and shook his head.

"But he comes in all the time. Takes his meals here. A big fella, from Ephes—"

"Oh, the sea captain! Why din'cha say so? Talks with a drawl like everyone else from there. Ephesus, right?"

I nodded like I knew.

"Been a regular here, twice a day for the last month or so, but come to think of it, he ain't showed up today. Not yet." Cato scratched his bald head on the side where it was dented. "Come to think of it, he din't show yesterday neither. Saved him a nice slab of mutton too. Orders meat, nothin' else. Likes it real rare. Plenty to drink too."

"He told us the other day to meet him here." By now, the lies were sliding off my tongue like custard.

"Well, customers come and go. But you got me thinkin'." He paused to suck in his upper lip again. "Tell you what: If he don't come in later, I'll tell the magistrate's soldier. He's a regular here too. Any news, I'll let you know."

And so, as long as we were there, we ordered a platter of boiled eggs garnished with olives, an assortment of breads and cheeses, and a salad of dandelion and spinach greens topped with figs and walnuts. We finished our lunch with a pot of lavender tea and bused the table ourselves, so he'd remember us.

By the time we left, our shadows were staining the pavement behind us, and I could hear the rhythmic tread of the torch lighters refreshing the wooden staves with a mixture of sulfur and lime.

"Your impression?" I asked, turning toward Miriam.

Her face frowned with concentration. "I think the news could be good. Maybe they met up in the agora yesterday, settled their business, and Demetra was too embarrassed to contact you."

But I knew better. I'd seen Demetra's face when she spoke about him.

Tuesday
Afternoon

Yes, I knew better, which meant I could no longer rely on Miriam to be much help. Oh, we parted with our usual round of hugs, but I could tell. Her mind was made up. Still, even if she was right and they'd gone away together, at the very least, I owed it to Demetra to call at her house once more.

As I made my way up her narrow walkway, a nippy gust of the sea breeze rippled the skirt of my tunic, and needling my face with grit, threw me into the stones lining it. Greased with sweat, a chill running through me, I trembled like the yellow corn marigolds as I tasted the bitterness of the dandelion greens rising in my gorge.

And then, even the wind hushed when I knocked on the door.

The peephole screeched open.

"Get lost, slut." Throbbing with menace, a thick drawl that could only be Helios's exploded through the security grid in an unabated stream of bile.

My own words rushing up my throat got snagged on my tongue. But swallowing twice and standing tall as if a block and tackle were lifting my shoulders, I squeezed them out with only a slight catch in my voice.

"I want to speak with Demetra."

"Not here."

"She told me to meet—"

"Gone to her daughter in Memphis."

"When will she be—"

The peephole slammed shut like a hard slap.

I was left to wonder whether she even had a daughter.

Tuesday
Late Afternoon

I didn't know whether Demetra had a daughter, but I could certainly find out whether she'd intended to go to Memphis. Everyone leaving the city, even if only to sail upriver, must apply for an exit visa. Though ashamed to admit it now, I was thrilled at the prospect of proving Miriam wrong. And so, just a few blocks from the Palace of Justice, I felt a naughty delight after the midday drowse and revival of commerce to be threading my way through the bustle of shoppers, hordes of slaves, and knots of tourists to get to its Public Records Office.

The Palace of Justice is a perfectly proportioned, three-story temple to Roman order. Entering through its vine-covered, wrought iron gate, I elbowed past businessmen and priests, artisans and bankers to mount the long shallow steps. At its granite-columned portico, I pushed open the doors to this maw of bureaucracy, inhaling its breath and hearing the clipped language of officialese.

A ferret-faced albino guard in scarlet livery squinted as I explained my business and pointing with a crooked forefinger to a potato-faced slave, thundered "Exit Visa Division." I was sure his imperious tone would hang in the air for hours. The slave lisped in a high-pitched whine, "Right thith way, madame" before ushering me into a cavernous hall and directing me to the end of a serpentine queue facing the booth of a thin, droopy-eyed clerk.

Taking my place, I was met with either indirect measuring looks, or vacant stares punctuated by sighs of impatience and the buzz of flies. I passed the time by mashing my purse and screaming mute profanities while watching the bars of light from the west windows lengthen, fade, and eventually merge with the gathering shadows.

When I heard the long-awaited "next" directed at me, I was startled. With my head lolling to one side, I'd already drifted to the edge of awareness. "Can you tell me, please," I asked with a phony smile and a singsong voice, "whether an exit visa was issued in the last thirty days for anyone going to Memphis?"

"No."

"What can you tell me?"

"I only accept visa applications."

"Well, what about visas issued?" I tried to disguise the distress in my voice. "Next booth."

"But no one's there."

"Only on Mondays." By now his voice had an edge, and those around me were throwing up their arms in impatience.

"But today is Tues—"

"Next."

"B—"

"I said 'next,' madame." This time there was no mistaking his tone. It was as sharp as a razor.

That's when I felt the rude nudge of the albino guard.

Tuesday
Early Evening

I shrank out of the building ablaze with indignation. Sobbing and sniffing, tears drenching my cheeks, I stumbled home reliving again and again the shock and shame of being thrown out like a common thief from that *kaka* temple of theirs. So, once again with a raw face, I asked my bearers to take me to Miriam, the only one who could give me some hard-earned sympathy and well-earned advice on how to continue my investigation. Frankly, I was stuck. I still didn't know why Demetra had missed our appointment or whether she was even alive. All I knew was her tenant was a nasty brute who, for some reason, was no longer going to Cato's, if in fact he was leaving the house at all.

When I found Miriam, she was in her study emptying a bag of salt over the layer of sheep dung spread out on her desk.

"What's going on?" I asked, though of course I knew the sharp stink of sheep dung. She was drying it for her furnace.

"Oh Pheeb, come here. You've been crying. "

Fresh tears of frustration and exhaustion spilled from my eyes as I folded into her arms inhaling short pieces of air. Then, as if stitched together, we rocked back and forth like a two-headed sailor to the soothing rhythm of her sweet murmurings until she arched her neck, and we slowly broke apart.

"There, there. Things can't be that bad," she said, pressing down the air with her palms. "Just tell me what's wrong."

So, I did. I told her all about Helios: how he addressed me with a foul tongue and said Demetra had gone to Memphis to visit a daughter I didn't even know she had. And then how I wasted most of the afternoon trying to verify his story. "But the worst part," I said, "was seeing those raised eyebrows, sly nods, and sidelong glances as I was thrown out of the Public Records Office like some kind of rabble-rouser—"

"Nooo—" Miriam's palm flew to her mouth.

"Or worse, like a traitor intent on destroying the empire."

"Oh, how dreadful for you."

I knew Miriam would understand. "So now what should I do?"

"Well, I've used up all my salt trying to dry out this sheep dung. Camel dung is just too scarce right now. So tomorrow I'll have to get some more to finish this project. Come with me. I'll bring the dog. We can set it loose in Demetra's yard to see whether her body could've been buried there. Afterward, we can treat the pooch to a bone when I get the salt from the butcher."

"Oh, Miriam, I knew you'd help. That's just what I'm afraid of, that he's buried her there."

I thought bringing the dog to search the yard was a great idea. I just didn't know what to hope for.

Wednesday
Early Morning

When I ventured over in the morning chill to Demetra's, even the slanting light of the new day failed to diminish my fears. Miriam, while waiting for me in the alley outside the gate, was cooing at the once-scrawny pooch as she rocked it in her arms like a well-cared-for baby. I figured she'd dismissed her bearers so they could polish off a hearty breakfast at Cato's or any of the other cookshops in the agora.

The rickety wooden lock on the gate needed to be replaced, if not before, then certainly after I broke into the yard. Gripping my satchel by its strap, I swatted the lock just once for the entire mechanism to splinter apart. Then, after Miriam gave the playful mutt a scratch behind its ears and murmured an encouraging word, it wiggled out of her arms and scampered through the gate.

My friend stood in the center of the yard, her eyes following the pooch as it sniffed the ground. At the same time, I checked the soil for any signs of disturbance, especially in the beds of white chamomiles and a pink flower I couldn't identify. We each took an expectant breath when the dog nosed the yellowed leaves at the base of a dwarf palm tree, but its interest faded quickly.

179

When we were convinced nothing had been buried in the yard, at least not recently, we passed through the gate into the alley, the dog bounding out after us. It jittered around Miriam before sitting on its haunches and looking up at her with its dark pearl-like eyes.

My friend patted its head. "Such a good little doggie you are. And just for that, you're going to get a treat."

I could swear the dog understood her every word, the way it tilted its head to one side, and as soon as she said the word "treat," it thumped its tail like a tribal drummer.

By now, I could feel the weight of the sunlight as it fanned into the alley. After an extravagant sigh, I asked, "Are we just spinning our wheels, Miriam?"

"No, I don't think so. We had to check her yard. Besides eliminating any possibility is progr—"

"*Shsh*, I said, gripping her arm like a vice.

"What is it?"

"The man on the roof across the street. He's watching us." I turned my back to the street and circled my thumb up and back. "See him?"

Miriam formed a visor with the palm of her hand as she looked up. "*Hmm*. He's been there since we got here. The magistrate's solder, Linus. I've worked with him before. He must be the regular at Cato's, the one Cato asked to keep an eye out for Helios."

When Miriam looked up at Linus with upturned palms in a gesture that said "Well?" he waggled his head.

She turned to me as if to translate. "So, Helios must still be in the house."

"Oh, Isis! I just knew it! He's got her chained up, and he's terrorizing her with a hot knife, threatening to rip open her belly and pull out her entrails like a thick sticky rope. Or maybe he's done that alrea—"

"Phoebe!" Miriam grabbed my shoulders with convulsive strength. "Stop it," she said in a gruff tone. "Your imagination is chasing away your good sense. We're doing all we can." And then, as if to distract me, she lowered her hand to point a long forefinger at the ground and said, "Look at that. The sun has caught one of your earrings and is throwing a circle of light."

Despite the blur of tears, I saw a perfect circle and knew it was a sign from

Isis. "These earrings," I said, fingering them, "belong to Demetra. When I borrowed them, she told me they're Etruscan coins. 'Eight hundred years old,' she said, 'and very valuable.'"

And that's when I got an idea.

Wednesday
Late Morning

Rather than jostle through the throng jamming the agora's West Gate, we opted to enter through the East Gate. And so, as we swerved and swayed toward Fulvius's Butcher Shop, around the knots of shoppers, tourists, gawkers, and hawkers, we had a chance to scan the alleys for Miriam's sedan chair.

Ruminating on the evidence, I spoke half to myself, surprised at the clarity of my thoughts. "There's no evidence that Helios either buried or took Demetra's body away. And we can conclude based on Linus's surveillance and Cato's observations, that he hasn't left the house. So, I wonder whether he could have burned her body."

I was surprised that Miriam, occupied as she was with the pooch, heard me above the harangues of hucksters, orators, and peddlers. Cradling it in her arms, treating it to a gentle belly massage, she murmured soothing words of praise, to which her cuddly friend responded with a doggie smile and a series of slow silent pants.

"I don't think so," she answered. "No furnace Demetra might have could get that hot. Besides, you'd have smelled or seen the black smoke anyway. The only thing I can think of is that if he killed her—and I'm still not convinced he did—he planned to throw her body into the sea. But with your watchful eye, he hasn't dared to."

Miriam couldn't have been more wrong.

We'd just passed the jeweler's stall where Demetra had bought the Etruscan coins when a flare of pain shot through my toes. "So, where's this butcher shop anyway? I want to unscrew my feet and give them a rest."

"That's because you insist on wearing fancy shoes."

"These? They're the pigskin *calcei* I always wear."

"Exactly, with those thick soles to make you look taller even when we're out searching for a dead body."

"Oh, Miriam, where's your sense of style?"

"Try loosening the straps."

"Good id—"

"Oh look, my sedan chair's over there." Miriam pointed with her chin to a slice of air between two buildings. "My bearers must be in that tavern. I'll just tell them to take the rest of the day off, that I'll hire a chair for me and the pooch to get home."

"And I'll go sit on that bench and loosen my straps." By now, they were biting into my flesh. My lips tightened with each step as I hobbled over, feeling crescendos of pain radiate through my swollen toes. As I loosened the straps and rubbed the burn each left, I hissed and moaned like a Nile crocodile until the sting eased to a throb.

"Are you ready?" asked Miriam with a chortle as the pooch, still in her arms, reached up to lick her neck. "Fulvius's stall is in the next building."

Thank Isis for that. But Miriam didn't have to tell me. As soon as we crossed the cobblestones, the reek of salted meat and the coppery stench of sour blood filtered up my nose.

Standing in the doorway, scratching his belly in the almost liquid light of late morning, a pleasantly ugly pudding face greeted us with a lopsided smile. Accompanied by the drone of flies, the man I assumed to be Fulvius signaled us in with an expansive sweep of the air.

"Welcome ladies," he said. Then, scooting behind the counter, he pointed to the racks of meat and entrails puddling the floor with blood. "What can I get you today?"

"Well, I'm looking for a bone for"—Miriam interrupted herself to kiss the wriggling pooch's ears—"Just a little longer, my sweet."

It responded with a throaty *brrr*.

"But I also need a few bags of salt. My bearers can fetch them tomorr—"

"You know, I'd be glad to give you a tasty treat for your pup, Miss bat Isaac, but I can't do the salt, not today and not tomorrow." He paused, drumming his fingers on the counter. "*Hmm*, maybe next week."

"Got some in yesterday—*hmm*, you know, it could'a' been the day before. Anyways, this new guy comes in, places an order with my son for every bag. Doesn't even ask the price, you know? Just takes out his purse and empties it in the kid's hands. Wants it delivered that day. So, I thought I'd borrow a few bags from the butcher near the West Gate, you know, to tide me over. No luck. Same thing happened to him. Go figure."

"Well, what did the man look like?" I prodded.

"You'd have to ask my son, but that knucklehead doesn't notice much these days unless it's a pretty girl."

But I knew. The man was big, built thick like a tree, and had a weathered face. And he spoke his foul words with a heavy drawl. The moisture gathered on my brow as I realized what I had to do.

"Phoebe, don't even think it!" said Miriam, stamping her foot while her eyes burned into mine like hot coals.

"No," I assured her. "You don't have to worry." But my voice was shriller than I intended.

Wednesday
Late Afternoon

I knew I had to get into that house and confront Helios. I just needed to scan my brain for any last-minute alerts Isis might have sent me about using the Etruscan earrings as a ruse. And at the same time, I thought about how I could boost any advantage I might have from taking him by surprise.

That's when Isis made me stumble because I slammed my sore toes into the stones lining the walkway to Demetra's house. A moment later, after sensing her plan, I closed my mind to the pain and slipped a few of the stones into my satchel. Then I slung the bag over my shoulder to balance the weight and knocked on the door, my arm twitching like the wings of a moth.

I gulped down my panic and knocked again.

And again.

The peephole screeched open.

Helios's thick voice howled through the grid like thunder. "*Ma Zeus*, you again, *shlut? Pigaíneis ston eaftó sou sta archaía.*"

Okay, so he told me what I could do to myself, and it wasn't nice, but I had a chance to notice from the slur of his voice that he'd had too much drink. "Listen," I said, "I have some jewelry of Demetra's, some earrings I promised to return."

"Already tol' ya', not here."

I put some flint in my tone. "Then I'll return them to you. They're too valuable to keep in my house."

"*Shlip* 'em through the peephole."

"The box won't fit through the grid."

"Leave it by the door."

"Can't. Promised I'd bring them in."

I could hear the desperation in my voice over the blood pounding in my ears.

"So come in, *shlut*, but make it fa*sht*." He dragged out every vowel and ended his offer with a hiss.

The latch lifted, and the door keened open, exhaling a familiar odor, but one I couldn't quite identify.

Then it slammed shut behind me.

"So, gimme the box."

"I need a place to sit down and open my satchel," I said, feigning a limp as I stepped into the atrium. But in truth, my toes were still throbbing so hard I could feel the veins fizz. "

"Hurry up."

That's when my eyes fixed on a trail of salt crystals leading toward the kitchen. As I hobbled along to follow it, I felt his eyes boring into my back. I shouldn't have looked over my shoulder, but when I did, our eyes locked, and I knew he realized what I was up to.

As soon as we were in the shadows of the kitchen, he repeated, "Gimme the box." He was close enough for me to smell the drink on his breath.

"What have you done to her?" I screamed.

"Oughta kill ya' right now."

I heard a low growl, but I wasn't sure whether it came from him or me.

We circled around each other.

That other smell was stronger now. It seemed to be coming from the terracotta urn on the table, its mouth heaped with salt.

His roundhouse swing caught me by surprise. It almost connected, but I lost my balance anyway, and the back of my head hit the wall as I slid to the floor.

I tasted blood dribbling out of my mouth.

Leaning forward, he crouched over me.

That's when I kicked him, the thick sole of my *calceus* aimed right at his crotch.

The pain in my foot raced up my leg like a wildfire.

His scream was guttural.

But then he got up.

So did I.

He rushed me, but I seized my satchel by the handle and swung its full weight at him.

He reeled, staggered, and collapsed sideways, scraping his shoulder against the edge of the table. The blow had knocked him breathless.

I crawled on top of him and scraped his bulging eyes with my ring, the one with the bird engraved on the carnelian.

And then I recognized the smell. It was the smell from the butcher shop coming from the urn.

I rushed to it, reached in, and pulled out the shriveled flesh and bone of Demetra's thigh, its length sufficient for me to keep my distance as I whacked him.

"You've been feeding on her, you *kaka* monster!"

His lips curled back baring his yellow curved teeth.

I kept clobbering him even after his eyes, glazed with pain, rolled into his head, and his groans faded to nothing.

The last thing I remember is screaming for the magistrate's soldier.

Friday
Noon

This time I didn't have to wait at the Flamingo's Tongue. My friend was already there, sitting on a plump dining couch, viewing the lighthouse and the hundreds of ships moored in the Great Harbor.

She'd likely been watching my reflection in the window because she turned and said, "Phoebe, you're limping!"

"My toes still hurt," I murmured.

"Oh, you poor thing," said Miriam, looking me over. "Come sit." She patted the cushions and added, "You can put your feet up here."

Relief melted into my toes like the wax of a burning candle.

"Hey, you're wearing a new pair of *calcei*."

"I ruined my other pair. Too much footwork." My lips formed a wry smile.

"Oh," she nodded.

I didn't know such a little word could carry so much sympathy.

For a while we watched the bumboats swaying in synchrony with the lapping tide.

"Say, Pheeb, I've been meaning to ask: How did you know Demetra's parts were in that urn?"

"Well, I figured Helios was the one who bought all that salt, and then, when I saw the trail of crystals on Demetra's floor, I was sure. But it was really the reek of salted meat, once I identified it. Just like in Fulvius's. So, I knew Helios was preserving her parts in there. And of course, Cato told us Helios liked his meat rare and had stopped showing up for meals."

"Yes, Linus told me the rest, and he said Helios was unconscious when he found him."

"So, what's going to happen to him, to Helios?"

"Well, he'll either be thrown to the lions or more likely, since there are no games this week, he'll be crucified outside the city gates. That'll be up to the magistrate, but my guess is he'll be left to hang until the only remains of him are a jackal's marks on his scattered bones."

Despite the sting of losing Demetra, I felt satisfied.

"And what did you decide to do with Demetra's earrings?"

"Well, you know I'm obligated to return them. So, I decided to sell them back to the jeweler and use that money to hire professional mourners for her funeral."

"Oh, Phoebe, what a fine tribute to your dear friend."

"Look, here comes the wait—"

"Listen, Pheeb, this lunch is on me. You've shown such courage and determination, as much as the best detective. So, before we order, I want you to have this cameo of Isis.

"Miriam, it's beauti—"

"And look, it's inscribed on the back."

Tears were blurring my vision, so asked Miriam to read it to me.

"'To Phoebe, my full-fledged partner.'"

I felt tendrils of pride spread through my chest. "You mean that? Not just your permanent number one deputy? After all, with a little help from Isis, I did exactly what you told me. I drew on my courage."

"Yes, I really mean that. Let's drink to our new partnership."

Glossary

Ad Aegyptum- literally "by Egypt," meaning that Alexandria was not considered part of the Roman province of Egypt. Instead, Alexandria belonged to only the emperor.

asclepeion- a healing temple dedicated to Asclepius, the first doctor-demigod in Greek mythology

bibliopōleion- a bookstore

Bruchium- the Greek or palace quarter of Alexandria

calends- the first day of the month in the ancient Roman calendar

calceus (singular), **calcei** (plural)- a Roman boot-like shoe with straps

Cardo Maximus- the main north-south thoroughfare in a Roman city

drachma (singular), **drachmae** (plural)- a silver coin of Ancient Greece

dulcia domestica- a chilled dessert made from pitted dates soaked in wine and stuffed with dried fruit, nuts, cake crumbs, and spices.

henket- a cheap Egyptian beer

himation- a mantle or wrap worn by men and women

horrei- warehouses

immune- a legionnaire trained as an investigator

kaka- the ancient Greek word for shit or shitty

kibotos- the small, square artificial port inside the Eunostos

kopraphagos- the ancient Greek insult meaning shit-eater

Khamaseen- a south-westerly wind that blows over Egypt in March and April

lectus- a bedframe

ludus- a gladiator school

Ma Zeus- an expletive equivalent to "Oh, Lord!"

opopanax- an essential oil with a warm, sweet, balsamic odor used in perfumes

peplos- an ankle-length tubular garment for women, like a sleeveless dress

phthisis- the name Hippocrates gave to a wasting disease known now as pulmonary tuberculosis

Pigaíneis ston eaftó sou sta archaea- Ancient Greek for "go f—k yourself"

posca- a cheap, watered-down, sour wine

pugio- the long straight-bladed dagger a *retiarius* uses to slit his opponent's throat

quaestor- the lowest-ranking regular magistrate in ancient Rome, whose traditional responsibility was the treasury

retiarius- the type of gladiator who uses a net and trident for his weaponry

Rhakotis- the oldest residential quarter in Alexandria where most of the Egyptians live

sacramentum gladitorium- the binding oath a recruit signs to become a gladiator

sella- chair

stoa- a long low building of shops with its columned porch facing the center of the agora

stola- a traditional outer boxy tunic worn by married women

synthesis- a fancy gown Roman men wore over a tunic to dinner parties

tiropita- a Greek pastry made with layers of buttered phyllo and filled with a cheese-egg mixture

tonsor- a barber

tunica interior- the garment worn under a stola

Via Appia- the Appian Way, the first and most famous of the ancient Roman roads running from Rome to Campania and southern Italy

Acknowledgements

I shall always be indebted to my academic mentor, Professor Jean Lythcott, for inspiring me to create Miriam bat Isaac in the image of Maria Hebrea, the legendary founder of Western alchemy who held her place for 1500 years as the most celebrated woman of the Western World. I continue to feel Jeannie's blessings on all my work. Moreover, I am grateful to Verena Rose at Level Best Books for her interest in Miriam's stories.

Every writer should have a family and friends like mine beginning with my twin sister and earliest reader, Gail Trop Kushner, who painstakingly edits all of my stories. My long-time friend, Professor Lewis M. Greenberg, a scholar of art history and culture, zealously checks the accuracy of my work. My newest support comes from Betsy Oden and Rondavid Gold, who encourage me as they gently critique my work, and from my web designer, Len C. Ritchie of LR Website Design, who happens to be the most patient man ever born.

And I thank my friends old and new for buying my books; inviting me to present my work at their book clubs, luncheons, and community fundraisers; and otherwise sharing their enthusiasm for Miriam's stories. And I thank you for reading *The Deadliest Deceptions.* I hope you enjoyed the book. Regardless, I'd be grateful if you'd post a review. Your opinion really does matter. I read the reviews assiduously to make my next book even better.

But most of all, I thank my husband Paul R. Zuckerman. He is always here for me. He believes in me, brags about me, and embraces my every goal as his own. In addition, I hope that Maria Hebrea, whoever she was, whenever she lived, and wherever she is, forgives the liberties I have taken with her persona in creating Miriam bat Isaac. May she recognize my profound respect for her spiritual quest and scientific accomplishments.

About the Author

June Trop has focused on storytelling her entire professional life. As a professor of teacher education, she focused her research on the practical knowledge teachers construct and communicate through storytelling. Now associate professor *emerita*, she writes The Miriam bat Isaac Mystery Series. Her books have earned a Readers' Choice Award, a Readers' Favorite Award, and praise from the Historical Novel Society. One was named a finalist for the Killer Nashville Silver Falchion Award, and another was recognized by Wiki Ezvid as one of the nine most riveting mysteries set in the distant past.

Living in New York's Hudson Valley with her husband, Paul Zuckerman, June is breathlessly chronicling Miriam and Phoebe's next life-or-death exploit. Be sure to visit her website at www.JuneTrop.com.

SOCIAL MEDIA HANDLES:
https://www.facebook.com/June-Trop-Author-1447548442142942
https://www.goodreads.com/author/list/7380932.June_Trop

AUTHOR WEBSITE:
www.JuneTrop.com

Also by June Trop

The Deadliest Lie

The Deadliest Hate

The Deadliest Sport

The Deadliest Fever

The Deadliest Thief